The Assist

Elizabeth Meitzler

First paperback edition October 2025

ISBN 979-8-9865455-4-7 (paperback)

ISBN 979-8-9865455-5-4 (ebook)

For the girls who faked it, feared it, and felt broken—

You were never the problem.

Baby, let the games begin.

To my family and relatives,

If you choose to continue reading after this page and choose to tell me about it, I highly suggest you only focus on the friendships created at Winger University. Please do not talk to me about any ... activities you read about that aren't related to hockey.

If you are going to turn the page, all I can say is I hope you enjoy this book. Except for you, dad. Stop reading immediately!

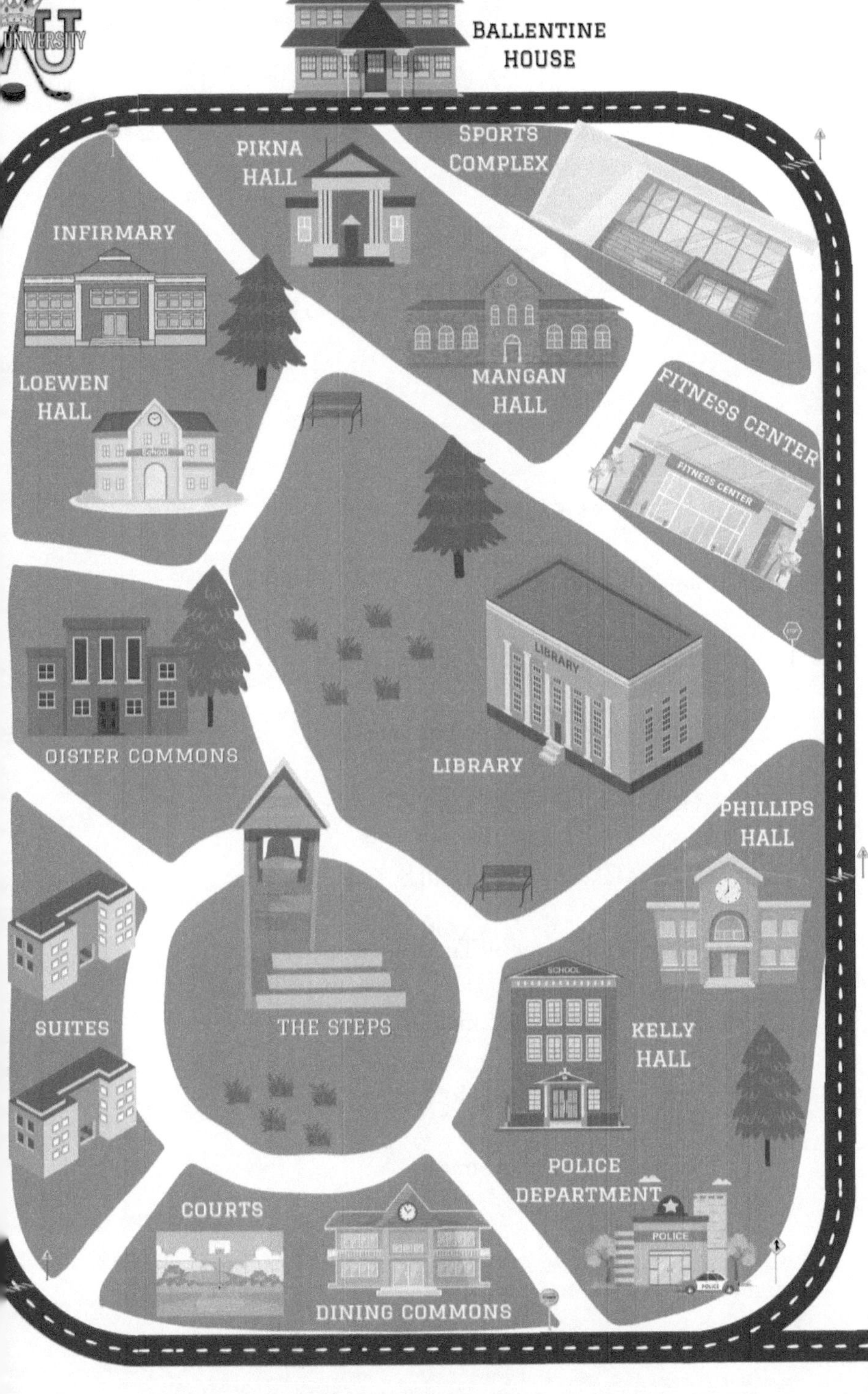
KU UNIVERSITY
BALLENTINE HOUSE
PIKNA HALL
SPORTS COMPLEX
INFIRMARY
MANGAN HALL
FITNESS CENTER
FITNESS CENTER
LOEWEN HALL
LIBRARY
LIBRARY
OISTER COMMONS
PHILLIPS HALL
THE STEPS
SUITES
SCHOOL
KELLY HALL
POLICE DEPARTMENT
POLICE
COURTS
DINING COMMONS

Playlist

1. APT. by ROSÉ, Bruno Mars

2. greedy by Tate McRae

3. Voices in My Head by Ashley Tisdale

4. feelslikeimfallinginlove by Coldplay

5. Heaven by Julia Michaels

6. What Makes You Beautiful by One Direction

7. Dirty Little Secret by The All-American Rejects

8. Dirty Thoughts by Chloe Adams

9. Slow Hands by Niall Horan

10. Stargazing by Myles Smith

11. Peer Pressure by James Bay, Julia Michaels

12. Like No One Does by Jake Scott

13. Hands to Myself by Selena Gomez

14. They Don't Know About Us by One Direction

15. ...Ready For It? by Taylor Swift

Contents

Chapter One

Jace

The semester hasn't even started yet and this asshat is already putting Ballentine at risk.

"Leave," Kai grunts, "while you're still able to walk."

Myself and a few other hockey guys are on the front lawn, strategically positioned around our team captain and my best friend, Kai Masterson, while he stares down this khaki wearing loser. To be honest, I have no idea who this kid is or the chick with him, but Kai said he needed our help, so we have his back. No matter how this situation ends.

The college kid who thought it was a good idea to show up to a Ballentine party in boat shoes tries to stand toe-to-toe with Kai. He's a few inches shorter than Kai and as his eyes dart around the lawn, I think it's finally dawning on him how stupid he is.

Kai grabs the girl and hides her behind his back and all I can think about is this could go one of two ways. Either the douchelord sulks away with his tail between his legs or the cops are getting called.

I'm taking a drink from my solo cup when the douchelord starts walking away. But then he turns back and yells, "She was a prude anyway. Couldn't give good head to save her life."

I snort into my cup, not expecting the balls on him. Kai takes his time as he walks down to meet the douchelord. I watch Kai closely and take a tentative step forward. I didn't plan on getting in a fight tonight, but shit happens. I've been friends with Kai for a while and he's never been the kind of person who would just stand by and let someone get spoken down to. Let alone someone he knows and cares about. I am curious about this mystery girl though. Kai's forced to lean down to threaten, I mean talk, to the guy, but when he turns to walk back to the party, the douchelord's face has gone pale and I'm pretty sure he just shit his cargo shorts. I'm not surprised - Kai's a scary looking fucker being 6 '3" and mostly made of muscle.

Kai walks back to the party holding the chick's hand. I follow them in, but when they head up the steps, I make my way towards the commotion in the kitchen.

Ballentine House is hosting its first party of the year and it's usually chaos mixed with a lot of booze since no school officials are on campus yet. It's a Victorian-style and is run through donations of old alumni who live vicariously through us. We only allow Juniors and Seniors to live here though because we're more mature. It's a mesh of guys from all different sports, which is kind of cool. The best part of the whole house is the room designated for video games, I mean watching game highlights.

I'm making my way through the crowd when I feel a hand tighten on my junk. I quickly turn and gaze down at a bunny. Oh, puck bunnies are the chicks that want to ride my dick just because I know how to play hockey. They like to hop from player to player. You know, like how a bunny hops? Whatever. I think it's funny. Major daddy issues and alcohol mean a great night for me. The girl, whose name I don't care to ask, stares up at me through lashes that have to be fake. They are thick and so long they almost touch her eyebrows. Come to think of it, they kind of look like peacock feathers. I chuckle to myself and she takes that as me accepting her unspoken invite.

"Another time," I yell so she'll hear me over the music and shimmy out of her grasp.

That's the problem I have with chicks. Most of them are hot, but they cover it up with all that caked on makeup and shit.

My head swivels back to the kitchen where the noise has gotten even louder. Not wanting to be left out, I push my way through the crowd. My jaw drops when I see what everyone is gawking at. Or should I say who.

Zoey Griffin is a thorn in my side. She's petty and annoying and the sexiest woman I've ever seen. She's also Kai's step-sister. His dad married her mom a few years back and I haven't been able to get her out of my head since. Zoey's a year younger than us, but chose to attend Winger U for God knows what reason. She could've gone anywhere, but had to show up here. I don't hate her, I just prefer not to be around her. Maybe it's because I know I can't touch her or maybe it's because she never stops fucking talking.

None of that matters now though. Not as my eyes are fixed on the thick thighs of the woman swaying her hips back and forth on our kitchen table. Her red hair is long and wavy and all over the place as she whips it side to side. She's wearing a white tank with a low neckline that pushes up her tits and makes my mouth water. And every other guy's mouth too. All I can think is what Kai would do to everyone if he wasn't upstairs busy with his girl.

I should do something. I should put a stop to it. Right? I mean, that's my obligation as Kai's best friend. But I can't move. She's hypnotized me or some shit and when she pushes her ass out, all I can think about is me standing behind her while she grinds that delicious ass over my hard cock. I look down at myself and realize I *am* fucking hard. Shit! I quickly adjust myself and am about to yell at her to get down when some guy swats her ass. I crush my cup and toss it to the ground as I make my way towards him. Even if she wasn't Kai's sister, you can't put your hands on someone without their consent. And her face tells me she definitely didn't like that.

Her facial expression is a mix of shock and anger and before I can even get close to the guy who touched her, she pulls back her fist and punches him square in the face.

Chapter Two

Zoey

OH MY GOD! I just punched someone in the face! I've never hit anyone in my entire life. I've never even thought about hitting someone before. And why did no one warn me how much it would hurt? To be fair, the asshole had it coming. My hand throbs and it feels like I broke a knuckle or maybe a finger. The party quiets down for only a moment. That is until the guy that smacked my ass turns back to me. His face is angry red with a small line of blood dripping from his nose.

"You dumb bitch!" he shouts.

I open my mouth to say—well, I'm not sure what—but I'm hoisted up and tossed over someone's shoulder before I can.

"All right, show's over," he announces.

"What?" I shriek. "Let me go!"

I pound my fists against his back, but he has a tight grip around my thighs.

"Put me down," I snap, but the stranger just keeps moving through the party and up the stairs.

I continue my assault on his back even though he's not bothered in the slightest. Finally, we walk through a doorway and once he kicks the door shut, I'm flung onto a bed. The bouncing makes my head spin and for a moment I think I might throw up. I didn't think I was that drunk, but then I register everything that just happened. I was dancing on the freaking kitchen table! Holy shit! I've never done something like that. Propping myself up on my elbows, my eyes focus on who saved me. And I groan, falling back on the bed.

Jace fucking Bennett, also known as my step-brother's best friend. Also known as the guy that hates me for no reason. Well, maybe not hate, but strongly dislike. I have no idea what I ever did to personally offend him, but ever since I met him, Jace has had a huge stick up his ass. He scowls every time I'm around. I don't understand what his deal is; Kai and I actually have a pretty good relationship. What's really unfair about the entire situation is that Jace looks like a God in human form. His dirty blonde hair and ice blue eyes are mesmerizing. Not to mention he knows how to use his charm. And I guess the strong jaw and muscles in all the right places don't hurt either.

"Not you," I moan, still shielding my eyes. "I'm hallucinating, right? I drank too much and passed out and now I'm dreaming."

"Nice to know you dream about me," he says.

I pop back up to a sitting position, but instantly regret it. The room sways, but I still manage to check his shit-eating grin as he leans against the door, arms crossed.

"Those would be called nightmares."

He shakes his head. "You'd prefer the hangover from hell over me saving your ass?"

"Saving me?" I stand, but then fall back onto the bed. "I had it under control."

Jace laughs at that. "You punched that guy. If anything, you only pissed him off more. Plus, I saved you from embarrassing yourself further."

My face falls and I don't know if I should start crying or just punch him in the face too.

This time, I push myself to my feet. Once the dizziness fades, I head towards him.

"And what exactly did I do to embarrass myself, Jace? I was having a good time. Would you have preferred one of your little puck bunnies on the table instead of me?"

I'm a bigger girl. I have rolls when I sit. Chub rub is real. I can't go anywhere without a bra. It's not a secret and it's not a bad thing. But if he's saying what I think he's saying, I'm going to go feral and tear his face off.

His brows pull together in confusion. "What? No. That's not what I was saying at all."

I scoff. "No, I get it. Who would want to watch someone who looks like me dance." I grab the door handle and try to open the door, but he leans his weight back on it. "Move."

Jace is well over six feet, so when he looks down at my 5'4" frame, I feel more intimidated than I should. Especially with his ice blue eyes boring a hole through me.

"No. Why the fuck are you so pissy all of a sudden?"

I try the door again, but when it doesn't budge, I sigh in frustration.

I turn to face Jace and that's when he realizes what he said. His hard features soften and he shakes his head.

"You think I was saying because of your size, you were embarrassing yourself?"

"Yeah! Because that's literally what you said."

He pinches the bridge of his nose like I'm the one exhausting him. "That's not at all what I said. You looked like you were shocked you hit the guy and wanted to apologize or some shit, even after he called you a bitch. I saved you from that embarrassment!"

I roll my eyes. "Bullshit! You're back pedaling and just trying to save your ass."

Jace lets out a growl and spins so he has me trapped against the door. I flinch when he slams his hand against the door next to my head, truly caging me in.

"You want to know what I think about your body?" he grits through his teeth.

My breathing picks up, but not because I'm scared of him. Because I've never seen him like this. Jace is always the calm, cool and collected guy. I know he would never hurt me in a million years.

"Jace?" He's so close and every time I try to inhale, my tits brush against his chest. In all the time we've known each other, we've never been this close. He stares down at me and for some reason, I can't look away.

His voice drops, low and rough, like the words are meant to touch more than just my ears. "You have one of the sexiest bodies I've ever seen."

Wait, what? That's it. I'm definitely hallucinating. I hate to admit it, especially since Jace decided that we weren't going to like each other when we met, but I've fantasized about him. Dreamt about him. I've never done anything about it and I would never tell anyone that, but it's true. So now that we're here, in this moment, I can't help but wonder if it's real.

Jace's hand that was on the wall next to my head slides down, landing on my shoulder. But he doesn't stop. I gasp as his hand continues to move south. His brow arches in question. Silently asking if he should stop or not. My voice has decided to stop working, so instead of talking I move my hands to grab his hips. When his hand finds my tit and squeezes, I toss my head back. If this really is a hallucination, I'm going to ride this high.

Jace rubs his nose against mine, again asking permission. What happens if we kiss? Will I wake up from this dream? As much as I shouldn't want Jace, I don't want this moment to end. So, I turn my head. The rejection doesn't phase him, because his lips land on my neck. My eyes flutter shut as he sucks and licks all the way down to the low neckline of my shirt.

He can't stop. I don't want him to. I want him to continue and stop asking me for permission every step of the way. I run my fingers through his dirty blonde hair, guiding his head further down. He licks a path to my cleavage, slightly pulling my shirt down.

"Yes," I pant.

"Yeah?" he asks, pulling his head back to look up at me.

"What? Why did you stop?" I hate how needy I sound, but if this is a dream, it doesn't matter as long as I can get off.

Jace stands, fixes my shirt and intertwines our fingers. He walks backwards, pulling me towards the bed furthest away from the door. Jace sits down on the edge of the mattress, silently guiding me to straddle his lap. Oh, holy crap! He's hard. Like really hard. Like how are his pants still containing him hard. Winding my arms around his neck, I play with the curls of his hair.

"Jace." I don't know why I say his name. It's all I can think of right now.

He runs his nose against my jaw, before whispering in my ear. "Ride me."

"I-I-I ..." I try to talk, but am unable to get even a syllable out.

A shiver runs through my entire body as Jace grabs my hips and starts moving me over his erection. Back and forth and back and forth. I grab onto his shoulders, steadying myself. We both are completely clothed and maybe it's the alcohol, but this feels a million times better than anything I've ever done while being naked with a guy.

"What if your roommate walks in?" I ask.

Jace laughs to himself. "I locked the door when I had you pressed up against it."

Jace's one hand stays on my hip, helping me, while his other hand slides up my body and into my hair. He tightens his grip, tugging my head back so he can access my neck better. A heat develops low in my belly and I close my eyes, determined to chase that feeling. This will not be like all the other times when my orgasm is so close that I can taste it, but vanishes before I can enjoy it. No. This will happen. And I can't believe I'm even thinking this, but it will happen with Jace Bennett.

Chapter Three

Jace

Holy shit. If you would've told me that by the end of the party, I would have Zoey Griffin dry-humping me on my bed, I would've said you need to go to an AA meeting. Given how good of a friend I am, I never let myself give in to the urge to fantasize about her. That's totally gone now.

Zoey's nails dig into my shoulders as she grinds down on my cock. I can feel how hot and wet she is, even through our clothes. I'm barely even helping her anymore, so I slide one of my hands up to grasp her tit. I pinch her nipple through the material of her shirt and her gasp has my cock twitching in my pants.

"You keep making noises like that, I might come in my pants."

"Don't talk," she breaths, "I like you better with your mouth shut."

I chuckle as I thrust my hips up while sinking my teeth into her neck. She doesn't push me off or tell me to stop. Instead, she runs her fingers through my hair and holds me in place. I lick and kiss my bite, feeling myself getting closer and closer to the edge.

"Fuck, Zoey. I really—"

My words are cut off when the little shit puts her hand over my mouth. That might be the hottest thing someone's ever done to me during sex. I quicken my pace while my fingers dive between us and rub circles on her clit. Her body convulses against me and I know she's moments away from her orgasm. My fingers grip her hip tight enough to bruise as my entire body stills, muscles going rigid as warm liquid coats my boxer briefs. I don't stop my movements until Zoey's crying out in pleasure, her hand falling from my mouth as her body goes limp in my arms.

I fall back on my bed, taking her with me. We're both still trying to catch our breath when all of a sudden, Zoey twitches and tries to roll off me. "Shit. Sorry."

I wrap my arms around her to stop her from moving. "Where do you think you're going?"

She looks up at me with confusion. "Um, I don't know. Let me at least get off you. I don't want to hurt you."

Sighing heavily, I sit us both up and force her to look me in the eyes. "I don't ever want to hear you say something like that again. Do you understand me?"

Her head jerks back. "Excuse you?"

"I guarantee my warmup weight is more than you, so I don't want to ever hear you say some shit like that again. To anyone. Ever."

Zoey rolls her eyes dramatically. "I was right. I like you better with your mouth shut."

Zoey gets up, I think to leave, but instantly starts to sway. I jump up and grab her before her head hits my dresser.

"I'm kind of dizzy," she mumbles.

"A little? Come here," I tell her, guiding her to my bed.

"No. I just left your bed. Why are you taking me back there?"

I chuckle to myself as I sit her on my mattress, take off her shoes and socks, and help her under the covers.

"Just close your eyes for a little and then you can go home whenever you're ready."

Zoey pulls my comforter up to her chin. "Fine. But only because your bed is weirdly comfortable."

I turn around when her eyes shut, thinking she's about to fall asleep. "And don't try any funny business either! I don't like you like that and you probably have dirty dick syndrome or something equally as gross."

Brushing the hair out of her face, I smile. "Get some sleep, my chocolate bar."

The next morning, I wake up feeling like I was hit by a truck. Not just because of the alcohol and weed combo, but because I slept on the floor. I didn't want to sleep on the couch downstairs because I didn't want to be forced to explain to Kai why I had his sister in my bed. After a few seconds of stretching, I manage to stand up only to find Conrad's bed made. Did that asshole not sleep here last night? Meaning I could've slept in my roommate's bed?

I groan, stumbling to my desk and grabbing some painkillers. I try to be quiet, but Zoey seems dead to the world. I stare at her chest for a few moments just to make sure it's actually moving. I sigh in relief when she takes a deep breath. I get ready for hockey practice in slow motion, the entire time re-playing what happened last night.

I essentially fucked my best friend's step-sister. Yes, we had our clothes on, but everything I felt was so intense. I've never done something like that before, but with her, I would do it again and again.

Oh, fuck.

Chapter Four

Zoey

The next morning, my eyes are heavy and I can barely open them. But once I do manage to not only open my eyes, but sit up and not vomit, I realize I'm in Jace's room. At Ballentine House. I'm completely alone as my eyes widen and I run a hand through my hair. Wait, last night wasn't an alcohol-induced dream? So that means ... that I got off while I dry humped the shit out of my step-brother's best friend.

Oh, fuck.

Two Weeks Later

"I don't kn-now if this is such a g-good idea," I mumble as I shift my weight. I clench my fists in frustration at my stutter. It chooses the worst times to come out.

"There's no reason to stutter," Corrine says. "It's just a party."

Maybe to my roommates it's just another party, but to an intro-vert who has a stutter? Corrine finishes straightening her platinum blonde hair before blowing a kiss to herself in the mirror.

I frown looking down at the outfit her and our other roommate, Becks, picked out for me. The platform heels Corrine gave me aren't the most comfortable. It probably doesn't help they aren't the right size.

"You look hot. I'd do you," Becks adds. She's finishing up her makeup look with metallic pink lipstick that goes perfectly with the gold jewelry in her nose. Becks has a very hippie-esque style versus Corrine who I would describe as more of Clubbing Barbie.

"I can't tell you the last time I wore a-a-a skirt." I take deep, calm-ing breaths and try to focus on what I'm saying. "I re-eally don't think—"

Corrine exhales sharply. "Seriously, you gotta cool it with the stutter. You're way over thinking tonight."

"Corrine!" Becks scolds.

"What?" Corrine looks confused even though we all know she isn't. Corrine is very blunt and doesn't hide her feelings well. "Everyone stutters sometimes. It's so not a big deal."

I bite the inside of my cheek to keep from stuttering again. Corrine is full of crap and she knows it. I don't have a slight stutter like other people. I have a speech disorder where I stutter when I'm nervous or anxious or upset or a thousand other emotions and it's frustrating as hell. Even more frustrating when the people around you trivialize what you're going through.

Corrine throws her hands in the air because she also loves to be the center of attention. "It doesn't matter. Leo is going to die when he sees you. I promise, this outfit will make him notice you."

I stare at my reflection. The smokey eyes, fishnet stockings, low-cut shirt. This isn't a good idea.

"I-I don't, um I don't know. This is, I shouldn't..." I fan myself as my skin heats up. When did the room get so hot?

Becks grabs my shoulders and turns me to face her. "Zo, you good? It's just a party. There's nothing to be scared of."

"It's not s-scaring me!" I snap. It's just the last college party I at-tended. I danced on the kitchen table, punched a guy in the face, got drunk off of god-only-knows what and then had an orgasm with my step-brother's best friend while we were both completely clothed. That was only two weeks ago and I hate that I still remember every single detail of that night. I was drunk. I shouldn't be able to remem-ber how his callused hands felt on my skin. Or how his lips were soft and warm and felt so good. I shouldn't ever be allowed back into a party or an event that involves guys and booze.

She rubs her hands up and down my arms. "How about we just go somewhere else? We can get a milkshake or something? Forget about the party?"

At Corrine's squeal of protest, Becks gives her a pointed look over my shoulder. Corrine and Becks have known each other for a while, so they have this nonverbal communication thing. As much as I like my roommates, Becks is definitely more tolerant of me.

"I guess I could go for a milkshake," Corrine mumbles while checking out her acrylics.

I look between the two of them, terrified I'm ruining their night. "I don't want you guys not to go just because of me."

Becks rolls her eyes dramatically. "I'm so tired of parties. The boys are always the same and a milkshake sounds delicious. Let's go."

Corrine holds the door and dramatically bows as if Becks and I are royalty. We each laugh as we pass her and walk into Cherry On Top.

Becks has been working here for a couple weeks now and being friends with an employee definitely has its perks. I'm all about 10% off milkshakes. Cherry On Top is themed like a 1950's ice-cream parlor and I feel incredibly underdressed compared to the employees in their vintage clothing. I try to tug my skirt down, hoping maybe it will cover at least some of my cellulite, but no luck. After placing our orders, the door chimes as a few guys walk in. Corrine pastes the biggest smile on her face and I turn away to hide my chuckle. I give Becks a nod signaling they can go flirt with them outside while I wait.

I'm standing at the pick-up window, waiting for my salted caramel vanilla milkshake when the bell over the door dings again. The sound of laughter fills the small shop and I turn to find some of the guys from Ballentine. I quickly look away, hoping they won't see me, when Jace speaks up.

"Little Griffin. That you?"

Not Jace. Anyone but him. It's been radio silence between the two of us since we … you know. I could say I haven't thought much about that night, but I'd be lying. Every time I close my eyes, I replay the memory of him guiding my hips over his hard dick while his sexy moans filled my ears. Maybe I can just pretend I don't hear him and he'll go away.

"Think she's ignoring you," Buzz loudly announces to the entire shop.

"Hm. I wonder why," Conrad deadpans.

I knew I wasn't that lucky. Squaring my shoulders, I turn and face the music.

"Damn, that skirt would look so much better on my bedroom floor," Buzz adds.

"Tell me honestly, what did you think my reaction to that would be?" I ask with raised eyebrows.

He shrugs like he doesn't have a care in the world then joins Conrad at the register.

Jace is just staring at me, so I finally acknowledge him. "Aren't you supposed to be at a party right now?"

He looks like he's going to respond, but then his eyes slowly scan down my body and I'm shocked that Corrine and Becks were right. The clothes really do work. Not that I want to attract someone like Jace, but he's a guy. And all guys are the same, right? As in they can only think with one head at a time. His gaze stops at my low cut shirt and I laugh because he's not even attempting to hide the fact he's ogling my body right now.

"My eyes are up here."

He chuckles nervously, rubbing the back of his neck. This might make me a bad person, but I'm taking a lot of pleasure in watching him squirm. I remember every single word he said to me that night in his bedroom. Does he? Or maybe he was just making up shit to try and get in my pants? That would make more sense, but he technically didn't get in my pants.

"We're heading to the house soon. Conrad just had to stop and get his girlfriend a pint."

I nod even though I'm not remotely interested.

Curious at how flustered I can make him, I twirl a strand of my hair around my finger and smile up at him. "That's very sweet of Conrad."

He sucks on his lower lip. "Yeah. I think it was pretty nice of us to come with him, too."

Is Jace seriously searching for a compliment? Fine, if he wants one, I'll give him one.

"I really like your shirt," I tell him, briefly brushing my fingers over his chest.

He sounds like he chokes on his saliva for a moment and I've never been so proud of myself. Freaking Corrine was right. Some confidence makes a world of difference when dealing with men. That and a short skirt. But if I'm being completely honest, I look damn good in a skirt and might start wearing one more often.

When my name is called, I grab my milkshake and go to leave but Jace is in my way.

"Are you coming to the party?" he asks.

Watching his pupils dilate, an idea pops into my head.

"Wasn't planning on it," I tell him.

Holding eye contact, I bring my milkshake to my lips, stick my tongue out and lick a dollop of whipped cream off the top. "Why? Are you inviting me?"

His Adam's apple noticeably bobs up and down. He clears his throat before pointing at my face. Jace sticks his hand out like he's going to touch me, then thinks twice about it.

"Um, you, you have a little something. Right there." He points to a spot next to his mouth.

"Oh." Using my thumb, I swipe the caramel and bring my finger to my mouth. He practically pants when I suck it clean. "Thanks."

This is actually fun. I've never had this kind of effect on a man before.

"Becks, Corrine and I were having a girls night. A party filled with stale beer and sweaty boys doesn't really sound fun."

"Jace! Let's go!" Conrad shouts from the door.

"I'm heading out too. I'll catch you around." Deliberately slowly, I wrap my lips around my pink and white striped straw before walking past him and out to my friends. I decided at the last minute to shake my ass when I walk and it doesn't disappoint. Jace runs in front of me to hold the door.

"Let me get that for you."

"Thank you, Jace."

Becks and Corrine's features are frozen as I approach.

"Hello?" I wave my hand in front of them. "Is anyone in there?"

Corrine wordlessly points to Jace, then to me, then back to Jace. It's kind of funny that me flirting with Jace has not only had him fumbling over his words, but my roommates too. If only they knew about what happened two weeks ago.

"Where are the guys?" I ask. They both are still staring at me with shell-shocked looks.

Becks finds her voice first as her smile takes over her entire face. "Were you just flirting with Jace?"

"Jace as in your brother's best friend?" Corrine adds.

I start laughing. "Step-brother. And not really. I was just messing with him."

"What if the guys tell Kai what just happened? They were practically panting watching you lick your finger," Becks tells me.

"It's not like Kai is my keeper. Anyways, I wanted to see if my new outfit worked and I'm pretty sure it did."

"Pretty sure?" Corrine looks behind me at the guys. "I'd say Jace has a little crush now."

I roll my eyes. "Whatever. I was thinking though, if the outfit worked that well on someone I don't like, what will it do to Leo?"

"Yes!" Corrine screams, throwing her arm around my shoulder. "Let's go get you laid!"

It's only when we're walking to Ballentine that I realize I didn't stutter when talking to Jace. Not once.

Chapter Five

Zoey

The walk to Ballentine takes almost twenty minutes, but I don't care because I'm still vibrating with energy. Flirting with Jace was fun. Even my ex didn't react to me the way Jace did. I guess that's why he's my ex.

Ballentine House is like an unsanctioned frat house. It's a mixture of different guys from different sports teams at Winger U. Most of the guys are seniors, but there's some mysterious ritual of how the housemates are determined. It's all very secret society. Majority of the parties are held here because it's right off campus which means campus police can't do anything and the town police just plain out don't care. The small front lawn is covered with students drinking out of red solo cups, some of them playing corn hole and a few of them making out. We all laugh at a couple sprawled out together in a bush. I can't tell if they're about to have sex or beat the shit out of each other. The three of us link arms and head up the cracked pathway to the door.

I almost trip at least twice, but Becks holds me up as we find the kitchen and the booze. And my step-brother. He's leaning against the wall, talking to someone when our eyes meet. He smiles, but looks extremely confused on why I'm here. Disentangling myself from the girls, I make my way over.

Kai wraps his arms around me, lifting me off the ground in a hug. When my mom and dad divorced, it absolutely sucked. Then she told me only seven months later she was re-marrying and I thought my life was over. Imagine my shock when Kai and his dad seemed like the perfect addition to our tiny family. Now Kai and I could not be more different, but he really is a great older brother.

"If you were dragged here against your will, blink twice," he jokes.

"Ha. Ha. Becks and Corrine were coming, so I figured I tag along."

His eyes quickly drop to my outfit.

Kai opens his mouth when I shake my head. "Nope. We are at a college party. No older step-brother Kai tonight."

He chuckles before telling me to enjoy myself, but not too much.

I find the girls with Becks holding up a shot glass to me. Not wanting to seem like a total loser, I take mine. We all cheers and then I toss mine over my shoulder. Someone behind me shouts and I realize

I've thrown my shot right at them. I wince, but as soon as he shakes his head off like a dog, he continues his conversation like nothing happened.

"Woo!" Corrine shouts. "Let's do another!"

"Let's take it slow," Becks says as she throws away our plastic shot glasses.

I smile and laugh but am content with the sealed water bottle I grabbed out of the refrigerator.

Corrine and Becks grew up in the same township. They knew of each other, but didn't actually become friends until they found out they both got into Winger U. Corrine likes to enjoy experiences and be in the moment while Becks likes to do the same, but responsibly. They are a match made in heaven. Originally, it was supposed to be just the two of them rooming together and me in a single dorm. I dealt with the roommates from hell my Freshman year, so I was so excited to live on my own my Sophomore year. The University must've felt differently because some filing error put the three of us together, but after a few days of shyness, Becks broke me and we all became friends. I can't even imagine what college would be like without them and we've only been here a short time. Crazy how you can know someone for such a small amount of time, but forget what life was like before them.

I'm fully invested in Becks' conversation with someone when I feel fingers brush my elbow. My eyes almost pop out of my head when I turn and find Leo smiling down at me.

"L-Leo? Hey. Hi. Hi."

"Little Griffin. You made it." His hand rests on my shoulder before sliding down my arm and I think I might combust right here in the middle of the party. Holy freaking crap! Leo Stanford just touched me. I don't think I can ever shower again.

It then hits me what he just called me, and I try not to cringe. Jace gave me that nickname back when we originally met a few years ago. Why did Leo have to call me that? The stupid nickname doesn't even make sense. Zoey would sound so good in his raspy voice. I'll never understand how anyone can play sports and smoke cigarettes. Normally, I would think that's a disgusting habit, but whatever brand he smokes smells good. Like a cherry pie, but slightly burnt.

"Yeah. I, um, my roommate br-brought me. I mean, I want-ted to come."

Dammit! Why am I stuttering so much? He's just a guy. A very hot guy. Come on, Zoey! You know how to make sentences. You know how to have a conversation with another human being. Okay, I can do this.

"How are, t-the, um." I freeze and am completely embarrassed. God, I want to cry. Instead I randomly shout, "The place looks great."

Leo laughs and nods. "Yeah, it does. I have to go grab some more ice, but I'll see you around. Yeah?"

I nod like a bobble head, not trusting myself to talk anymore.

I continue to nod as he walks away and then mentally smack myself. What in the hell was that disaster? It's like I lost all my conversational skills. He's never going to want to talk to me again after that. I don't want to talk to me again after that.

Downing the rest of my water, I walk through the crowd in search of Becks and Corrine. They wandered away when Leo approached and I need to talk to them. I think I have to get out of here. I need to preserve at least some of my dignity. If I don't find them in five minutes, I'll send them a text and bolt.

Chapter Six

Jace

I snuck off for some peace and quiet. This is the second party we've had this week, and I'm so over it. Normally, I'm the one pounding drink after drink, but after Coach tore me a new asshole at practice, I'm choosing to be responsible and not get drunk. Just high.

My attention shifts when the door to the laundry room bursts open. Of course it has to be her. My cock twitches like some muscle memory response to what happened the last time Zoey and I were alone in a room together.

Her eyes narrow on the joint in my hand and she scoffs, "Classy."

Really? She's going to judge me?

"That was some grade A shit you just pulled with Stanford."

She's about to retreat back to the party, but freezes at my jab. To add insult to injury, I smile like the asshole I am.

Finally shutting the door, she takes a few hesitant steps towards me.

"Don't tell anyone about that."

Zoey trying to be the authoritative one is cute.

"Chill, Little Griffin. It was classic entertainment. But I'm not some chick who likes to gossip, so your secret is safe with me."

Zoey narrows her eyes. "Why are you being nice to me?"

She thinks this is nice? Jesus.

"You have a low threshold for what you consider nice."

I hop up to sit on the washer and bring the joint to my lips.

"I thought Kai said the guys were supposed to stay sober during the season."

My shoulders shake with laughter as I flick my lighter and inhale deeply.

"A little weed never hurt anyone."

I extend the joint to her as I blow smoke out of the corner of my mouth. I may be an asshole, but not all the time. She shakes her head and I shrug, taking another puff.

"Tell me something. What the hell was that? You have no problem talking to me but Stanford comes along and you stumble over every word."

A shadow comes over her face like I said something wrong, but I don't know what.

"It's called a stutter asshole! Jesus. First Corrine and now you. It's an actual speech disorder in the DSM—"

I jump down, covering her mouth so I can get a word in. "I didn't know you had a stutter."

Zoey jerks her head away and crosses her arms. "Because you don't know everything about me."

I stare her down, in true awe that I had no idea she had a stutter. I've known her for a few years now and have never once heard her stumble over her words.

"It doesn't happen all the time," she adds. "My shitty SLP told me it just happens when I'm nervous or can't think. It's like my brain isn't connected to my mouth."

So I don't make her nervous. Interesting.

"The hell's an SLP?"

"Speech Language Pathologist. It's a therapist who was supposed to help me with my speech problem."

I scoff. "Sounds like they didn't know how to do their fucking job."

Zoey narrows her eyes. "Well, it was the therapist insurance would pay for, so I didn't exactly have a say in it."

After a moment of silence, I say, "That really sucks."

"It's fine." A wide smile spreads across her lips as she stares off into space. "I'm going to be a better one."

"That's what you're majoring in?"

She nods. "Yep. I'm going to be the therapist little Zoey needed back when she was seven and could barely speak two words without stuttering." Zoey chews on her bottom lip, stuck in her head again. "Kids can be really mean."

A sudden burst of anger rushes through me at the thought of little shitheads making fun of Zoey which probably made her stutter even worse.

"I would've kicked their asses for you."

Zoey giggles at that. "Well, apparently I still have issues because I sounded like an idiot out there."

I groan in disgust. "How do you like Stanford of all people? That guy's such a tool."

"Don't say that about him. You don't even know him."

"And you do?"

Zoey opens her mouth to speak, but nothing comes out. It's like she wants to defend Stanford, but she can't. Because even though she won't admit I'm right, deep down she knows it.

She rolls her eyes. "Okay. Fine. Maybe I don't know him that well, but at least he's nice to me. And what's the harm with a small crush?"

Licking my lower lip, I take a step closer. "So you're busy making fuck-me eyes and showing off your short skirt for me, but not him? I don't think you really like him that much."

"I wasn't—"

"Yeah, you were. You were seeing if you could get a rise out of me. I'm man enough to admit that you did. But what I don't get is why you didn't suck on your finger for him?"

Zoey's jaw clenches in anger. I've pushed her too far. I know I have, but I don't want to stop. She goes to spin away, but I grab her arm to stop her.

"I know that I just humiliated myself," she snaps as she turns back to me, "you don't have to rub in it."

"Woah, I wasn't saying that at all."

Shimmying out of my hold, she takes a step back. So I take a step forward. Like the world's weirdest dance, we keep doing this until her back is pressed against the door. Her eyes dart around like she's looking for a way out before she makes the decision to straighten her spine and face me head on like the ball buster she is.

"No? So then you were just making fun of me for your own personal pleasure?"

My eyes rake down her body and get stuck on her tits that are almost spilling out of her top.

Bringing my eyes back up, I tuck a lock of hair behind her ear. "Making fun of women isn't what I do for personal pleasure."

Her breathing is sporadic and every deep breath she takes has those glorious tits rubbing up against my chest.

"Then what do you do?" She looks just as surprised as me at the words that just left her lips.

Propping my arm above her head on the door, I lean down and run my nose up her neck, stopping when my mouth is centimeters from hers. Painstakingly slowly, I glide my fingers up the outside of her bare thigh and chuckle when she gasps. I continue moving up, over the denim of her skirt, purposefully bunching the material of her shirt around her waist before wrapping my arm around her and pulling her flush against my body. And my very hard cock. Zoey licks her lips as her eyes bounce back and forth like she doesn't know what to focus on. Fuck, I need to kiss her. Claim her mouth and let her know that she belongs to me. Only me. I wonder if she knows that she's owned every part of me since that party? Every moment—awake or asleep—I haven't been able to escape her. Then Kai, my stupid best friend, pops into my head. And it's like a bucket of ice cold water is dumped on me. Fuck, I can't do this to him.

Changing tactics, I whisper, "That."

Her brow furrows as I stand to my full height, peering down at her.

"Excuse m-me?"

"I take pleasure in satisfying. Knowing wherever I touch or tease, you would be begging for more. Knowing I made my partner feel something she's never felt before."

Her brows pull together. "I don't understand."

"Your pupils dilated, heart rate increased, breathing slowed. Your mouth went dry at the thought of me kissing you. Of me doing other things to you. Even though I barely touched you, I know that made you feel good."

Zoey clenches her jaw in defiance. "That's not true. You didn't make me feel any of that."

I chuckle, knowing she's such a liar.

Leaning down, I whisper in her ear, "You can tell yourself that lie while you're touching yourself to the thought of me later."

Two hands shove at my chest and I only step back because I wasn't expecting it.

Her face turns into a grimace. "Stanford isn't the tool. You are."

And then she walks out the door.

Chapter Seven

Zoey

My fist is raised and I'm about to knock on the door when it flies open. A red hoodie runs past me in a blur and before I think I shout, "Is Jace home?"

"His room I think," the guy yells before sprinting in the opposite direction.

I wait a couple moments, peering in the house to see if anyone else is home. When the living room remains empty, I step over the threshold, close the door and head up the staircase to my right.

This is a bad idea, right? After storming out of the party last night, I tossed and turned all night. Stupid Jace. He would be so much easier to hate if my body didn't like him so much. I replayed our interaction over and over and every time I came to the same conclusion: that I must've been way more drunk that night than I thought and that's why I thought it was so amazing.

Regardless, he was right. I stuttered like an idiot in front of Leo, but not him. As much as I don't want to admit it, I'm comfortable with Jace. I don't worry about if he thinks I sound weird or if he's embarrassed talking to the fat girl. It sucks because I actually like my body. It's the rest of the world that has a problem with it. Mainly men. Every guy I've ever dated—fine, the two guys I've dated—always made comments about my body. It made me feel like shit.

But Jace isn't like that. So at around three in the morning, I came up with a plan. I'm not entirely sure how good the plan is, especially since I conveniently didn't tell my roommates for fear of them talking me out of it.

Whatever. I'm here now. There's no going back.

There's three levels to Ballentine House and I'm just realizing how big it is. I've never actually been here during the day before. It looks so much bigger without college kids stuffed into every corner. Out of the eight rooms on the third floor, only one door is closed. It was early and I was pretty hungover when I stumbled out of Jace's room the morning after we hooked up, so I can't exactly remember which room is his. I quickly peek in the other rooms before taking a deep breath and knocking on what I'm hoping is Jace's room.

"Jace?" I ask. When he doesn't answer I knock again.

"Jace?" I say a little louder. "Can I talk to you? It's Zo—Little

Griffin."

Still no response. After counting to ten in my head, I reach for the handle and twist.

"Jace? Are you in here? Is this your room? Oh, God. Please be your room," I whisper-yell.

The door creaking open is the only noise in the entire hallway. I look around wondering where everyone else is? Aren't there like a hundred guys living here? Why do I feel like I'm in a horror movie right now? Ignoring my inner voice yelling at me to turn back, I walk in and shut the door behind me. If I remember correctly, Jace is roommates with Conrad. And I have to give Conrad props because his side is immaculate compared to the bomb on the farther end. Conrad's side has a bed that has been made, a dresser with a small television on it and a desk with some homework on top that looks like it's been organized. My eyes then travel around the gigantic mess that should most likely be condemned, to a bed in the corner. Jace is snoring and shirtless, one hand above his head and the other under the sheet that is way too low. Like if he makes a quick movement, I'll see everything.

"Jace?" I try one last time.

He sleeps like the dead. I clap my hands loudly and smile when I'm finally successful. Jace startles awake and the sheet slips. It's like the next few seconds happen in slow motion. I don't close my eyes fast enough and am greeted with little Jace. Wait, that's anatomically wrong. Big Jace. Huge Jace I would say. How is it even possible that he's that big? I thought all men were relatively the same size. I'm now realizing that was another obvious lie from my stupid ex. He just didn't want me to know the truth. That he was waaay below average. My mouth falls open as Big Jace is standing to attention. Oh, God! I need to look away. Why am I not looking away?

Jace scrambles for the sheet, holding it to his groin. "What the—Little Griffin? What are you doing in my room?" He looks down and then back at me. "Did I drink last night?"

My shoulder slump. "Are you such an alcoholic you can't remember when you do and don't drink?"

"Are you such a brat that you can't be nice to someone after you break into their room and wake them up from a peaceful sleep?"

For some unknown reason, my eyes drift down to where he's clutching the blanket. And where it's starting to move.

Jace follows my line of sight then shrugs. "Take a picture, it'll last longer."

"Jace! Put on some clothing or something!"

"It's called morning wood. Every guy gets it."

"Well put it away!" I shriek.

He chuckles to himself before sarcastically saying. "Sure. I'll do that right away."

I look around, unable to talk to him when he's completely naked. Grabbing a pair of basketball shorts I find on the floor, I toss them to him.

"Put these on. And maybe a shirt too."

"Bossy little thing. I like it."

I scrunch my nose in disgust. "Gross."

He stands up and is about to drop the sheet when I quickly turn around.

"So why are you here?"

"Huh?" I squeak, fully aware there is a completely naked man standing only a few feet behind me. A completely naked man whose penis I can now picture in my brain.

Jace clears his throat, "You can turn around now."

"Are you sure? Because if this is some stupid trick—"

"I'm covered. Now why are you in my room, Zoey?"

I slowly turn back around. Once I find Jace's bottom-half covered and him sitting on his bed, I relax.

"And a shirt?" I ask, but he sighs dramatically. "I wanted to talk. I have a ... " My words fade away as I watch him. Thinking about this proposal was one thing, but having to ask him actually seems crazy. He looks so laid-back and calm sitting on his cream sheets. In his room. In his bed. Holy shit! I'm in Jace's room. This was a mistake. This was a bad idea. Why didn't I tell Becks and Corrine my idea? They would've talked me out of it for sure! Well, Becks would. Corrine would probably pay money to see me proposition Jace.

"You know, I-I-I should go. You look like yo-ou need to take care of your," I gesture to the lower half of him that is still standing up straight, "situ-uation."

I quickly turn around and am almost to the door when a still-shirtless Jace runs in front of me. I jump back, nervous his downtown area might invade my space.

"No, no, no. You came here for a reason. And you woke me up from a very, very nice dream, so you might as well tell me."

My eyes are wide as I stare at his chest. How many muscles does he have? Why are they so big? Are they supposed to be that big?

"Hey," Jace grabs my chin with his thumb and forefinger, guiding it up to look at his face, "my eyes are up here."

I roll my eyes and sigh loudly. "It's nothing. It was stu-upid and I shouldn't have come. I'm sorry to have woken you up. Now, can I pl-please leave?"

I'm feeling embarrassed and now I'm stuttering. It's like I'm a masochist or something. An extremely familiar burning sensation is happening behind my eyes and I blink frantically to keep it at bay. I hate that I cry when I'm upset. It makes me look weak and pathetic. Another thing Jace doesn't need to see.

"Zoey?" Jace's finger traces my jaw, his tone oddly soft. "Are you okay?"

I swallow the little bit of pride I had. "I came to ask you to help me, but it was a dumb idea."

His brow furrows. "Help you with what?"

I take a step back and he drops his hand. "I know you think I'm pathetic, but you were the only person I thought I could ask."

"Jesus, Little Griffin. Spit it out."

"I flirted with you the other night. It was easy and I didn't feel uncomfortable or awkward and I didn't stutter." When he smirks, I add, "And I know it's because I don't like you." His smile falters. "Is that supposed to be a compliment?"

"I feel nothing towards you, so I had nothing to lose if I made a total idiot of myself."

"I can't possibly see why you're single when you have such a way with words."

"Exactly! With Leo, I looked like a total goof. I couldn't even ask how he was doing. I freaked out. And instead of having diarrhea of the mouth like I usually do, I had the opposite happen. And I think I need help."

Jace stares blankly at me. "Did you just use the phrase 'diarrhea of the mouth'?"

When I stare blankly at him, he continues. "I still don't know what you're asking of me."

I bite my lip nervously. It's time to rip off the bandaid. Jump into the deep end. "I want you to teach me what guys like. Teach me how to talk and flirt and be someone who can attract a guy like Leo."

His expression doesn't change. He looks confused. Maybe mad? No, that's not it either. It's a solid ten seconds before I snap my fingers in front of his face.

He runs a hand through his messy hair. "Are you asking ... wait. I need a minute."

Jace walks around me, falling down into his computer chair. He leans forward, elbows on knees and head in hands. I know what I just dumped on him, so I allow him a minute to process. I silently count to sixty in my head, the only noise in the room the incessant pounding of my heart. When he still doesn't look up, I can't take it anymore.

"I know it sounds crazy which is why I didn't want to tell you, but you wouldn't let me leave. Can I just go now?" I point to the door when he lifts his head.

Jace finally lifts his head with a huge grin. "Would this make me like your sex guru?"

"So that's a yes I can go?"

Jace stands up and starts pacing. "What exactly would I do?"

"I know this is a dumb idea, you don't have to make me feel worse by making fun of me."

He freezes and looks up at me. "I'm not making fun of you. I'm genuinely asking."

My jaw hits the floor. He's actually considering this? He prompts me again and I stay silent. I never expected to even get this far in the conversation, let alone him want to go along with this ridiculous idea. When I still don't say anything, Jace starts talking.

"You were pretty rough with Leo. Maybe you just need to tune up your social skills. When was the last date you went on?"

Silence.

"Have you ever been on a date?" he continues his questions.

"I'm sorry, are you actually considering saying yes?"

He rubs his hand over his scruff. "Is this the kind of crap that's in those romance novels girls are obsessed with?"

"I have no idea what you're talking about."

"Like you're fake dating me but then are going to discover you're in love with me by the end of the book?"

I narrow my eyes. "Um, I don't think so."

He chuckles low in his chest. "All right, Little Griffin—"

"Don't call me that."

"—But I don't do anything half-ass. You want me to teach you how to be a girlfriend, we're going to do it right."

My voice shakes when I ask, "What does that mean?"

Walking up and stopping inches from me, Jace smiles almost like a predator. "You're my girlfriend. I'm your boyfriend."

"What? Ew. No. Did you not just hear me say I like Leo?"

"Your first lesson. You don't need to say every thought that comes to mind. You could give a guy a complex." Jace taps my nose with his forefinger.

Instinctively, my hand flies out to smack him on the shoulder.

"I meant," he continues, "if you want me to show you the way, I need to see what I'm working with."

"Meaning?"

Jace walks around me and opens his bedroom door. "Meaning, I'll see you tomorrow at seven."

I'm walking down the hall in a daze, feeling like this can't be real life. Did I really just ask my brother's best friend to teach me how to get a guy? Oh, shit. I did.

"Zoey?"

I freeze in place as Kai says my name. And the front door is right there. It's so close.

I was so focused on Jace that I didn't even think of the possibility of running into Kai. In the place he lives. God, I really am an idiot.

"Morning," I turn around with a bright smile on my face.

"What are you doing here?" he asks between sips of coffee from a Looney Toon mug.

I hold up my wrist. "Bracelet. I lost my," I clear my throat to hide my stutter, "bracelet last night. Thought I would come look for it."

Bracelet? Why would I choose that lie? I don't even wear jewelry.

"Oh. I didn't think you wore jewelry."

Of course he would know that. Well, there's no way I'm admitting to being up in Jace's room only a few seconds ago. I'd rather just run for the door and pray Kai doesn't come after me.

Luckily, Kai just shrugs. "I'll tell the guys to keep an eye out. What's it look like?"

"What's it look like?" I pause, feeling my stutter. "That is a great question. It's—"

Don't stutter. He'll know something is up. Don't stutter!

"Found it."

Mine and Kai's eyes fly to the stairs to see Jace coming down, holding a blue bracelet in his hand.

He holds it out and it takes me a moment to move.

"I picked it up last night outside. If I knew it was yours, I would've given it to Kai."

"Yes. That is mine."

I take it quickly, but hide it behind my back. Because whoever this bracelet belongs to has way skinnier wrists then I do.

"Okay then. B-bye."

I finally can breathe normally once I'm at least a block away from Ballentine.

Chapter Eight

Zoey

I know Jace is going to say something about my outfit. He said he wanted to take me out, so I put on the only nice dress I have. My shoulder's slump as I stare at my reflection. My mom meant well when she bought it for me. Too bad it's a size too big, resembles a potato sack and was non-refundable.

"That's not seriously what you wear on a date, is it?" Jace asks when I open the door.

"What are you doing here?"

Jace looks at his wrist ... that has no watch. "It's seven. I told you I'd pick you up at seven."

I shake my head. "No, you said you'd see me at seven. I assumed I was just meeting you at your place."

"Then you're late." Jace pushes past me to get in my dorm. "Now go put on clothes you'd wear on a real date."

"But this isn't a real date."

His shoulders slump and he sighs dramatically. "I know this isn't a real date. You know this isn't a real date. What this is, is a practice date. I am going to be treating you the way I would treat a girl I actually want to date—"

"Rude."

"—And you are going to be acting like I'm the guy you're trying to get into your bed."

"Gross."

Jace rubs a hand down his face. "Listen KitKat, can we just take a break because you're exhausting me."

You know that unamused emoji with the line for both eyes and the mouth? That's my face right now.

"Oh, come on! That was funny," he laughs.

Walking past me, Jace heads into my room with purpose.

"You're not allowed in there!"

He ignores me and starts looking through my closet.

"Do you own any clothes that were made in the last decade?"

I push him out of my closet. "Fine. I'll change. But get out of my room while I do it."

"Are you sure? This could be the perfect opportunity."

"For what?"

"You said you're doing all this to get Leo to notice you. Why don't we take a look under the hood and make sure everything's good?"

Grabbing the pillow off my bed, I whack him over the head before pushing him out the door.

Jace

Thinking back, I probably could've been a tad nicer when Zoey opened the door. In all honesty, she could wear a brown potato sack and she would look amazing. But that's not why she asked for my help. And if she wore that baggy dress on a date, I don't think there would be a second.

When she opens the door ten minutes later, she's wearing dark blue jeans that look painted on, a black tee with a low V-neck giving just a glimpse of her incredible cleavage and black heeled boots. I wonder if she wants me to give her lessons in the bedroom too? Would she wear those boots and nothing else for me?

Dammit, Jace! Focus. This is not about you and your dick's need to be inside Zoey.

"How's this?" she asks sarcastically while doing a twirl.

I start to slow clap before she rolls her eyes and walks past me.

Once we're out in the hallway, I place my hand on her lower back and feel her slight shiver. I'm barely even touching her.

"What do you think you're doing?" she asks, stopping and taking a step away.

I chuckle, wrapping my hand around her and guiding her to the elevator. "We're supposed to be going on a date. If you were someone I was interested in, I'd start the night with small touches. First, your lower back. Next up would be holding your hand on the way to dinner."

"And what would happen after that?"

Am I delusional or did that sound a tad breathy?

Leaning down so my lips brush her ear, I whisper, "That would depend on how dinner goes."

Flirting with Zoey is way too easy. This entire situation is a bad idea. But I'm not the least bit sorry.

Zoey's eyebrows shoot up in surprise when I open her car door for her. Jesus, what kind of dicks had she dated? Wanting her to enjoy this "date," I let her pick the music and of course she picks fucking

Taylor Swift.

"Of course you would pick Taylor Swift. Are you one of her followers? What are they called? Swifters?"

"You mean 'Swifties'?" Zoey corrects me.

"I bet you like pumpkin spiced whatever Starbucks sells too, huh?"

"Do you judge all your dates like this?"

"Just the cute ones."

She'll never admit it, but Zoey likes our back-and-forth banter. The evidence is in the smile she's currently trying to hide behind her hand. The ride is quiet as I rest my hand on her knee. I've never sat in comfortable silence with a chick before; it's kind of nice. Out of the corner of my eye, I see her hand jerk like she wants to push me away, but she doesn't. I bite the inside of my cheek to hide my smile.

When we pull into the parking lot of a restaurant on the outskirts of town, I say, "I figured you'd want to do this somewhere we wouldn't run into Kai."

"Thanks. That's actually really thoughtful of you."

My head jerks back in surprise. "Actually? Psh, I'm always thoughtful."

I help her out of the car and hold her hand all the way to the corner booth we're sat at. She grabs a menu and starts perusing, but like the creep I am, I can't stop staring at her.

Her eyes look up, catching me. "Why are you staring at me?"

"I can't figure you out."

"Most guys can't," she says returning to the menu, "that's probably why I'm chronically single."

Folding my hands, I lean closer to her. "Why did you really want to do this? And why pick me of all people?"

She runs her hand through her hair and exhales sharply. "I told you. Flirting with you was surprisingly easy and it's wasn't with Leo—"

"That should probably tell you something," I interrupt.

"—And I have never been good at dating. I've never even had a serious boyfriend before. I'm not good at this kind of stuff and I just thought maybe I needed a little help. That's all."

"Oh, Jelly Bean."

Her face pinches together. "No. You are not calling me Jelly Bean. Pick a new pet name."

I can't help laughing. She's cute and funny. What the fuck is wrong with Leo that he doesn't see that?

"So, no serious relationship. Have you dated before?"

She exhales sharply. "Do we really have to talk about this?"

"Newsflash, popsicle. People talk about themselves on dates. They share details of their lives with the other person in hopes of getting closer to them."

Rolling her eyes, she sets her menu aside. "My last few dates was with a guy named Tommy—"

"You dated one of the Rugrats?" I tease.

She stares blankly at me like she has no idea what I'm talking about.

Once I stop laughing, she continues. "As I was saying before I was so rudely interrupted, Tommy and I didn't end very well. And I haven't had the desire to go out with anyone since. That was a few years ago."

"Years?" I almost shout. Shit, I didn't think it had been that long. "Sorry. What happened?"

My foot accidentally bumps hers under the table, but she doesn't move away.

Zoey looks down at her lap. "It was like our fourth date and I thought it was going well. But then I went to the bathroom and came back to an empty table and a $75 tab."

"The fuck?"

She shrugs. "I just had to wash my hands and when I came back, I saw him running out the door. Like actually running. It was humiliating."

The silence is heavy. She refuses to meet my stare and my knuckles are white as I grip the leather seat under me. I wonder if pressing would get me Tommy's last name. And maybe his address. Kidding. Kind of. Instead of doing something a crazy person would do, I reach across the table, my fingers brushing over hers.

"That's really shitty. I'm so sorry. But any dude like that isn't worth a millisecond of your time."

She finally looks up at me as I rub my thumb back and forth over her knuckles. Her skin is so soft, but I would definitely freak her out if I told her that.

Her eyes are shiny with unshed tears and she clears her throat before saying, "Thank you for that. I know I'm not the best with guys, but I don't think I'm that bad."

I chuckle and hold eye contact. "You definitely aren't. And I'm not going anywhere."

Once we place our orders, the comfortable silence is back. I really don't mind it.

"What's your favorite sport?"

I'm taking a drink of my water and stop mid-sip. "Seriously?"

She giggles nervously. "I mean like to watch? Do you like other sports or is your whole life just hockey?"

"Uh, pretty much just hockey. My dad coaches for our high school back home, so I was born into this life."

"Not a bad life to have. Parties every weekend. Girls every weekend."

Is she fishing?

"Games and practices every weekend. Five AM wake calls every weekend." She looks at me like she's waiting for me to comment on the girls. This time I decide to put her out of her misery. "And there's only girls every weekend if you're interested."

Zoey bites her bottom lip, letting the silence hang between us. "And you're not interested?"

I'm not stupid. I know my reputation. But rumors are a bitch and not even 40% of the girls who claim they've slept with me ever entered my bed. A smile spreads across my face and I lick my lips. Is Zoey Griffin ... jealous?

"Depends on the person."

Zoey

Jace once again helps me out of the car and I find it rather sweet.

Until he doesn't move and I'm trapped between the car door and him, forced to look up.

"I had fun tonight," he says low enough so only I can hear.

"Um, yeah. Me too. Dinner was really good." I shake my head when I realize what I just said. He's trying to be all hot and heavy and I tell him 'dinner was really good'? I may need more help than just a pretend date.

His fingers tug on the hem of my shirt. "I like this. Looks really good on you."

"It was on the clearance rack at Target."

The clearance rack at Target?! What is wrong with me?

Jace slides his hand around my back, pulling me into him. When said hand slides down to rest on my ass, I gasp. Our lips are so close I would barely have to move to have them on mine. My breathing slows and I struggle to swallow. This is what he'd do if we were on an actual date. This is all pretend. This isn't real. None of it is real. He's so close, I can smell his — wait, did he put cologne on for our fake date? Nope, I'm not going to read into that. However, I can't help melting when the hand currently not on my ass comes up to cup my face. Featherlight touches skim my jaw, just before his thumb brushes along my bottom lip. My eyes flutter shut all on their own.

"And this is where I would give you the best goodnight kiss you've ever had. A kiss so good, you'd have to touch yourself just to relieve the ache. But when that wouldn't work, you'd come crawling on your hands and knees to me. Begging me to make it all better. And I would."

I didn't realize Jace was practically holding me up until he backs away and I wobble on my feet, blinking rapidly because what the hell just happened? Did I really think Jace was going to kiss me?

"Now, my little butterfinger, if anyone ever ends a date with you and you don't instantly have the desire to get off at the thought of them. I promise you, they aren't the right one."

"Classy," I say, straightening my t-shirt and walking away from the car.

Jace shrugs. "It's the truth. You may be able to have good conversation, but if there isn't that spark, it's a lost cause.

"Not everything has to be about sex," I inform.

"Since you're saying that, I'm going to go out on a limb and guess that you've never had really great sex. You know, I could add that to the lesson plan?"

I cringe and smack his chest. "I'm not a prostitute."

Jace laughs like I'm the most ridiculous person he's ever met. "Goodnight, my Milky Way."

When I get home, Becks and Corrine are in the middle of watching some movie. I still haven't told them about my experiment with Jace, so I pretend to be on the phone and sneak off to my room. Once I'm completely alone, Jace's words replay in my mind over and over again.

"And this is where I would give you the best goodnight kiss you've ever had. A kiss so good, you'd have to touch yourself just to relieve the ache. But when that wouldn't work, you'd come crawling on your hands and knees to me. Begging me to make it all better. And I would."

And that's the first time I touch myself to the thought of Jace Bennett.

Chapter Nine

Zoey

I'm about to resort to getting down on my knees as I beg. "Please. Please. Please. Please."

"Digging in the dirt really isn't my thing," Beck shrugs unapologetically.

"You won't be! They'll probably have us picking up litter or power washing the sidewalk."

Becks' expression is almost impossible to read. I swear, she has the best poker face.

I signed up for the Good Neighbor Program because I had some free time and wanted to give back. But then I found out the Head Coordinator is my roommate from Freshman year. I'm not sure if she still hates me, but Regina always hated the fact that I wasn't a clean freak like her. Like I'm sorry I forgot to take my old milk out of the mini fridge. It really wasn't that big of a deal. Plus, the smell went away eventually.

If begging won't work, maybe bartering will. "I'll buy you coffee."

Her arms are crossed over her chest as she slowly blinks.

"All week? I'll buy you coffee all week?"

Becks rolls her eyes before grabbing her wallet off the side table. "No dirt."

"No dirt!" I assure her.

With a smile I know is fake, Regina holds up two shovels for Becks and me. "You two can start digging up all the weeds. The township wants this lot ready for the playground soon."

I look around at the empty lot the Good Neighbor members are standing in. It's the future site for an accessible park and needs a lot of work. Weeds make up most of the lawn, graffiti needs scrubbed off benches and there's trash everywhere.

"You better get started," Regina continues, "and make sure to clean up after yourself."

I roll my eyes at Regina, but then register Becks' glare from beside me. I turn my head slowly to her, hoping she isn't too mad.

"It's for a good cause," I plead.

"You told me no dirt! I just got my nails done."

I grab a pair of gardening gloves from one of the bins of tools other volunteers brought and hold them up. With her eyes narrowed, Becks dramatically sighs as she takes them from my hands. "You're lucky I love you."

I grab a trash bag and another pair of gloves for me and get to work. Some of the weeds are really stuck in there and when I go to pull one out, I lose my grip and fall back on my ass. Becks laughs as she easily removes her weeds.

"So, I heard you went out with Jace Bennett."

I freeze, wondering if I don't move, maybe she won't see me.

"And then I heard some ... noises coming from your room last night. Care to comment?"

Avoiding eye contact, I mumble, "Nope. Not really."

I jump to my feet and quickly head to a different section. I start working faster because I cannot afford to think about last night. Or what I did after Jace walked me to the door. I definitely won't think about how the steam from the shower surrounded me as my hand slid down my soft belly. How my eyes fluttered shut as my finger grazed my clit. And how with every thrust of my fingers, I replayed Jace's words over and over again. Nope. Definitely won't think about that.

Becks' laughter follows me. "You really don't want to talk about how you went on a date with your brother's best friend?"

"Step," I correct her. I bend down and continue cleaning the lawn when I notice Becks sitting there. Not doing anything. Just staring me down. "It's not going to work." I try to focus, but it's like her stare is drilling a hole through me. I look away from her, but can feel every thought she's probably having. How I'm an open book and tell her everything. How I'm acting cagey even though there's no reason for me to be.

"So-"

"We're just friends." The words spill out of my mouth at lightning speed. Her raised eyebrow tells me she knows something is up, so I take a deep breath and repeat myself, but this time slowly. "We found that we have things in common and are friends."

"Friends?"

I nod.

"With Jace?"

"Y-yes."

I wince at my nervous stutter and see the corner of Becks' lips tug up in a smile, knowing that she caught it too. That's the last we talk of Jace. I probably could tell Becks, but I don't want her to judge me. I guess she wouldn't, but if Corrine found out, she definitely would. As surly as she is, Becks has this way about her that everyone likes. Me and my stutter? Not so much. We spend the next hour weeding and are sore as hell by the time Becks and I stumble home.

Jace

When Zoey asked me to help her, I thought it was a joke. But then I heard her stutter. Zoey has never had a stutter around me before. So I said yes, but then my stupid ass almost kissed her. My best friend's step-sister was looking up at me like she wanted me to do way more than just kiss her. And fuck, did I want to. I haven't thought about her like that since the move-in party. I can still remember what she felt like as she rode me. Who cares if we were both wearing clothes. It was one of the hottest moments of my life.

I should do the responsible thing and stay far, far away from her. Instead, I sent her a text that I was stopping over after practice to de-brief. I stripped out of my gear, jumped in the shower and was the first one out of the arena.

My fist rasps on their dorm door and I wait. And wait. The faint sounds of whispers drifting from their room make me chuckle. I lean my ear closer to try and hear what they're saying.

"Just answer the door!"

"Is it Jace? Why is he here? What aren't you telling us Zoey?"

"Nothing! He's just a friend."

"I'm going to answer the door."

"No, I will. Stop being so weird."

When the doorknob turns, I jump back. Zoey's smile is shaken at best and it takes all my control not to laugh.

After a few moments of just staring at each other, I ask, "Can I come in?"

She blinks like she was day-dreaming and nods. "Yeah. Of c-course."

She's stuttering again. Interesting.

"T-th-" Zoey clears her throat. "These are my roommates. We can talk in my bedroom."

I go to wave at them when Zoey grabs my hand and drags me through the open doorway to my left, slamming the door behind us.

I lean back against the door, taking her room in as she frantically grabs clothes off the ground. It's a typical dorm room: twin bed, dresser and desk covered in thick textbooks. Nothing out of the ordinary.

"So, you, um, you want-ted to talk?"

"Why are you doing that?"

Her brow furrows. "Doing what?"

"Stuttering." No point beating around the bush. "You don't stutter in front of me."

Zoey runs a shaky hand through her hair. "I wasn't ..."

She lets her sentence fade away, knowing that she can't talk her way out of this.

I take two steps closer, relishing in the fact that she stands her ground. "I don't want to make you nervous. That's the whole point of this, isn't it? Just take a deep breath."

I put my hands on her biceps and rub up and down. "Breathe in and out."

She slowly inhales through her nose.

"That's good. Now exhale through your mouth," I say quietly. Zoey does as I say and my next words slip out before I can stop myself. "Good girl."

Clearing my throat, I walk over to her bed, and fall down before kicking off my shoes. "Now, can we talk about what an amazing boyfriend I am?"

Within seconds, I feel her walls crumble and the sassy, take-no-shit Zoey is back.

She rolls her eyes, "Were you born as an insufferable prick, or do you just come by it naturally?"

I look down my body as I spread my arms, "I'm all natural, banana bread."

Zoey's fighting a smile as she walks over to the bed to join me.

"Give me that," she says as she grabs the pillow from under my arm and places it in front of her stomach. "You wanted to talk?"

I grab the pillow from her and toss it out of reach. "I thought we could talk about our date."

"That was rude."

She goes to stand when I practically jump on top of her.

"Jace! Get off me, you neanderthal! What are you doing?"

"I will get off you only if you promise not to pick up that pillow again."

"What?" Zoey's hips buck underneath me and I have to give little Jace the talk that this is not the time or the place. "Your gigantic weight is crushing me!"

"That's not even remotely true."

She's squirming beneath me and I'll give it to her, she's got some strength behind her. "Promise me you won't pick the pillow back up."

Zoey finally stops fighting my hold, blowing a lock of hair out of her face. "Why does it matter if I pick it up or not?"

"Because you're using it to hide from me. And I don't want you to ever think you have to hide from me. Do you understand?"

Zoey's breathing begins slowing down, but she still doesn't answer me. I lean down closer to her, running my nose along hers like I did the night of our date. "I asked you a question and when I ask a question, I expect an answer."

"Y-Yes. I understand," she pants.

Satisfied, I crawl off of her. Zoey remains frozen until I nudge her legs with my foot. She sits up, running a hand through her disheveled hair before turning her attention back to me. "Okay. So, about the, um, the date."

I can't help my smile. "Let's just get right into it. You suck at dating."

Zoey's mouth drops open and before I know it, she's jumped up, grabbed the pillow off the ground and smacked me across the face with it.

"You promised!"

"That was before you were a dick," she taunts.

"Look," I place my hands up in defense, "it's not your fault. From what I saw, it seems like you've been taken out by some losers. Opening of car doors and picking you up at your front door? Things like that are things men should be doing for you no matter what."

She shrugs, but doesn't meet my eyes.

"It's kind of unspoken rules of being a gentleman."

"A word I never associated with you," she mutters.

I chuckle to myself before looking over at her. "What did you just say?"

"Nothing," she shakes her head, trying to hide her smile.

"No, I definitely heard you say something," I say as I crawl over to her side of the bed.

Zoey starts to back up, but I grab her calf and drag her back down.

"Jace, don't!" she shouts, just as I start tickling her ribs.

"Don't what? I can't hear you."

"Stop! I can't breathe!" she laughs.

I let up when tears start falling down her cheeks and collapse on the bed next to her. We both are laughing so hard, we can't catch our breath. I turn towards her when the air around us suddenly turns serious. Without thinking, my hand comes up and I wipe away a lone tear with my thumb.

"You should always be treated like a princess," I tell her, continuing our conversation from before, "and in turn you should treat your man like a prince. And I don't mean buying big and expensive gifts or anything like that. Little gestures go a long way."

I tuck a strand of hair behind her ear. "It might not seem like it, but all the little things women like, so do men."

Her brows pull together in confusion. "What do you mean?"

"Being little spoon, holding hands even if it's just from the driveway to your house, texts throughout the day to let them know they're on your mind. Relationships and sex don't have to be complicated. People make them complicated."

"You make it all sound so easy." With us being so close, Zoey's fingers are mindlessly playing with the neckline of my shirt. I don't think she consciously knows what she's doing and I'm not bringing attention to it.

"If there's anything our date made me realize is that you need to be wined and dined by a real man sometime."

Zoey's eyes are now closed, but she still softly laughs. "Sometime."

And when Zoey falls asleep, I don't leave right away like I should. I stay for a little longer because I don't know if we'll ever have another moment like this again.

Chapter Ten

Zoey

Becks, Corrine and I are sitting in our common room, watching reruns on TV. Personally, I have no motivation to do anything that involves getting off the couch.

"I'm so bored," Corrine whines, tossing her head back dramatically.

"We could go get some food?" Becks offers.

"Pass," I say. "I don't really want to move."

"What about going for a walk in town? It's nice out," Becks tries again.

"You really want to leave this room, huh?" Corrine teases.

Our boredom continues as we stare at the same blank four walls we still have not decorated. Maybe we should hang up some pictures or something? It does look kind of depressing in here.

Corrine starts to laugh to herself.

"What's so funny?" I ask.

"Remember when the girl's volleyball team pranked that one guy from the rowing team?" she asks Becks.

Becks' shoulders start to shake. "That shit was funny."

"Wait, what did they do?" Even though Corrine and Becks went to high school together, they try hard to keep me from being left out of any inside jokes they have.

"Nothing bad. They just told a bunch of people he was doing an art project about how much trash we use in a day."

My brows pull together. "I don't get it."

"They only let it go on for like a day or two," Beck adds, "but people started leaving bags of trash in front of his locker to help. That section of the hallway reeked."

"That's so mean," I say, but can't hold back my own laughter.

Becks shakes her head. "I promise, it wasn't. Our school was kind of small, so the entire senior class was basically pranking each other all year long. Nothing too harmful, though. The teachers hated it, but it was awesome."

"You know," Corrine lets her words hang in the air before turning to me. "We could always prank a house full of guys. Ones that just happen to live right off campus."

Realization sets in and I immediately start shaking my head. I haven't told them anything about Jace, but they clearly have eyes and aren't stupid.

"No. Jace and I are j-just friends."

Dammit, you stupid stutter!

"Oh, come on! We won't do anything bad. I actually have a few good ideas." Corrine falls to her knees in front of me.

Becks quickly joins her.

"Don't be a party pooper," she teases.

I scoff. "Take that back."

"Every party always has a pooper and this time it's you," Corrine sing-songs.

"Shut up," I laugh, pushing them away so I can stand up.

Jumping up, Beck grabs my shoulders. "Do you not want to because you're hiding something from us?"

"Yeah," Corrine sidles up next to her. "Are you hiding something from us? Something like a guy with an 8-pack and an 8-inch d—"

"Oh my God! Stop talking," I shout, quickly covering her mouth. "There is nothing going on with me and Jace."

She pulls my hand away from her mouth and asks, "Who said I was talking about Jace?"

And that's how we end up at Walmart buying all the supplies needed.

Jace

"I'm not sure if you all were practicing for a hockey game or Disney On Ice out there, but it was pathetic. Sloppy passes, shitty stick handling and Bennett, what the hell was up with you? Was it not clear that you were left wing? I apologize then. I just assumed you knew what fucking position you were. Everyone go home and get out of my sight."

It's like the entire locker room finally starts breathing again the second Coach walks out the door.

"What the hell is up Coach's ass?" Beaver asks, but in a quieter tone. The entire team might look big and tough, but Coach could probably kill us all with a paperclip. Instead of college, he joined the Army and I'd put money down that he knows some obscure ways to torture people who piss him off.

"Can you really blame him? We played like shit out there," Kai says. Everyone who was chirping a second ago calms down.

"It was just practice," one of the underclassmen chimes in.

"Yeah. And then it turns into just one game and then just one season and then we're all hosed. Let's all get cleaned up and get some rest. We obviously need it."

The big, bad captain has spoken.

I walk up to Kai nudging his shoulder with mine. "Not all of us are trying for the NHL, man. Lighten up on the kid."

Kai exhales sharply. "Facts are, Coach was right. We need to stop fucking around out there."

I nod, rubbing the back of my neck. "You're right. But don't take whatever weird shit is going on with you out on the rookies."

Back in the summer, Kai met this girl. And she turned his fucking world upside down. I have no clue who she is, but I'm not really in a position to judge.

Once we're all showered and the locker room is cleaned up, Kai, myself, and the rest of the guys from Ballentine head home. The walk is fucking miserable and my legs want to give out. Jesus, I need to get back to the gym. I've been taking some "me" time and it's gotten way outta hand. I'm walking behind the other guys and bump into them when they come to a sudden halt.

"What's going on?" I ask.

Moving around them, I see the last thing I ever expected to. The entire front lawn of Ballentine House is covered with flamingos. Big and small plastic pink flamingos.

"What the ..."

Kai walks up to a sign attached to a wooden post and chuckles.

"What's it say?" I ask, walking up next to him.

To the boys of Ballentine. The war has begun.

"What war?" someone asks from behind.

I don't answer though, I just smile. Because I know exactly who's writing this is. I grab my phone out of my pocket and take a picture of the sign.

J: *pic* You sure you want to start this?

Z: Bring it on

Chapter Eleven

Jace

I go to open the door to my room, but stop after a few inches.

"What the - Conrad! Open up, man."

"Sorry. Hold on."

After a few seconds, the door swings open and when I walk in I see why it was blocked. There are moving boxes everywhere.

"I know I smell sometimes, but I'm not that bad of a roommate," I joke.

Conrad forces a laugh, "I'm not going anywhere. It's actually the rest of my stuff."

"What stuff?"

He scrubs a hand down his face. "From home. I, um, I'm not going back."

Tossing my backpack on the ground, I collapse on my bed. "Your parents kicked you out?"

A slight nod is all I get.

"Fuck," I breathe.

"Yeah. Look, I know I should've asked you before I brought all my shit here, but—"

"Ask me what? It's your room too. Of course you can bring the rest of your stuff here. As for where it's going to go, that's a whole other conversation."

Conrad smiles tightly in thanks.

I reach him in a few strides and wrap my arms around him.

Conrad chuckles, "I'm fine. Really."

"Just shut up and hug me back. Don't make this weird."

Conrad stiffly wraps his arms around me and just as we're about to break apart, Caleb and Buzz bust through the door.

"Well, shit. What did we interrupt?"

"So much for not making it awkward," Conrad mutters.

After a few hours, Conrad, Caleb, Buzz and myself find a place for most of Conrad's stuff. There were a few boxes he refused to let us near which I'll be sure not to forget about. A bunch of the guys are now downstairs watching some baseball game. I join them, but end up scrolling through my phone most of the game. And then somehow I end up on mine and Zoey's texting thread. The fiery redhead flashes through my mind and it's only when my thumb is hovering over the send button that I realize I typed out a message to her.

J: What are you up to?

What the hell? Delete! Delete! Delete! I toss my phone on my lap and scrub a hand down my face. Not even something sexual like 'What are you wearing?' What do I care what she's up to? It's not like we're friends or something.

Beaver bumps my shoulder with his, "You good?"

I nod. "Yeah. Why wouldn't I be?"

He shrugs it off. And as I stare down at my phone's blank screen, the only thing going through my mind is that I am totally fucked.

Zoey

"Where's Corrine?" I ask Becks as we sit down. We laid out a blanket on the lawn near the science building. It's sunny and warm and we're trying to soak it all up before the weather turns to cold rain.

"Meeting for some class project."

I make a gagging noise. "I swear the only thing class projects teach me is that I can only rely on myself."

Becks giggles. "Dark. I like it."

I close my eyes, trying to tune out the sound of noisy college kids. My body slowly begins feeling lighter and I'm about to drift off to sleep when Becks' hand gently smacks my arm.

"Why'd you hit me?" I complain.

"I forgot to tell you. I met someone."

My eyes shoot open and I sit up. "What? Who? When?"

She giggles and has the biggest smile on her face. "His name is Trent and I ran into him at work one day. Like physically. I was carrying a tray of milkshakes and he got up from his table quickly. It was a mess."

"Sounds like it." Holy crap, is Becks blushing?

"He was so nice. He helped me clean it up and then offered to pay to have my uniform dry-cleaned."

"Becks! He sounds so sweet. Have you guys gone out yet?"

"Not yet. We were—"

Her sentence is cut off by her ringtone. It's one of Miley Cyrus's new songs. She always picks a song she likes for her ringtone so when telemarketers call her, we have an impromptu dance party. This time I don't think that's going to happen.

"Answer it," I whisper-yell.

She jumps up and walks away before answering and I lay back down.

I haven't known Becks for a long time, but I know she hasn't had the easiest life. Seeing her smile like that warms my heart.

I swear, Becks just doesn't want me to take a nap because the next time I feel like I'm about to fall asleep, a shadow falls over me.

"I thought you were on the phone. What happened?" I ask, but then open my eyes.

It's not Becks looking down at me. It's Jace.

Before I can even ask what he's doing here, Jace nudges my leg with his foot. "Move over, funnel cake."

"What is it with you and the weird nicknames?" I ask as I scooch over.

Jace just shrugs. "Why are you sleeping by yourself on the lawn? It's kind of weird if you ask me."

"Well, it's a good thing no one did. And I'm not alone." I gesture over to where Becks mindlessly walks back and forth. "Becks is on the phone. I was just trying to relax for a little. Thanks for ruining it."

"Don't act like you aren't happy to see me," he says with a wink.

"Why are you never in classes? Every time I see you on campus, you never even have a backpack with you."

Jace chuckles, closing his eyes as he drops his head back to get some sun. "I have a lot of early mornings. Classes at odd times."

I run a hand through my hair as I glance over at him. "I don't think I even know your major."

"Is that you asking?"

I shrug, weirdly curious. "I guess so."

"I'm majoring in Veterinary Technology."

I'm not sure what I thought he would say, but it wasn't that.

"You want to work with animals?"

Opening one eye, he peaks over at me. When he doesn't say anything, I ask, "Why are you looking at me like that?"

"I was waiting for the "You would fit in perfectly" joke."

Jace's normal smirk is nowhere in sight. He looks almost sad. As if that joke bothers him more than he wants to admit.

I fake laugh. "I don't know. You might fit in with the cuddly cats."

I teasingly pinch his cheek and he sits up straight, shaking me off. But I smile when I get him to laugh.

Comfortable silence takes over and it's the exact moment I notice a guy carrying a plastic pink flamingo across campus. Is that ...?

"Yes," Jace answers, reading my mind.

"Yes, what?"

"We didn't clean up the flamingos because practice was a bitch. When we woke up a few of them had been stolen. I've already seen a few placed around campus."

Freaking genius. I love college.

Out of the corner of my eye, I see Jace smile. He totally thought our prank was amazing.

As we people-watch, I feel a slight brush against my pinky finger. Jace slowly moves his finger back and forth causing goose bumps to pepper my skin.

"What are you up to later? Ready for your next lesson?"

"You know, some people actually have to work."

Jace's brows pull together. "I didn't know you had a job. Where do you work?"

"Have you ever been out past the edge of town? It's that little gym off Crest."

Jace sits up a little straighter, his hand moving away from mine. "Out past the stadium?"

"Yep." I nod.

He runs a hand through his hair as he stares off into space. When he doesn't say anything, I continue talking.

"I worked there all summer. To accommodate my classes, they have me on the closing shift."

"And you work there voluntarily?" His tone is clipped and judgmental.

My head jerks back in surprise. "Uh, what are you talking about? It's not a bad place to work."

"The place might be, but the area isn't. You can't work there."

"Is that a demand?" I tease, trying to lighten the mood because there is no way he is serious.

Jace turns to face me head on. "Zoey, I'm serious."

Wait, did he just use my real name?

"Not only is that area littered with drugs and shit, but it's a good walk from campus."

"Jace," I sigh heavily. I'm so sick of having this discussion. First with my step-dad, then with Kai and now Jace? "It's really not as bad as you're making it seem."

"Zo—"

"No," I interrupt. "It's my decision where I want to work and I like North Side. It's a nice gym and the owners have been beyond amazing with working around my school schedule."

"One day you're gonna be put in a shitty situation because you work at that hell hole." He shakes his head as he brushes some dirt off his pants. "No, I'm not letting you work there."

"What?" I start laughing out loud. Is he joking? "Did you say you're not *letting* me work there?"

Jace scrubs a hand down his face. "That's not what I meant."

"So what did you mean then? Because the last I checked, you're not my dad, not my brother and certainly not my boyfriend. So what the hell gives you the right to think you can *let* me do anything?"

Jace and I are still in an unwarranted staring contest when Becks comes bouncing back over. I'm glad at least one of us had a good conversation.

"What's going on?" she carefully asks.

"Nothing," Jace says before standing up and replacing his scowl with his typical smirk. "I'll catch you guys around."

Becks waves goodbye, but I don't. How dare he think he can talk to me like that. We've been friends for all of ten minutes and now he thinks he can tell me what to do?

"Are you okay?" Becks asks as she places a hand on my shoulder.

I nod, turning around to see Jace approach Kai and tackle him from behind. The two walk away laughing while my blood continues to boil.

Chapter Twelve

Zoey

I'm currently studying at Oister while eating lunch when Kai approaches me wearing his Royals captain shirt.

I gasp dramatically and clutch my chest. "Oh, wow! The big and important hockey captain has graced me with his presence. What ever have I done to deserve such an honor?"

Kai sits down opposite me, tossing his sandwich on the table. "Flamingos? Really?"

I can't help but laugh.

"Don't give me that stern look. I know you thought it was funny."

Kai's exterior has always been hard. But I know he's a big softie inside. I also know he found it funny because Jace told me. Kai shakes his head and takes a bite out of his sandwich to hide his smile.

"What's been going on with you?"

"Coach has been crazy lately. Practices have run over and the rookies don't know the difference between their left and right. I do think we have a new grinder on the team, so that's something?"

I shake my head. "I don't know why I talk to you about hockey. It's like you're speaking a different language?"

"What did I say?" he asks through a mouthful of food.

My phone chimes next to me and I smile as I quickly silence it. There's only a handful of people I text and I'm sitting across from one of them. Ever since Jace and I exchanged numbers, I get paranoid that Kai is going to see his name on my phone and freak out. Not that he has any reason to. All we did was go on one fake date and he gave me some pointers. Nothing bad at all. But I still don't want Kai to know. It doesn't matter because I don't want to talk to the asshat anyways.

When I look up, Kai is staring at my phone.

"You can answer that."

I shrug. "If it's an emergency, they'll leave a message."

Avoiding his eye contact, I try to continue my homework. I know he's still looking at me.

"So," he clears his throat, "I've seen you and Jace hanging out more. You guys friends?"

I force myself to take a deep breath so I don't stutter. Nothing is happening between Jace and I anyways. So it doesn't matter.

"Friends?" Calm down, stupid pulse. "I mean, it's a small school. We've just been running into each other a lot lately."

Kai nods slowly like he doesn't believe a word I'm saying. "You seemed annoyed."

"When?"

"The other day. When I saw you and Jace on the lawn. He do something to piss you off?"

When he was giving me shit about having a job? Yeah, he was pissing me off.

"No. I wasn't mad."

"What were you two talking about then?"

"Work." I'm trying to keep my answers short and concise, hoping Kai will get the hint and drop it.

"And what about work?"

"Um, he just didn't like that I worked at North Side."

"Because it's a shit hole." Kai doesn't even finish chewing the bite of food he has before diving back into this fun topic. "I told you, I can find you another job. Somewhere on campus."

I sigh, partly because I'm sick of having this conversation but also thankful we're not talking about Jace anymore. "Believe it or not, I actually like working there. My coworkers are awesome and the clientele is great. Also, you're never going to find a girlfriend if you can't learn to chew with your mouth closed."

"I also leave the toilet seat up after I pee. And who says I don't have a girlfriend?"

I lean forward, immediately wanting to know every detail. "Do you really? What's her name?"

Kai just shakes his head and continues eating. "Nice try. But all I'm saying is don't come crying to me when North Side gets attacked by a nuclear bomb or something."

I roll my eyes. "Laying it on a little thick today, huh?"

We both chuckle, but stop when Caleb appears.

"Masterson," they bump knuckles. "I'm heading to the gym soon and need a spotter."

"Aw. Are you two arranging a little date? How cute."

Kai flips me off, making me laugh. Then he cleans up his food and he and Caleb disappear while I'm left to think about why Kai was so concerned about Jace. Jace is just helping me out to be nice, but I can't even begin to imagine how that conversation would go with Kai. We just need to be more careful in the future.

Jace

With Kai and a bunch of the other guys busy, I decide it's time for Zoey's next lesson. And for her to stop being ridiculous. This is my third call in the past two days and I don't call people. Why would I when texting is such a better form of communication? I swear to God, if she lets this go to voicemail again, I'm going to march over to her dorm and—"

"What do you want?" Fuck, she's still pissed.

"It's time for your next assignment. We're going out tonight."

"Oh, are you *letting* me go out?"

I blow out a breath, my entire body sagging. I knew I screwed up the other day on the lawn, but she's delusional. There's a reason people stay inside the town's limits. She's being stubborn and hardheaded and it's gonna get her in trouble.

"I shouldn't have said that," I admit, tucking my tail between my legs. "I'm sorry. It came out wrong."

"You bet your ass it did," she says without missing a beat.

"But you've got to see where I'm coming from. That area is bad and just because you're some pretty girl, doesn't mean those assholes will leave you alone."

"You think I'm pretty," she jokes and I can hear her smile.

I smile back, probably looking like a fool. "You already know what I think. So, I'm forgiven?"

"This time. But there won't be a next time."

"Yes, ma'am." I salute, even though she can't see me.

Something weird happens then. It's like a weight has vanished and my shoulders don't feel as heavy as they did a moment ago. Weird.

"Well, now that all is forgiven and forgotten—"

"I didn't say it was forgotten."

"—I need you to get dressed."

That has me pausing in my steps. "Do you walk around the dorm naked?"

"No, you perv."

Oh. Damn.

"I'm coming over in thirty and be ready to go to the bar."

She starts to protest, but then I end the call. This will be good. We'll go out and Zoey can meet someone to practice on. Someone who isn't me.

I take Zoey to a bar closer to the edge of town, where I know the hockey guys won't be. Mainly Kai. The bar is packed when we enter, all dim lights and sticky surfaces. Zoey stays close to me as we make our way through the crowd, her fingers wrapped around my shirt so we don't get separated. Shit, I kind of like that.

I grab a beer for me and a cider for Zoey. She hates the bitter taste of beer. Wait, why do I know that?

"Listen up, red velvet," I turn to her, offering her the cider, "it's time."

"Time for what?" she asks before taking a drink. Her pink painted lips part as she swallows sip after sip. I don't realize I've zoned out until Zoey snaps her fingers in front of my face. "Time for what?"

I clear my throat and down half my bottle. "Time to show me your moves."

Her eyes dart around the room in confusion. "What moves?"

"You know, your moves," I say with a wink.

"I don't have moves."

"Everyone has moves."

"Not me. At least, I don't think so."

As fun as flirting with Zoey is, we've known each other for a while. I'm familiar with her. She needs fresh meat to practice on. And maybe having her practice with someone else will show me that she's just a good student. Jesus, who am I kidding? Searching the crowd, I spot some guys huddled in the corner. Definitely under-age because they look scared as hell, but they'll do.

"See the guy over there in the red shirt?" I gesture in his direction.

Her eyes bounce between me and the guy. "What about him?"

"Go ask him to dance."

She's mid-drink when I tell her what to do and ends up in a choking fit. Once she's got herself calmed down, Zoey starts frantically shaking her head.

"N-no. I can't. I'm go-oing to stutter. Fuck!"

Not going to lie, I don't even notice her stutter most times. I do know it pisses her off though, so I try to keep her calm.

I step closer to her so she can hear me over the noise. "The reason I picked those guys is because they're random. So what if you stutter a little bit? Unless you want to, you'll never see them after tonight."

Zoey tips her chin to look up at me. "I don't want them to make fun of me."

I tuck a curl that's fallen out of her ponytail behind her ear. "Chocolate chip. Trust me when I say if I ever see someone making fun of you, I will personally see to their demise."

My fingers are still resting on the side of her neck and I don't know what the fuck is happening anymore. Her pulse is beating a million miles a minute under my thumb and she's looking at me like —"Go," I nudge her in their direction. "I believe in you."

Zoey rolls her eyes, then turns away and starts walking.

What in the actual fuck is going on in my head? I slam the rest of my beer and order another from the bartender. She's blonde, big tits, and my type. But instead of trying to get her number, I toss a tip on the bar, grab my beer and turn back in the direction of the guy in the red shirt. The guy who is smiling down at Zoey as she places her hand on his bicep. I taught her that move. I clench my jaw when they both start laughing. He looks like the least funny person in this room.

Just as I'm about to go over there, an arm brushes against me. Striking blue eyes stare me down.

"You look lonely. Can I buy you a drink?"

Forward. I like it. At least, I usually do. Instead I look back in Zoey's direction and she's still laughing. What the fuck is she laughing about? He looks like he works at fucking Old Navy. Stupidly, I chug my beer and slam it down on the bar.

Wrapping my arm around her waist, I whisper in her ear, "How about we just get out of here?"

Her tongue licks her bottom lip and she nods. I guide her out of the building, but the second we turn the corner, I stop. I didn't tell Zoey I was leaving. What if she looks for me and wonders where I went? Releasing the woman whose name I don't even know, I run a hand through my hair wondering what the hell I'm doing.

"Everything okay?" she asks.

"This, fuck, I can't do this. I gotta go."

And like the dick I am, I leave her standing on the street corner. Alone.

Chapter Thirteen

Zoey

Harry is nice. Cute. Kind of funny. His fraternity brother's dragged him out tonight. He's said all the right things at the right times. And the best part is, I haven't stuttered once. The worst part is, all I want to do is go home. Or go back to the bar and have a drink with Jace — which is a thought I never thought I would have. Harry tells me he likes my hair for the second time and I smile politely while scanning the room. I look back to where Jace and I were a few moments ago, but no Jace. I keep looking until I see him walking out of the bar. With a girl.

My smile falters and I feel ... disappointed. Disappointed that Jace left me for some random girl. But that shouldn't matter. I can do this on my own. Except when I turn back to Harry and he's smiling down at me, all I want to do is go home and snuggle under my covers.

"So, can I buy you a drink?" he asks, stepping closer to me as he places his hand on my waist.

My entire body shivers and not in a good way. I almost feel icky where he touched me. Like he's covered in slime or something.

Wanting to still be polite, I smile and take a step back. "I actually think I'm going to call it a night."

His smile is tight, but when I turn to walk away, I don't give him a second thought. Once I'm outside, I grab my phone from my side purse. I want to hurl it across the alley when I see I have no missed text messages. It shouldn't bother me that Jace left the bar with someone. It shouldn't bother me that he left *me* alone at the bar. We're not even friends. I glance around the dark, empty alley as I tuck my phone away and try to blink back the tears that have clouded my vision. There's no way I'm crying because Jace chose getting laid by some random girl over staying at the bar with me.

So why do I feel so sad right now?

I wake up in the morning, feeling hungover even though I never finished my drink last night. Something I didn't even ask for. Which is weird because how did Jace know what I prefer to drink? I've always hated the taste of beer because it's too bitter.

I stare down at my phone, wanting to check for missed messages. I went to bed, fighting to keep the tears at bay, but woke up pissed off. Part of me hopes Jace isn't the total asshole I think he is and he sent me a text about how there was some emergency and he didn't mean to ditch me. That the girl he left with came down with a sudden case of tuberculosis and needed to be rushed to the hospital. But I know that's not the case. So instead of checking my phone, I jump in the shower and get ready for the day.

The Good Neighbor Program has another meet up at what will soon be the new local park. Corrine typically refuses to come volunteer, but Becks rolls her out of bed and forces her to come with us. With the promise of stopping to get breakfast sandwiches at Michelle's first.

"I'm dying. The sun hurts. Why are we up so early?" Corrine complains.

Becks and I both laugh. "It's ten."

"Yes. But it's a Sunday. Ten o'clock on a Sunday is like eight o'clock on a Tuesday."

"I think you'll survive," Becks tells her as we all link arms and stroll into Michelle's.

Michelle's is a small café on Main Street with the best breakfast sandwiches. It gives the true vibe of a small town. There are a few scattered tables throughout the café along with some loveseats and chairs to relax in. My eyes instantly fall to the ground when I see who is in one of the loveseats.

"I think we're going to be late," I say, wanting to be anywhere but here. In reality, I shouldn't be mad. I shouldn't feel sad at practically being abandoned. But he's the one who asked me to go out and told me to go talk to Harry. And then just freaking left.

"If you expect me to do any manual labor today, I need my caffeine."

Corrine is ordering when I feel a presence behind me. I close my eyes, praying that I have some magical powers that just never developed and all of a sudden, I can disappear without a trace.

"Hey, gummy bear."

Damn. This is almost as disappointing as when I turned 11 and didn't get my Hogwarts letter.

I want to ignore him, but that would be petty. So instead, I do the only logical thing I can think of. I turn towards the door and power walk out and don't stop until I'm a few stores away. I've never been good with confrontation. I'm more of a stew-until-you-get-over-it kind of person.

But apparently Jace isn't.

He finds me in no time, chuckling like he thinks this is funny. What is wrong with him?

"You okay—"

"What is wrong with you?" I snap

His brows pull together. "What are you talking about?"

"You ditched me!" Okay, so confrontation it is. "You took me out and then sent me off like some mail-order bride. Did you even check to make sure I was okay with that random guy before you went home and hooked up with a bunny?"

He inhales slowly through his nose before stating the obvious. "You're mad."

I roll my eyes so hard I think I'm going to give myself an aneurysm.

"Of course, I'm mad. You didn't even let me know you were leaving. Don't you know girl code?"

"I've heard of it, but—"

"You don't just leave someone alone with a freaking stranger while you go and get laid!"

"First off, I'm not a girl." At my unamused expression, Jace rubs a hand over the back of his neck. "Okay. You're right. It was a dick move."

"Yes. I know it was."

His smile is slow and I have to bite the inside of my cheek to keep from reciprocating it.

"I'm sorry, tootsie roll. I didn't think of it like that. But you are right. That shit won't happen again."

I stare down at my nails, picking off the polish on my thumb nail.

"I hope you at least got lucky, because I sure as shit didn't," I say. Not sure why though.

"What did red shirt do?"

I look up and his normal cheerful expression is nowhere to be seen.

"Did he touch you or—"

"No. Nothing like that. Just not a love match or anything," I chuckle.

His shoulders seem to relax as he takes a step closer to me. "But you did it."

"Did what?"

"Used your moves. That guy was about to start drooling over you. You're a very good student."

I'm not sure what is happening, but Jace is standing way too close and something feels different. The air feels charged like one spark might set everything on fire.

Until Becks and Corrine start walking towards us. Corrine is the complete opposite of who I saw only minutes ago.

"Coffee works that fast?" I tease, taking a step away from Jace.

"Three shots of espresso does," Corrine sing-songs as she skips towards us. I don't think I've ever seen anyone over the age of five skip before.

Becks' eyes travel up and down Jace. "Did we interrupt something?"

We both shake our heads.

"Come on," Corrine jumps up and down, "let's go build a playground or carry some heavy shit or whatever before my caffeine high dies."

Jace salutes the three of us before turning around and going back to Michelle's.

"Kill me," Corrine whines.

"It wasn't that bad," I giggle.

"Don't even bury me six feet under. I don't have that much time left."

Becks rolls her eyes as she pushes the door open. I love Corrine, but she definitely should be part of the drama club.

"It was just a little bit of weeding," Becks adds.

"It was just a little bit of weeding," Corrine mocks.

"After a shower, I think we should all nap," I say and everyone agrees.

We just finish the trek up the stairs to our room, but stop at our front door. There's a note on our whiteboard that wasn't there when we left.

"Merry Christmas, Reese's Pieces? What the hell does that mean?" Becks says.

With slight hesitation, I swipe my key and open the door. Our mouths collectively fall open as we take in our living room.

"I know I was being dramatic, but were we really gardening for that long? How the hell did someone have time to do all this?"

Not someone. Someones. Because there is no way Jace alone individually wrapped every single item in our living room in Christmas themed wrapping paper. And I mean everything! Our television, the couch, even the hangers and coats in the coat closet.

For the next few minutes, all three of us just stare in awe. How did they even get in here? Who all helped? And where the hell did they get all this Christmas wrapping paper in October?

Jace

I smirk when my phone rings. I watch it vibrate on the desk for a few seconds before finally answering.

"Hello?"

"Christmas wrapping paper?" She sounds out of breath and I chuckle.

"Hello? Is someone there? I can't hear you."

"Oh, you mean you can't hear me over all the freaking wrapping paper we've spent the last hour dealing with. Jesus! Did you buy the entire section of tape at Walmart?"

Yes. Yes I did.

"At least it wasn't three dozen flamingos. And before you comment, I should let you know that they are all coming back."

"What do you mean coming back?"

"Whoever stole them before is now bringing them back and hiding them in our yard."

A laugh bubbles out of her, but then stops suddenly like she's covering her mouth.

"It's not funny. Do you know how hard it is to get rid of big, plastic flamingos? The garbage man won't take them!"

This makes her laugh even more.

I wait until she calms down and the sound of paper crinkling stops.

"So what are you wearing?" I tease.

"I paired my chastity belt with some thigh high boots."

"Now that I need a picture of."

She's laughing again and it makes me smile. Shit, do I need to punch myself in the balls for thinking something like that?

"You should come over, cupcake. I have an idea for your next lesson."

"I can't. I work tonight."

I groan, speaking my next words without thinking. "You should quit tonight instead."

Ignoring me, she gasps. "Oh shit, what time is it?"

"Almost three."

"Crap! Crap! Crap on a cracker!"

"That's an expression I haven't heard before," I say through a laugh.

"I gotta go. I'm gonna be late."

"Just call them and tell them you can't make it in. Tonight and for the rest of time."

"God," she mumbles. "You and Kai are like the same person."

"What does that even mean?"

"He won't get off my ass about North Side either. I get it. You don't like where I work. Let's move on."

Not wanting to piss her off again, I concede. "Well, if you survive work, come over tomorrow after class. I have a break from eleven to two."

"You can't see, but I'm giving you the middle finger," she tells me and then is gone.

I know I'm being a dick about North Side, but I don't give a shit. That place is sketchy as fuck and I'm glad Kai is on my side.

Chapter Fourteen

Jace

The next day, I'm icing my shoulder when Zoey barges through my door. I guess we're past knocking now.

She's only a few steps in when she freezes, her eyes narrowing on my shoulder. "What happened? Are you okay?"

"Fine," I grunt. "Took a hard hit at practice yesterday and woke up sore."

"We can do this another day. I don't mind—"

"I'm okay," I say. "Really. It's just a few bruises."

Taking a deep breath, I toss the ice pack on my desk and stand up. Her forehead crinkles as she stares at my shoulder. Is she worried about me? Her brother plays hockey. She knows how physical the sport can get. So why is concern etched all over her face?

She turns back around when the door flies open and in walks a half-naked Conrad.

"You're naked," she shrieks as she quickly turns back around to face me.

He chuckles. "I have a towel covering the important bits. I think the question I should be asking is what are you doing in my room?"

"Our room," I correct.

Conrad stares me down over Zoey's shoulder. He's not stupid and as much as I wish he was like every other guy here and just ignored Zoey and I hanging out, I know that's not happening. He thinks something is going on between us and that Kai's going to find out. But he's wrong. I'm just helping her out.

Clearing my throat, I say to Conrad, "Zoey needed help with homework, so I'm just lending a hand. You should probably put some clothes on now."

"I'll do that."

Conrad grabs a few items from his dresser and disappears out the door. He won't be back for a while.

"Um," she runs a hand through her wavy hair, "so what am I doing here?"

This probably isn't the best idea I've ever had. But Zoey asked me to help her, so I'm going to help her.

"How long has it been since you kissed someone?"

Her face falls and she looks like she's a moment away from running. Putting my hands up in surrender, I step closer to her.

"I'm not trying to make fun of you or embarrass you. You asked for my help and I'm just trying to help you."

We didn't kiss. That night a few months back, when I tried to kiss her, she turned away. I want to say I don't think about it all the time, but that would be a lie.

She avoids my stare and mutters, "A while."

"Exactly how long is a while?"

"I don't want to tell you. It's embarrassing."

"Well, now you have to," I tease, hoping to ease some of her tension.

Zoey looks away as she walks towards the door and continues picking at her nails. She mumbles a few words.

"We both know I couldn't hear you."

She exhales heavily. "He said I was weird. That it was weird."

"Like the kiss was weird? Wait, is this that fucker from the restaurant?"

Zoey lifts one shoulder. "Kind of. We would give each other little pecks on the lips, but we didn't make out that much."

She pauses, but I don't push. I know this has to be hard for her to talk about, but it's clearly something holding her back. "He said it felt awkward and that I just needed to relax, but I couldn't. If anything, I started thinking even more about everything."

"Everything?"

"Like where to put my hands or if my tongue was doing the right thing. And then it ended. The kiss and the relationship. He didn't want me anymore."

Closing the distance between us, I grab her chin with my thumb and forefinger, forcing her to look up at me.

"If you ever are with someone and it doesn't feel right, whether it's kissing or having sex or just holding hands, you can say no. You can stop it. You have that power, Zoey. Always."

"Thank you," she whispers.

Our mouths are close now. Probably too close. But then she says something I've only ever fantasized about.

"Will you teach me?"

It takes me a second to process her words. "You want to practice kissing with me?"

She nods. "For lear-lear-learning purposes?"

Staring down into Zoey's big blue eyes, I slide my hand around to the back of her neck, tangle my fingers in her hair and then pull her closer. Then I do something I have fantasized about for weeks. Our kiss is soft and slow. Just a slight brush of our lips. I'm not sure exactly what she wants here and I wasn't just making up shit earlier. She has all the power here and I want her to know that. A shiver runs through my entire body when Zoey's hands slide up my chest and link behind my neck.

"Is this okay?" she asks through a whisper.

I nod, not moving an inch. Wanting her to determine how fast or how slow we go. Just when I think she's going to back away, she raises up on her toes and presses her lips to mine.

I want to go slow. I want to help her. But, fuuuuck, she tastes so good. Better than I ever imagined. Zoey pulls me closer to her, pressing her tits against my chest and I can't help myself. My tongue swipes against her lips, silently asking for permission and when she opens her mouth, I'm fucking done for. I don't just kiss her. That's not even possible. I devour her. Wanting and needing to taste every inch of her.

My other hand grabs her hip while a moan escapes her as I tug lightly on her hair and I'm not ashamed when my dick hardens. Does she not see how she's the real life definition of sexy? Needing to touch more of her, I slide my hands down, grabbing her ass and hoisting her up. She instinctively wraps her legs around my waist, but then quickly pulls her mouth from mine. Zoey feels me between her thighs and I don't think I've ever been this hard before. Especially not from kissing alone.

"You have all the power," I tell her through panted breaths.

She swallows hard as she slides her hand up and into my hair ... and then pushes my head towards her neck. Fuck, yes!

I lick just over her pulse point, then suck, testing her boundaries. When she doesn't object, I nip at her skin, just enough to have her squeezing her legs together.

"Jace," she pants.

My hand brushes up along her side, stopping just under her tit. Clearly tired of waiting for me, she guides my hand up. Her big, full tits feel like they were made for my hands. Is there anything that's not perfect about this woman? I thrust my hips and am rewarded with a gasp of pleasure, so I do it again and again. I could listen to her moan all night long. I think it might be my favorite sound in the entire world.

Suddenly the door behind us is being pounded on.

"Hey! We're all heading out now. You coming or what?"

Zoey's eyes widen in fear. It's Kai. God Dammit! Asshole could not have worse timing. Zoey looks like she's about to have a panic attack, so I bring my finger to my lips to tell her to be quiet. We both can't be freaking out right now. She nods, but the fear in her eyes is palpable.

"Just give me a minute."

"Jesus," he chuckles, "it's the middle of the day. Put the lotion and tissues away and get out here."

Zoey and I stay frozen until we hear Kai's footsteps disappear down the hall. We're both still breathing heavily as I gently let her go and she slides down my body. Neither of us knows what to do. How to process what the hell just happened between us.

"Thanks for the le-lesson."

I nod slowly, resting my forehead against hers. I have no idea what would've happened if Kai tried to open the door just now. But, we both know that was way too close.

"I hate the words that are about to come out of my mouth, but wait five minutes before you leave."

She nods, understanding that Kai can never find out about this. If he does, I'm fucking dead.

Chapter Fifteen
Zoey

It's been over 48 hours with no contact from Jace. This shouldn't bother me. But it does. He kissed me. I kissed him. Oh crap, we kissed! And it was sooo good. It was probably the best kiss I've ever had. And it can never happen again.

How is it possible that over a dozen guys live in the Ballentine house, but my freaking step-brother was the one to almost catch us. As much as I don't want to be the girl glued to her phone, I haven't had it out of my sight for more than a few minutes these past two days. I don't know why. It's not like Jace is going to call me up and talk about how amazing of a kisser I am. That might sound conceited, but I know what I felt. And his cell phone is not nearly that big.

"Plans tonight?" Corrine's leaning against the wall, probably wondering why I've been staring at a blank word document on my laptop for five minutes.

"Nope. Nothing planned. Just some homework."

"Yeah, you look super invested," she teases.

"It just isn't holding my attention."

Becks walks in and tosses a shirt on my lap. "I know what will."

I hold up the long sleeve and roll my eyes. There's a hockey game tonight. Kai asked if I was coming and like the coward I am, I told him I was busy. Jace hasn't reached out and I don't want him thinking I'm some clingy bunny by showing up at his game.

"I really don't want to go."

"How come?" Corrine chimes in. "Something going on you want to tell us?"

I open my mouth, but nothing comes out. My gaze jumps between the two and I know there's no way I'll get out of this unscathed. With a heavy sigh, I stand up and throw on the gray long sleeve with Winger U's hockey emblem in the dead center. WU are in large letters with two hockey sticks making an X in front of it with a crown on top for the Royals.

The crowd is packed with students and townies and a decent fan-base from the away team when we get to the Winger Sports Complex. I'm a bad hockey sibling. I mean I like hockey. It's a cool sport, but the puck goes from one end to the other. Back and forth and back and forth. What's so special? We find a row of available seats and sit down on freezing cold metal benches. I now see why Becks brought a blanket with her. I thank her at least three times when she spreads it out over the three of us.

"Who are we playing?" I kind of have to shout because of how loud it is and the players haven't even come out of the locker rooms yet.

"Shouldn't you know this? Your brother's the hockey star," Corrine says, sounding a tad judgmental.

"Cyprus," Becks answers, tossing another piece of popcorn into her mouth.

She passes the bucket over for us to share when the Royals jump onto the ice. Each guy runs out and it amazes me that they never trip or fall. A few of them skate straight to the bench while some of them start stretching.

The blue jersey with yellow letters spelling out "Bennett" has his back to us. He drops down, spreads his legs and practically starts humping the ice.

My mouth slowly falls open. "I don't think I've ever realized how—"

"When they stretch they look like they're raw-dogging the ice?" Corrine casually says.

"We're in public," I scold her all while Becks laughs.

Corrine rolls her eyes. "Lighten up. Maybe one of the hockey players could do that to you and remove whatever stick is up your butt."

Woah. That was ... harsh.

I narrow my eyes at her. "Seriously?"

Corrine sighs. "Sorry. I haven't slept great lately."

There are a couple claps from the opposed side when the Squids emerge and start their warm-up routine. A timer is set on the scoreboard for five minutes and I spend that time trying to focus on anyone who is not Jace. It doesn't work; not even a little bit.

The sound of a whistle fills the arena just as the timer expires and it's that moment Jace chooses to look up in the stands. I'm not sure if he sees me yet, but I sure see him. I see him run his hand through his shaggy hair as his tongue comes out to wet his lips. I see him look through the crowd. And I see what looks like disappointment when his eyes don't find who he is looking for. Was he looking for me?

Something hits the side of my face and I turn towards Becks and Corrine. They're both laughing, throwing a few more kernels of popcorn at me.

"See something you like?" Becks teases.

I join them in laughing as I roll my eyes

Okay, fine. I'll admit, it was a great game. Kai kicked major ass and I guess Jace did okay. Not that I was watching him or anything. Because that would be weird. I internally groan, wanting to slap some sense into me. It was just a kiss. A really fucking hot kiss, but a kiss none the less.

Looking around the benches, I ask, "Should we try and find Corrine?"

After the first period Corrine got a text message and with a quick wave, disappeared. We haven't heard a peep from her since.

Becks shakes her head. "She's a big girl and can fend for herself."

"Okay, let's go then."

I grab Becks' hand and try pushing past a few people to get out. Why is everyone moving so slowly?

"Woah," she pulls back her arm. "Where's the fire?"

"No fire. I just want to beat the crowd. You know, traffic?"

Her brows pull together. "Traffic on the walk back to the dorms?"

I nod with a smile. Her eyes widen and it's probably because I look crazy. I feel a little crazy.

She definitely doesn't believe me, but I can't exactly tell her that I know some of the hockey players change fast and I want to be nowhere near this building when they exit the locker room.

Becks looks over my shoulder and waves. "I think I see Trent. You good to get back home by yourself?"

I nod, thinking I'll move even faster on my own, and dash for the door. Well, I try to. This older couple in front of me can't seem to pick a side to walk on. I'm finally through the rink's double doors when I hear, "My little sour patch came to watch me."

I slowly turn around and find Jace smiling down at me. Shit.

I roll my eyes as I walk up to him. "More like I came to watch my step-brother. Family support and all that."

His grin continues to grow. "Yeah. I'm sure."

Neither of us speak. Or move. It's like the world's weirdest staring contest.

"I saw you," he continues. "In the stands. After I score, I like to point to the stands for my celly and imagine my surprise when I saw you."

I cross my arms over my chest in an effort to appear nonchalant. "I told you. I came to watch Kai."

"It was a nice surprise."

My head is so far back, my neck starts to hurt. Holy shit. When did Jace get that close to me? And why is he looking at me like he wants to devour me?

"Work," I shout.

"What?" he laughs.

"I have to go to work. I'm going to be late."

I turn and run like my ass is on fire before I can hear his response.

I'm almost to the door when I feel a tug on my elbow.

"Zo? I thought you were busy?"

Of fucking course Kai would be out here already.

"Finished early."

"Finished what early?"

"Homework. Um, I'm late for work. I'll talk to you later."

I try to walk away, when Kai grabs my wrist to stop me. "Is everything okay? You're acting jumpy."

I shake my head. "Nope. Not jumpy. Bye."

I finally make it out of the sports complex and to work. I was praying work would be a distraction, but it's a boring shift which usually isn't a bad thing. Tonight, however, I spend all my down time thinking about Jace's smile. And how happy he seemed when he saw me.

Chapter Sixteen

Zoey

Becks, Corrine, and I are huddled together behind a row of trees. We decided not to wear black because we didn't want to look too suspicious, so now we just look like straight up bunny stalkers.

"Everyone understand the plan?" Becks asks.

Corrine and I nod.

"Pull and run," I say.

I stick my hand in between us and Becks and Corrine place theirs on top of mine. We press our hands down, count to three and then shout, "Boys suck," as we raise our hands.

The door to Ballentine is unlocked, which is pretty standard, so the three of us are able to sneak in easily. I talked to Kai earlier and he said that he and some of the other guys were staying in tonight to watch "the game." Like I knew which one he was talking about.

I plaster my body to the wall as I side step my way down the hall. Becks tilts her head in confusion.

"This is what they do in movies to hide," I whisper-yell.

"Are we in a movie now?" she asks, in a totally normal volume.

Straightening to my full height, I roll my eyes and walk over to the entertainment room. Jace is sitting in the corner of the couch, focused on the hockey fight on TV. I find myself admiring his side profile when Corrine jumps next to me with a crazed look in her eye and shouts, "REVOLUTION!"

Holding the febreeze I brought in one hand, I tighten the zip tie around the nozzle, toss and run. Becks and Corrine do the same and all hell breaks loose. Kai jumps up and shouts, Conrad grabs a throw pillow and covers his mouth and just as I think I'm going to get away, my eyes connect with Jace's. His grin is an evil promise and I think I can make it to the door. The only problem is big, burly guys take up the entire hallway and I can't get through.

A shriek escapes my mouth when hands grab me from behind and pull me into a closet. We're back to chest and I'm about to scream again when Jace slams his palm over my mouth. His breath is hot against my ear as he whispers, "And just where do you think you're going?"

My chest rises and falls rapidly and I can't seem to catch my breath with him being this close to me. His voice is all low and dark and husky, just like that first night when he walked me to my door after dinner.

He doesn't remove his hand as his nose skims up the side of my neck. Somehow I find myself leaning my head to the side to give him better access. I hear his sharp inhale as something deep in my belly twists into a knot. It's only when my entire body relaxes do his lips land on my neck and his other hand, the one not covering my mouth, slides from my hip to the front of my leggings.

"Do you think you're funny?" he goads, his fingers drifting back and forth on the skin below my belly button.

He removes his hand from my mouth and I laugh breathlessly, "It was kind of funny."

"Wrong answer."

His hand covers my mouth again as his other one drifts lower. My moan is muffled as he cups me through my pants. His chuckle is low and dangerous as he presses his hard dick into my ass.

"Why are you so wet? You weren't expecting me to catch you? Or were you?"

He continues to rub me through my pants and without thinking, I grab the hand that's slowly torturing me, drag it up to the top of my pants and guide it under the fabric.

"Greedy little thing," he mumbles.

But I don't care. I need him to touch me. I need to feel his fingers against me before I combust. Jace's fingers dip into my pants and just when I think I'll finally get some relief, we hear, "Has anyone seen Zoey?"

A sigh of disappointment leaves both of us as Jace removes his hands from me. With a sweet kiss to my temple, he says, "Go. I'll wait."

And just like that, what I thought was about to be some incredibly hot fooling around, vanishes. This is the second time my step-brother has cock-blocked me. Or whatever the girl version of that is. Clam-jammed? Cliterference?

I step out into the hallway and run to the bathroom, which is luckily empty. I turn the faucet on, count to ten, turn it off and head back out where I run into Kai.

"I thought I lost you in the chaos," he chuckles.

I shake my head. "Just had to use the bathroom."

"Or you were hiding out from the assholes who now smell like Tommy Bahama's nut sack?"

"Gross. Try Hawaiian Breeze from Walmart."

I pretend to gag as I steer him away from the closet Jace is still hiding in. When we round the corner into the kitchen, I look back and see Jace sneaking out. He spots me and holds his forefinger to his lips. My smile never falters; not when I have a drink with Kai on their back porch, not when I get home and certainly not as I tuck myself into bed.

Chapter Seventeen

Jace

The last thing I want to do today is go to practice. I barely slept last night, classes sucked, and I've been skipping the gym way too often. I'm the last one to arrive at practice and the slowest one to get dressed which means I get the dirtiest looks when I manage to make it out of the locker room. I don't know what everyone's so pissed about considering the Zamboni is still on the ice.

I'm knocked off balance when Caleb nudges my shoulder with his. "What crawled up your ass and died?"

"Just an off day."

He nods and I think we're cool until he says, "Just make sure you don't bring that shit on the ice."

Wait, what the fuck?

"Who do you think you're talking to? I'm not some rookie-ass

Freshman you can push around."

He chuckles to himself. "I don't mean it like that. But if you take whatever attitude you have out on the ice, Coach is gonna take it out on all of us."

The rink doors open and all that pent up energy the guys were holding back is unleashed. Caleb gives my back a slap before he joins them. Shit, Caleb's right. He's one of my best friends and I almost just bit his head off for no reason. I roll my neck, ready to leave all that shit behind, and run out onto the ice with everyone else.

I'm going through my stretching routine when visions of Zoey rubbing her ass against my dick fill my brain. Of how wet she was for me and how eager she was for me to touch her. I will never understand how she doesn't see herself as the sexiest thing on Earth. I'm stretching my hips when little Jace decides it's time to wake up. Fuck, that's painful.

"Shit," I mutter to myself as I fall over on my ass. A hard-on with a cup at hockey practice is one of my nightmares.

"Bennett!" Coach yells. "Get the hell up! If you want to sit so badly, you can sit on the bench for the next game!"

"Sorry Coach," I holler back.

Quickly I jump into another stretch and think of literally anything to get this situation to calm down.

Spider monkeys, Christmas lights, diet coke, the little mustache dude from monopoly, Totoro.

Okay. I think I'm good. Shit, I think I already sweat through my pads and practice hasn't even started yet. I actually flinch when Coach blows his whistle and start counting the seconds until practice is over.

After practice, I'm the first one out of the shower and dressed because I don't want to wait around for Coach to yell at me some more. He can do that tomorrow. On my walk home, I grab my phone and text the woman who has been on my mind for the past two hours.

> **J: Next lesson: Confidence**

Her response comes almost immediately.

> **Z: Seriously? I have a freaking stutter. If I didn't have confidence, I would never leave the house**

> **J: Come over tomorrow after anatomy and physiology**

> **Z: How do you know my class schedule?**

I'm not sure if telling her that I simply paid attention would either freak her out or flatter her, so for now I leave that question unanswered.

Zoey

Halfway through class, I got a text from Jace saying he would meet me at my place instead. No explanation needed or anything. I wanted to ask questions, but the idea of him in my space was too tempting. I've barely set my bag down when I hear three knocks on my front door.

"Where's Becks and Corrine?" Jace asks, walking in like he's right at home.

"Becks is working and Corrine is out with some friends."

He nods slowly, heads into my room and over to my closet.

I laugh to myself as he starts looking through everything. "What are you doing?"

"Confidence is the number one key when trying to attract someone." Jace audibly swallows. "Like Leo."

He says Leo's name like it's a bad word. Like it was painful for him to say it. Even though Leo is the reason for this entire arrangement.

"Oh. That's why you wanted to come over." Because of course that's why he wanted to come over. Why else would he want to?

"Which of your clothes makes you feel sexy?"

I looked down at my joggers and oversized sweatshirt and start laughing, but quickly stop when I realize he's serious.

"Um, I guess none of them. I'd rather be comfortable than sexy. Hence my outfit."

The corner of his mouth quirks up. "Do you not think you're sexy in that outfit?"

This time I don't stop laughing. Because that has to be the biggest joke I've ever heard. "I've never really considered myself sexy before."

"What did you just say?"

I shrug. "It's not my fault. Practically every girl I know has a flat stomach with abs that come out of nowhere. Most guys don't want to see a girl with a lot of extra padding."

"What the hell are you even talking about? All right, brownie bites. Let me see."

Jace crosses his arms and stares down at my chest with furrowed brows.

"See what?"

His eyes gesture down my body and I shake my head.

"What? No!" I say, covering my chest even though he can't see anything. "I'm not putting on a strip tease, you perv. And your nicknames are getting weirder by the way."

Jace stuffs his hands in his pockets. "I'm here to help, right? So let me see what we're working with."

"Uh, this is so stupid," I grunt, lifting my shirt over my head and dropping it on the ground.

Jace's eyes instantly fall to my chest, which is unsurprising since he is a dude. But it's bringing back unwanted memories. Memories of his hands all over me, his tongue in my mouth, the feeling of him pressed between my thighs. I shake my head to forget and when the silence stretches on, I go to pick my shirt back up.

"I told you this was stupid," I mutter.

"Woah, woah," he grabs the shirt from my hand. "I just need a moment."

"A moment?"

"Yes, to, uh," he clears his throat, "to form my opinion."

I place my hands on my hips. "You're trying to form your opinion on my nude bra with straps so wide they could part the red sea?"

Jace's eye's never waver, but when he still doesn't say anything I try to grab my shirt back.

"Jace, just—"

"Can you just shut up for a moment?"

My mouth falls open. "Excuse me?"

The tips of Jace's ears turn red. Is he ... blushing?

"I, I, um, I'm an ass man. I love asses. It's kind of my thing. But you have the sexiest rack I've ever seen in person."

"In person? Like you watch fat people porn? Is that your kink?"

He exhales heavily, rubbing a hand down his face. "Jesus Christ, you can be annoying when you want to. All I'm saying is you have really nice tits and whatever guy gets to touch them or put their mouth on them isn't going to give a shit about your granny panties."

Okay, I don't know if I should be calling Jace a pig or be flattered about his praises. It does feel kind of good to hear someone, besides myself, talk positively about my body for once.

I look away as I scratch my head. "I've um ..."

"What?"

"I've never been fully naked with a guy before. I know my size and I have no problem with that, but other people seem to have issues with it."

Jace steps closer to me, tucking a stray hair behind my ear. "Zoey?"

"Yeah?"

"Out of all the things I would think to call you, fat wouldn't even make the list. Beautiful would though. Strong and sexy."

He's too close again. This is dangerous territory for us. We've already discovered that. Trying to swallow the sand in my mouth, I ask the only logical thing to break whatever trance we're in.

"Can I have my shirt back?"

Chapter Eighteen

Jace

The second I made my way onto the ice for practice, I knew something was different. A brief scan of the stands was the reason why. Zoey and her roommates sat side by side waiting for us. For me. I couldn't help my smirk when my eyes met hers. Was it my most productive practice? According to Coach, no. But did I have fun showing off my skills? Hell yes. I could hear her roommates laughing over Coach's shouting and every time she rolled her eyes it made me want to work harder for her smile.

Once Coach was done tearing me a new one in the locker room, Kai and I headed out to the lobby to find Zoey waiting for us.

"You coming out with us tonight, DumDum?" I ask Zoey without thinking.

She narrows her eyes at me and I have to suppress my laughter.

I sober when Kai speaks first. "What did you call her?"

Uh, I kind of forgot he was right here.

"DumDum? You know, like the lollipop." At his blank stare, I continue. "What? She likes the funny nicknames I give her. It's our schtick. Right, Kinder Egg?"

Zoey tosses her head back with a dramatic sigh. "This conversation is not making me want to come out in the slightest."

Kai looks around, confused. "Where did your roommates go?"

Zoey shrugs. "Becks met this guy that she's been attached at the hip with and Corrine just wanted to go home."

Caleb chuckles, walking up with his arm wrapped around Millie. "I bet Kentucky would love the company."

"You'll come to trivia night?" She shimmies out of Caleb's embrace and runs over to link arms with Zoey.

"Woah. Way to abandon ship, babe."

Millie rolls her eyes. "Please say you're coming? Trivia night is always filled with too much testosterone and stale beer."

"Well, when you put it that way, how can I say no?" Zoey deadpans.

We all start heading towards the parking lot when Kai comes up next to me, "And stop giving Zoey nicknames. It's weird."

Hiking my hockey bag higher on my shoulder, I shrug like the nicknames I give her are no big deal. "Nah, I think she likes them."

Kai drives Zoey and I back to Ballentine to drop off his car and then we walk to Mixed, a bar on Main Street. It's only a few blocks from campus and the weather isn't too bad today. Kai and Zoey are walking together on the sidewalk with me trailing behind them.

"Is it going to be a problem that I don't have a fake?" she asks.

Kai shakes his head. "They don't check ID's on Trivia Night."

"Why do you think we like to come? You didn't actually think we played Trivia, did you?" I tease.

She sneaks a peak over her shoulder and I don't even try to hide the fact that I've been staring at her ass the past few blocks.

We head into the dimly lit bar and I grimace when my shoes start sticking to the floor. The only thing going for this place is the cheap ass drinks. A large wooden bar sits in the middle of the room with half the room littered with high top tables and the other half a dance floor with an elevated DJ booth. Kai, Caleb and I snag a couple tables and push them together for when the rest of the guys stop by later.

Kai and Caleb head to the bar to grab drinks, but I hang back with Millie and Zoey who grab seats. My hands itch to pull Zoey's chair out and I ball them into fists. What the fuck is wrong with me? Millie's eyes bounce back and forth between us like she's at a tennis match.

"I should probably go help them, huh?"

"It would be the gentlemanly thing to do," Zoey says.

With a nod, I join the guys at the bar. Pretending to rub my neck, I glance behind me. Zoey's biting her lip and staring at my ass. I'm not sure what they're talking about, but I nod in acknowledgement, as I eavesdrop on Zoey and Millie. Unethical, probably. Do I care? Not even a little.

"There's just a vibe." Millie tells her.

"A vibe?"

"Yes, a vibe."

"Between who?" Zoey asks.

Millie scoffs. "Considering the only three schmucks we're out with tonight are the doofus who won't stop flirting with me, you're stepbrother and Jace, I'll give you one guess."

I look over my shoulder again and Zoey is still staring at me. Her gaze doesn't falter when our eyes meet. I'm the first to break away and it's only because the bartender interrupts us.

"Are you waiting for something?" he yells over the crowd.

"Water and whatever you have on tap."

Conrad, Buzz and a few other guys from Ballentine enter the bar chanting about Trivia Night, so we all grab our drinks and head back to the table. Walking behind Zoey, I set the water in front of her and place my hand on her lower back. Her shirt has ridden up slightly, so we're skin to skin.

"Thanks," she mutters. As she takes a sip of her drink, my fingers rub back and forth on her back. She coughs, spilling some water on her chin.

"You okay over there?" Millie asks with a raised brow.

Zoey nods frantically. "Fine."

"You good?" Kai asks, appearing by her side.

"Yeah," she clears her throat. "Just went down the wrong pipe."

I look down at the drink Kai sets in front of Zoey.

"I got you a cider, but I guess Jace already got you something?" Kai is talking to Zoey, but his eyes are trained on me. Shit, am I about to be in my first bar fight? And with my best friend of all people?

"Yeah," Zoey says loud enough for the entire table to hear. "Millie and I were talking, so I asked him to grab me a water. But thank you. For the cider."

"Sure." Kai nods, but his eyes still don't leave mine as he backs away. Almost like a warning or something.

Millie's eyes dart from Zoey to mine and there's something threatening in them. Jesus, what has Caleb gotten himself into?

In order to stay, we actually have to take part in Trivia Night, so we split into two teams: Kai, Conrad, Buzz, and Zeke vs. Zoey, Caleb, Millie, and me. The DJ quiets the music and we all patiently wait for this week's theme.

"We've got a pretty decent crowd tonight and as always we have the benders for the Winger U's Royals—"

"Boo," all the guys shout.

"What's a bender?" Zoey turns to me and asks.

I bend down closer to her ear, so she can hear me over the noise. "A shitty player."

She giggles as she leans into me.

"You know I'm just fucking with you," the DJ continues. "Let's get this all started. The theme for the night is pop culture. So, all of you Taylor Swift bitches better be ready. You all know the rules. You have thirty seconds to write down the answer. Once you do, your whole team must put their hands in the air. And wave them around like you just don't care." He pauses for dramatic effect. "Wow, tough crowd tonight. Now the important rules. No phones, no cheating, and no getting so shitfaced we have to call an ambulance for you."

"Think he's talking to you," Caleb says, slapping Buzz on the shoulder. Buzz takes this as an invitation to jump on Caleb and put him in a headlock.

"Jesus, it's not even midnight yet," the DJ mutters.

Caleb shakes Buzz off and they both cheers before chugging their beers.

Separating into our teams, we huddle around the round tables and get ready for our questions.

"Listen up." The smiling Millie from moments ago is gone and in her place is a competitive monster who could give Marty McSorley a run for their money. "I play to win. So, if you're like Caleb and you're just here to fuck around, sit back and shut it, okay Jace?" Millie says.

Zoey's and my eyes widen. Damn, I think I'm a little afraid of this chick.

"Uhh..."

"Down, girl," Caleb teases, but instantly shuts his mouth when Millie turns her fury on him.

"First question of the night," the DJ announces. "How many children does Nick Cannon have?"

Millie grabs the pencil, but freezes just above the paper. Does she actually know this shit?

"Do you actually know the answer?" Caleb mutters.

"Shut up. I'm thinking," she snaps.

Zoey shrugs. "I'm out. I know he has at least two with Mariah Carey, but that's it."

"You have five more seconds," the DJ warns.

"What?!" Millie shrieks. "There's no way it's been twenty-five seconds already!"

"Five. Four. Three ..."

"Ah! Um, shit!" Millie scribbles down something and then tosses her hands in the air. We all follow suit.

"The answer was twelve. If you wrote down twelve, you get a point."

Zoey nods at our sheet, "What did you write down?"

Millie's mouth is open in horror. "I wrote down five. Who the hell has twelve children?"

Caleb chuckles into his beer.

"Raise your hand if you got the answer right," the DJ says.

Millie's expression turns from awe to pissed off when she sees most of the room got the question correct.

"This is common knowledge?!" she shrieks.

"Alright, next question," the DJ continues. "What animal does Britney Spears famously carry on her shoulder during a performance?"

Zoey practically jumps out of her seat, about to shout the answer before calming back down. "A snake. It's a snake. I think it's like a big yellow one or something like that."

"Are you sure?" Caleb asks, then nervously glances at Millie. "Like 110% sure?"

She nods. "Positive. Whenever her songs come on the radio, my mom grabs a toy snake and pretends she's a pop star."

Millie sucks in a deep breath before writing down our answer.

"Five, four, three, two, one. Hands up."

We do as the DJ says and wait.

"Congrats to those of you that said snake! Raise your hand and give yourselves a point if you said snake!"

"Holy shit! Go, Zoey," Millie says, giving her a high-five.

Not sure when I became such a sap, but seeing her smile is warming something inside me.

"Are we ready for the next one? Which Taylor Swift song has a lyric that's often misheard as "Starbucks lovers"?"

I laugh to myself because this shit could not be easier. "Blank Space."

Zoey turns to me. "What did you just say?"

The smile falls from my face. Did I just say that out loud? "Hmm?"

"You just said something."

Maybe if I play dumb, she'll forget she heard anything. "No, I didn't."

"Yes, you did. Did you say the answer?"

Why the fuck did I think playing dumb would work? Zoey doesn't let shit go. Her eyes are burning a hole through me while Caleb and Millie try and think of different Taylor Swift songs.

"And that's five, four, three—"

Zoey turns away from me and tells Millie, "It's Blank Space. Hurry up and write down Blank Space."

Millie writes it down and we all put our hands up just in time. When the DJ reveals the answer, I don't miss the mischievous look Zoey tosses my way.

Chapter Nineteen
Zoey

"This isn't fair," Millie complains. "We're at a huge disadvantage being at this table."

"It's just a game, Kentucky. We're only one point behind Kai and them." Caleb tells her.

"Want me to tell you that the next time your shot goes wide just because you were a smidge too far away from the net?"

With a resigned sigh, Caleb turns to Jace and me, "How do you guys feel about shifting closer to the DJ?"

We haven't even opened our mouths to answer before Millie starts walking away.

Millie might be crazy competitive, but she's not wrong. With more people making their way here, it's almost impossible to hear the DJ clear enough back in this corner.

"Oh no," Jace feigns shock, but his smirk gives him away, "we've been left alone. Whatever shall we do?"

I giggle to myself but tense when his hands come around me from behind, caging me in against the table.

"What are you doing?" I ask over my shoulder.

"It's a dark corner back here. And the bar is getting busy. I don't want anyone getting too close to you. Plus, Kai is busy playing Trivia with his team. There's no one else here to watch out for you."

I roll my eyes, slightly relaxing into him. "I think I can watch out for myself."

His chuckle is deep and husky. "Keep telling yourself that."

I move my elbow back to nudge him in the stomach, but he steps closer. I gasp when I feel him press against my ass. All of him.

"Jace," I breathe. All the moisture has disappeared from my mouth and I can't for the life of me swallow the lump that has lodged itself in my throat.

"Yes," he sing-songs next to my ear.

"Wh-what are you do-doing?"

There's a moment of silence and I'm nervous my stuttering might have scared him off.

"Tell me to stop and I will. Tell me to back off and never touch you again and I will." One of his hands leaves the table to grab my hip. "You are in complete control of the situation. Always. Do you understand?"

I can't speak. I'm either too stunned or my stutter has completely taken over my speech.

Jace squeezes my hip. "Use your words."

"Yes," I say without hesitation.

"Yes?"

"Yes. I understand." I turn my head, meeting his intense gaze. "And I don't. Want you to stop, that is."

The hand that was on my hip slowly—so painfully slowly—begins traveling up my stomach. "You don't?"

I shake my head and close my eyes, letting my body relax further into him.

"I've been thinking about you lately," he continues, just as his hand meets the underside of my tit.

This is so not a good idea. I should put a stop to this. He said I could. I easily could. All with one simple word. I open my eyes to do a brief scan of the room and when I find that no one is even remotely looking our way, I give in.

"Were you touching yourself when you did?"

Jace's groan ignites something in my stomach and I swear I could come with just him looking at me. Well, I could at least try.

"Fuck, you're perfect."

A shriek escapes my mouth when he pinches my nipple through the fabric of my shirt. I can't do that again, but holy God does that feel good. Without thinking, I shift my stance which moves my ass back and forth. Jace grunts and I'm not entirely sure if it's a good grunt or bad grunt.

"You hustled me, didn't you?"

My forehead creases in confusion. "What do you mean?"

"There's no way you needed help in getting a guy. The way you just shook your ass against my cock proves that much."

"Jace—"

"Have you fucked yourself to the thought of me yet?"

When I don't answer immediately, the hand that was cupping my boob, pinches my nipple again.

"Ahh, shit."

"You know I like it better when you use your words."

We're not even looking at each other, but he's towering over me and so demanding and I'm way too excited to be in a crowded bar.

I can't tell him. He's going to think I'm a pathetic loser if I tell him the truth. I asked him to help me with Leo and after we went on one measly date, I couldn't help but finger-fuck myself to thought of Jace taking me from behind.

"You first," I blurt out, trying to avoid the inevitable.

He chuckles, running his nose up the side of my neck. "That's not even a question. Have you seen the way you look? God damn delicious. Fucking edible. When I can't sleep at night, I stay awake wondering what you taste like."

"Oh my God," I whimper.

"Would you do that for me? Let me taste you?"

He takes my earlobe between his teeth and gently bites. My eyes look around, once again pleased to find no one noticing us.

"We're in a room full of people, Jace."

Jace's hand that was still on the table slides over to rest on top of my hand. He interlocks our fingers and guides my hand off the table; I go willingly.

"What if someone sees?" I ask.

Toying with me, he uses my fingertips to lightly run back and forth over the sliver of skin above my pants. My body starts shaking, I'm so pent up. This is absolute insanity and I should've stopped it a long time ago.

"Do you want me to stop?" When I don't answer, he groans my name in my ear.

"No."

Jace guides my hand down my pants and into my panties. His finger helps mine swipe against me and I shiver. I need so much more. I try to break from his hold when the hand that was on my tit is suddenly on the front of my neck.

"Now, now. Let's not get greedy."

"Please," I beg. "It hurts."

"I know, baby. I know."

This entire time, neither of us have made eye contact. Maybe that's why we haven't stopped. But I can't not see this. Never letting go, Jace takes my hand out of my pants and brings it to his mouth. He stares at it for a moment. Admiring it. And then he sucks it clean. Every single inch of it. Jace's satisfied smile is unbelievably hot and just when I think he might actually kiss me, a large body bumps into

Jace from behind, bursting our private bubble.

The reality of what we just did hits me all at once and I vaguely hear Conrad say to Jace, "The fuck do you think you're doing? He's right over there."

Sweat forms along my hairline and the room starts to spin. I need to get out of here. I push away from the table and run as fast as possible towards the exit. I don't stop running until I'm safe and sound back in my own dorm room.

Chapter Twenty
Jace

Everyone is doing their pre-game rituals and I'm sitting in the locker room, trying not to get a fucking boner. I have not been able to get the taste of Zoey out of my mouth since last night and it only makes me want more. She was shy at first, but then turned to putty in my hands. It was easily the sexiest moment of my entire life and I didn't even get off. Fuck, I need to taste her again.

"Bennett!"

I snap to attention when Coach yells my name. "Yes, sir?"

"Are you here with us?"

I nod. "Yes, sir."

"Then get your ass on the ice!"

I look around and realize I'm the last one in the locker room.

"Shit," I mutter to myself.

I'm the last one on the ice and join the rest of the guys skating around in circles, taking shots at Rodriguez in net. My puck goes wide and I skate to find another when I'm nudged from behind.

"Someone have a little too much fun last night?" Kai taunts.

I chuckle nervously as I pick up a puck with my stick and bounce it a few times.

"Seriously, man. You ran off early. What's her name?"

I miss the puck and it drops to the ice, the noise like a gunshot to the heart. My eyes fly to his wondering if he knows what I did to her. What I made her do. Wait, did I make her do it? She went willingly. It wasn't like I forced her to do it, right? Oh, shit. I need to talk to her right now.

I turn to skate away when Coach chooses that exact moment to blow his whistle.

We all pass the pucks in, letting the rookies on the team gather them together. I rush to the bench quickly, wanting to be the first to Coach.

"Hey Coach. Can I run to the bathroom real quick?"

"That's a joke, right?"

I wear my best smile. "You know, when nature calls."

"Tell it to wait. We've got a game to play."

I sit my ass down and once the entire team is back at the bench, Coach gives us one of his pre-game motivational speeches.

"It's time to get your heads out of your asses and play like I know you can."

"Coach, did you just compliment us?" I say, unable to help myself.

"Can it," he quips.

I smirk as the rest of the guys chuckle.

"We're playing FSU who is known for their defense. Stay vigilant and for the love of all that is holy, stay out of the sin bin."

Straight off the face-off, Beaver takes it down center only to be knocked on his ass in seconds. Beaver is one the bigger guys on our team. I'm talking bigger in height and width. I would've thought a hurricane couldn't do damage to Beaver. But watching him lying on the ice within the first minute of the game tells me one thing. We are totally screwed.

You would think being on a power play would work to our advantage, but their defense is insane. A shot from the point hits the goalie and bounces off his pad, resulting in a scramble around the net where Gomez kicks the puck to his stick. He tries to score on the rebound, but is cross-checked in the upper back. Our entire bench protests, very loudly, but the shitty refs stay completely silent.

"Hey ref, does your wife know you're fucking us?" Caleb shouts.

I look up at Coach and see his stone cold face twitch slightly. As tough as he tries to be, I know he finds us all funny and enjoyable to be around. He just hides it. Very deep, deep down.

The buzzer sounds, ending our power play and we have nothing to show for it except a pissed off Beaver. Caleb, Beaver, and I jump the bench when it's time to switch lines. I man an FSU player while Caleb goes to establish a forecheck; Beaver doesn't give two shits and goes after the mammoth who took him down. It all happens fast, but within seconds the benches are cleared and both teams are fighting on the ice. The FSU player I was watching grabs my jersey and tries to sucker punch me, but I head butt them before they get the chance. I love wearing helmets. The sounds of multiple whistles echo throughout the arena while the two refs do what they can to break it up.

Once everything calms down, Beaver and the mammoth are ejected and four players from each team are sent to the sin bin. Since I was on the ice when the brawl happened, I'm unfortunately one of them. The only good thing that comes from it, is while I'm in there, I look around the crowd and see her. Zoey's here. Her eyes are focused on the ice, watching Kai control the puck. But she's here. She wouldn't be here if what we did, what I had her do crossed an unforgivable line. Right?

I nervously chew on my mouthguard, wanting this whole shit show of a game to just be over. At least get us to the end of the period so I could text her or something. I just need to make sure I didn't hurt her. I can't have her thinking I would ever hurt her.

I'm the first one in the locker room once the period ends and even though Coach's stare would kill me if it could, I fire off a text to Zoey.

> J: Are we okay? Did I fuck everything up last night?

> Z: What are you talking about?

> J: You ran out of the bar. I never meant to force you to do something you didn't want to do

My phone starts vibrating in my hand once Coach walks in. Shit. If I answer this, he's going to actually kill me. I act like I'm stretching my back and turn away from the door, quickly answering the call.

"I can't talk," I whisper.

"You didn't do anything wrong," she says quickly. Five simple words that relax my entire body and make me feel like I'm not the worst human being in the entire world.

"Bennett! You with us?" Coach yells more than asks.

"Thank you," I mumble and hang up the phone, dropping it to my side before turning back to face the music.

Knowing I haven't completely fucked things up between Zoey and I, the second I'm back on the ice, I'm a totally different guy. I pick the pocket of some jagoff and rush the puck past their offense with ease. One of their defense backs up the closer I get to the net. With a shit-eating grin on my face, I deke right then go five hole.

If you've never played hockey before, you'd think after you'd score a goal all you'd hear is loud chaos. The echo of the fans celebrating another point to add to the board. Not me though. I just hear silence. And if I close my eyes, I can pretend the crowd isn't even here. At least I can before my teammates tackle me. Heading back to the bench, my head feels like it's in a fog. The skates slicing through ice, sticks slapping the boards, knowing the crowd is cheering and chanting my name, but not being able to hear any of it. It's almost peaceful. Kind of crazy to think about it that way since hockey is one of the most brutal sports out there.

Feeling the heat, I sit down on the bench and rip my helmet off. I shake the sweat from my hair and flip it back. A sigh of relief escapes me when a rush of crisp air washes over me and the combination of hot and cold sends a shiver down my spine. Or maybe it's the way Zoey's eyes are trained on mine right now.

Zoey

I left quickly after the game, not waiting around for the guys. I figured they could celebrate their sweep with just the team. Jace scoring the only goal of the night was incredible to watch and I've had a smile on my face ever since. Once I'm home and watching a movie in bed on my laptop, I plug my phone into the charger close by. You know, just in case anyone decides to call me.

My eyes are refusing to stay open and I let out a defeated sigh moments before my phone starts ringing. The scramble of pillows and blankets as I try to find my phone is a tad embarrassing. I swear to God, it better not be Kai.

"Hello?" I answer, a tad out of breath. I push a tuft of hair out of my face realizing I never looked at who was actually calling.

"You sound out of breath. Were you thinking about me?" Jace asks. I can hear the smile in his voice.

"Maybe I was," I giggle, "or maybe I lost my phone in my blankets and was struggling to find it before the call went to voicemail."

Jace's deep chuckle has me relaxing back onto my pillow. "I saw you tonight. At my game."

I feel my cheeks burn as I remember how he looked at me after he scored that goal. "It was a nice goal. I cheered for you and every-thing."

"I thought I heard a loud redhead in the crowd."

"Shut up," I giggle like an idiot.

"You sound tired. Are you in bed?"

I nod, my eyelids drifting shut. "Mm-hmm. My eyes don't want to stay open."

"I can stay on the phone with you until you fall asleep if you want?"

Never in a million years would I have pegged that kind of a question coming out of Jace Bennett's mouth.

"I'd like that," I say with a smile so big, my cheeks start hurting.

The next morning when I wake up, my phone battery is down to 12% and I have one missed text message.

J: Sweet dreams cinnamon roll

Chapter Twenty-One

Zoey

I'm just closing my eyes when I hear faint knocking at the front door. There's no way I'm getting out of my blanket cocoon to answer it. The pull of sleep has me in its grasp when the sheets are suddenly yanked off of me.

"What the hell?" I shriek.

"Let's get lunch," Kai says with the biggest grin.

"Get lost," I mutter, grabbing a pillow and placing it over my head to block out the sun. When he tries to grab it, I refuse to let it go, but he uses his stupid hockey strength against me and easily wins.

"Come on. I'm buying."

"He's says he's treating," Corrine eagerly shouts from the doorway.

I groan the entire time Kai drags me out of bed, helps me into my shoes and practically pushes me out the door with my roommates.

Kai's weirdly chatty with Corrine and Becks while I walk behind them through town. I'm not entirely sure what's happening, but something about this situation seems off. I mean Kai's a nice guy, but why is he all of a sudden so buddy-buddy with my roommates?

We walk to Pizza Pub, a small pizza joint a few blocks away from campus. It's a cute little bistro with an Italian vibe to it. Once we get our food and we're all sat down, things start to feel even weirder. The polite chit-chat from before is gone and now it's just awkward silence.

"So," Kai rubs his hands together, "this looks incredible."

He got pizza with, like, five different meats on it.

"Why did you insist we come to lunch?" I ask, my suspicions finally getting the best of me.

Kai finishes chewing the bite in his mouth before saying, "Well, I invited you. Corrine invited herself and Becks."

Becks smacks Corrine's arm. "You little liar! You told me we were invited."

Corrine shrugs. "He said the more the merrier."

"Because he was being polite." Becks directs an apologetic look in our direction.

I angle my body towards Kai and lower my voice, "What did you want to talk about?"

His smile slowly starts growing. "I, uh, I applied to this camp a while back. I didn't really think much of it, but I got in."

"That's awesome. What kind of camp?"

He shrugs like it's no big deal. "It's kind of like an amateur hockey league thing. Some guys from the NHL volunteer their time to come and Coach us a little bit. Give us an edge up for when scouts come to our games."

My food freezes on its way to my mouth. "Kai! Are you serious? That's freaking amazing! You were accepted?"

He nods a few times. "I had to send in an online application and then a video submission. They only take a handful of guys and someone must have messed up and sent me an acceptance letter."

"Messed up? Shut up!" I gently smack his arm. "This is so cool. Have you told your dad?"

Kai's phone vibrates and he quickly checks it. "Uh, no. But I think I'm gonna go do that now."

"Now? We just sat down a few minutes ago."

Standing up, he fishes his wallet out of his pocket and hands me his credit card.

"I'll catch up with you," are his parting words.

"Seriously?" I say more to myself as he races out the door.

"That was really weird, right?" Becks asks.

Like non-weirdos, we stay and finish lunch. I do get a to-go box for Kai's pizza though because even though he ditched and was acting super shady, he did treat us. Becks, Corrine, and I are walking down the hall to our room when we stop at our door. I swipe my card key to enter, open the door, but stop when I hear the first crunch. Lifting my foot, I look down to see what I stepped on.

"Why aren't you going in?" Corrine whines. "I have to pee."

I open the door wider and show them why I can't go any further.

"Those little shits," Becks laughs.

"Screw it, I'll pee outside," Corrine says and runs down the hall.

"Will she really?" I ask Becks and she just shrugs.

"How do they keep getting in here?" I shout.

My eyes scan the living room where every inch of carpet is covered with little plastic cups filled with water.

"Should we just walk through it?" Becks asks.

"We could, but then our floor will take forever to dry. We could drink it all?"

"Do we trust they got the water from the faucet?"

I pretend to gag. "Scratch that idea. I guess we can tiptoe around it?"

Becks nudges my shoulder. "You first."

I stare in disbelief. "Why me?"

"Because you're the reason for this prank war."

"You two aren't exactly innocent bystanders."

I groan even though she's right. I scan the floor and when I find a spot that looks like I could set my foot down, I make my move. A terrible move because I instantly lose my balance and when I go to grab for Becks, I fall immediately. And am now laying on the floor, completely soaked. Becks and I are laughing our asses off, but she makes sure to take a picture of me with my thumbs up. Once I'm all dried off, I send it to Jace.

Z: *sends pic* Using my brother as a decoy? I didn't know we were playing dirty. Guess the gloves are coming off

J: I think I like this version of you

I wipe a bead of sweat from my brow as I dramatically lay down on the ground. It is ungodly hot out today and I've only been outside for thirty minutes. Becks said she was going to meet up with me to continue helping make this lot safe for a playground, but so far she is nowhere in sight. I close my eyes, pretending I'm on a beach. The waves are crashing against the shore and I'm getting a tan while listening to a new audiobook. The heat is way better when I'm on a beach.

"What are you doing? That doesn't go there!" Regina shrieks at someone, ruining my fantasy.

I prop myself up on my elbows and squint into the light.

"Did you pass out?" Millie asks, concern all over her face.

I groan. "No, but I might. Why is it so hot today? Isn't Winger U supposed to be cold 90% of the year?"

She laughs, sitting down next to me and handing me a water bottle.

"Don't remind me. I hate being cold. Anyways, how can I help?"

My new friend gets to work picking up trash with me. It's mostly cigarettes and I kind of want to gag.

"So, where's your guy?" Millie asks.

"My what?"

"Jace? Aren't you two together?"

"What?" It comes out as a shriek and I cough to cover it up. "I mean, no. W-W-We aren't together."

Her smile widens. "Oh. Okay."

Millie finds some more trash and tosses it in her trash bag that she's carrying around. If Millie thinks we're together, then what does Kai really think? I'm probably just being paranoid. Millie's a girl and we tend to pick up on cues that boys don't. Right? Right.

"I don't know which is worse," Becks says, strolling on over to Millie and me, "weeding or picking up trash."

I grab the pair of gloves in my back pocket to hand to her. "Take it up with Regina."

"The last thing I want to do is get on Regina's bad side."

"Hey Becks," Millie says as she walks past.

"You two know each other?"

Becks nods. "She works at Cherry On Top with me."

"I could so go for a cold milkshake right now," I moan

"I wouldn't step in that building on my day off for a million dollars," Becks grunts.

Becks pulls on her gloves before getting another trash bag to help. A smile tugs at my lips when she doesn't make any more snarky comments. I love my Becks.

"Is lover boy coming?" Becks asks.

I hate my Becks.

"You see it too?" Millie chimes in. "I thought they were already together."

"There's no lov-ver boy." When Becks smiles at my stutter, I flip her off and move a few feet away from her and Millie.

"You guys here to lend a hand?" Regina asks and I turn to see who she's talking to.

My jaw hits the floor. Jace, Kai, Caleb, a girl who looks eerily similar to Caleb, Conrad, and Buzz are all sweaty and panting.

"We could always use more volunteers. Especially ones with muscles," Regina flirts.

"Put me and my muscles to work," Buzz announces. Regina grabs his hand, walking him over to the broken cinder blocks that need hauled away.

Caleb winks at Millie. "Hey, Kentucky."

"Gag," Becks whines before walking away.

"I'm Bonnie, Caleb's twin. I absorbed half of his brain in the womb, so that's why he's so stupid."

Caleb gives her a pointed glare and I wave to her as she walks away with the guys.

"Bonnie's funny," I tell Kai when he steps in front of me.

"Yeah, she's something."

"What are you guys doing here?"

Kai shrugs. "Ask Jace. It was his idea."

It's not exactly a scowl, but Kai doesn't look thrilled to be here as he walks over to help another group.

Jace saunters up to me and I try to bite back my smile, but I can't. He's here. And he brought help.

"What are you doing here?"

Jace quickly looks around, then takes a step closer, tucking a lock of my hair behind my ear. "It's a nice day out and Ballentine is behind on their philanthropic hours."

I raise my brows skeptically. "And you just happened to end up here? At my organization?"

"Oh? This is your organization? I had no idea."

I roll my eyes. "You know what I mean."

Jace shrugs one shoulder. "Didn't really feel like spending the day inside."

I stuff my hands in my back pockets. "That's the only reason you're here?"

"The only one. Why? Oh, did you think I was here because of you?"

I shake my head, about to turn around and walk away, when his hand catches my wrist.

"You never told me you were a part of The Good Neighbor Program."

I shrug. "I don't help out as much as I want with school and work being so hectic, but I like to donate my time when I can."

Jace claps his hands then rubs them together, "Just tell me where to go, boss."

Chapter Twenty-Two

Zoey

I'm sitting in my ged ed class, bored out of my freaking mind. The only reason I chose this class was because I was late picking my classes last year and am hard-core regretting that right now. We're in a lecture hall and I'm sitting closer to the back of the room, so when my phone vibrates with a text message, I grab it out of my bag.

> **J: Next lesson, my young Padawan is the art of sexting.**

My eyes widen in surprise. Jace and I have been flirting more and more lately, but we haven't talked about anything like that. I look around the room at everyone focused on their notes and curse him. He couldn't have picked a worse topic at a worse time.

> **Z: I'm in class. Later.**

> **J: School waits for no one!**

I had to cover my mouth to hold in my laughter. There is no way we're talking about this right now. I'll just text him back later. I go to put my phone away when it vibrates again.

> **J: Sexting is like dancing. You don't want to go too fast. You want to slow down and enjoy the moment.**

Awe. That was strangely poetic for Jace.

> **J: It's like a fart. If you force it, it's probably shit.**

There he is. A laugh escapes my lips and the professor zeros in on me. She points to my phone and shakes her head. I nod and place it in my bag at my feet. I continue taking notes when my watch vibrates.

> **J: I don't even get a laughing emoji! That was funny**

My shoulders silently shake and that's when I hear the soft padding of heels coming towards me. Quickly I silence my watch and start writing.

"Ms. Griffin? A moment?"

Putting on a smile, I follow the professor on shaky legs towards her desk. I'm going to kill Jace.

"You know you are only allowed your phones out for educational purposes in this class."

"Yes."

"Not frivolous texting and snap chatting and whatever applications are out there that kids like to use these days."

"Yes, I do."

She folds her arms and I can't tell what is going to happen next. I pray to anyone that will listen that she doesn't ask to see my phone or ask what was making me laugh so much.

"Next time I see your phone out, I will be confiscating it."

I nod, taking a deep calming breath. "Y-Yes. Of course. It won't happen again."

I walk quickly back to my desk, but am stopped when she clears her throat.

"And Ms. Griffin?"

"Yes?"

She points to her wrist. "Leave the watch at home too."

When class is over, the rest of the day is very blah. So once I get home, I make myself a blanket cocoon and hide in it while mindlessly playing on my phone. I stop scrolling through my photos when

Jace's name appears on the top of my screen.

"What are you smiling at?" Corrine asks from the doorway, making me jump in surprise and drop my phone on my face.

"Ow." I rub my nose and groan. "I didn't hear you come in."

"Must be texting someone really good if you didn't even hear me."

She's staring at me like I'm going to spill all my secrets, but instead I click my phone shut.

"I was just looking at pictures. What's up?"

She definitely doesn't believe me.

"Yeah, I totally don't believe you. But Becks is out with Todd or Tank or whatever his name is and I'm hungry. Come eat with me?"

"Sorry. I just had a big snack and am pretty tired, so I planned on relaxing the rest of the evening."

Without even a backward glance, Corrine is walking out our front door "It's fine. I'll just eat by myself."

Okay, then.

Picking my phone back up, my thumb hovers over the notifications, wondering if this is a smart decision. Taking a deep breath, I click the message.

J: I didn't get you in too much trouble earlier, did I?

I should just ignore the message. Or at least wait a little to text back. I can at least pretend I'm out doing something fun instead of rotting in my bed.

Z: What would you do if I said yes?

Clearly, I have self-destructive tendencies.

J: If Professor Never Smiles puts you in detention, I'll break you out. Scouts honor.

Z: Somehow I don't believe you were in boy scouts

J: I plead the fifth. You interested in resuming our lesson?

My heart stops and I re-read his message about seven times. Part of me thought he was just screwing with me earlier and that's why it didn't make me nervous. I've never sent a dirty message before. There was never a reason to.

Z: Show me what you got big boy

J: What? Like a picture?

Z: *rolling eyes emoji*

J: Here's your tip of the day my Chips Ahoy. Guys like to be edged too. Make him beg for it. You're worth it

I feel my entire body warm at those last three words. They're not even dirty, but maybe that's the point? When I don't answer, he messages back.

J: I had a dream about you the other night

Z: Seriously? Why?

J: Class has started...

Z: Oh. Okay.

After fifteen seconds of radio silence, I realize that I'm supposed to continue the conversation.

Z: Right. What was your dream about?

J: We were back in the laundry room at Ballentine.

Instantly, I'm transported back to that small room where I was trying to hideout. I had just made a fool of myself and felt like complete shit. And in a very un-like Jace way, he made me feel slightly better. The memory brings a small smile to my lips.

J: You were wearing that short little skirt and when you bent over, I could see your panties

My mouth falls open as I recall my clothes. I was wearing a jean skirt, but it wasn't that short. I know he's trying to teach me, but if he's using a real scenario, he should at least be accurate.

Z: No you couldn't.

J: Wanna bet?

J: Blue, with little white and yellow daisies. I've thought about those panties a lot.

I gasp because I'm wearing those exact same panties right now. He really did see them that night. I'm supposed to answer him, but what the hell do I say back to that? I wipe the sweat off my palm, stop thinking and start typing.

> **Z: You mean the ones I'm wearing right now?**

His response is instant.

> **J: Pics or I don't believe you**

> **Z: *middle finger emoji***

> **J: We were back in the laundry room. But this time, I didn't let you leave.**

Closing my eyes, I let myself travel back to that room. The scents of that evening invade my nostrils. His blueberry and vanilla smelling weed, the perfect amount of cologne that made him smell fantastic. A feeling I rarely ever feel starts forming in my belly. It's hot and heavy. Wait, am I getting turned on just by reading his words?

It's been a few minutes and I haven't answered. I don't want him to think I'm chickening out. I take a deep breath and shut off my mind. He's saying he didn't let me leave. He's trying to take control. And … I think I like it.

> **Z: What did you let me do?**

J: That's my girl.

Oh. I like the sound of that.

J: I wanted to take my time with you. But the thought of those panties made it impossible.

I try to swallow, but my mouth is too dry and when the hell did it get so hot in here? I toss off my blankets and sit up. Why does this not feel like a hypothetical situation? I have no idea why my brain isn't connecting to the rest of me, but my fingers have already typed out a message before I can stop myself.

Z: I didn't want to go slow.

J: No you didn't. You started the dryer and jumped up on it like you'd done it before. But you haven't, have you? I was the first guy who ever turned you on enough that you couldn't wait to get to a bedroom. Couldn't wait to have me inside you.

Oh, dear God. I keep reminding myself this is all imaginary, just a lesson. But as I close my eyes I can see every dirty detail Jace is describing. Me sitting tall, him between my parted thighs. His calloused hands running up my bare legs, leaving goosebumps in their path. My phone hasn't buzzed in a few minutes, so I take the initiative.

> Z: I didn't say to stop. I wrapped my legs around you and pulled you closer, ripping that disgusting joint out of your mouth and tossing it to the ground. You laughed, but I knew you didn't think it was funny.

> Z: I'd never been punished before, but I couldn't help moaning when you gathered my hair and tugged it hard enough to expose my neck. Your lips were soft and I liked when your teeth scraped against my skin. You'd barely touched me and I was already so...

He did say to make him beg.

> J: So...what? Please tell me, baby. I need to hear you say it.

At this point, the fantasy is real. I close my eyes and I'm fully back in the moment and can feel everything. I remember how his lips felt against mine when we were in his room and my hand dives between my legs.

> Z: I was so wet for you

J: And you were so tight. I'm fucking hard just thinking about it.

My toes curl and my fingers shake as I pull the small amount of fabric to the side. I'm warm and wet and it's all because of Jace. I can't think too much about it or else my body is going to shut down on me. Squeezing my eyes shut, I try to picture the finger sliding into me is his. My thumb circling my clit is his. It feels so good that I forget about my phone for a moment.

J: Be a good girl and tell me what you're doing to yourself. Tell me what you're doing and who you're thinking about while you're doing it.

I'm aching and hurting and no matter how I touch myself, I'm just out of reach. I need him here. I need his help.

Z: It's not the same

J: What isn't the same?

Z: It feels good when I touch myself, but it's not the same as when someone else does it

J: When who does it?

Z: When you do it

J: Are you imagining me sucking on those big, perfect tits while you come all over my hand?

Z: You didn't like that I ruined your joint and to show me you were in charge, you pulled me off the dryer, turned me around and took me from behind. My hand slipped down the front of me and the combination of my hand and your cock had me seeing stars

J: Fuck

Z: I'm so close, Jace. I'm so close.

J: I wish I could taste you right now. Come for me, baby.

I curve my finger and it feels so good. Sweat beads at my hairline and that feeling I've been chasing, that itch that so desperately needs to be scratched starts to fade away. Again. I pull my hand away and lay there in silence. God dammit! What the hell is wrong with me that I can't even make myself come? I look down at my phone, knowing he's going to text back soon. I don't want to ruin this for him, but I also don't want to lie.

Z: Wow

J: You're lucky my buddy borrowed my car tonight or else you'd be in serious trouble.

Z: Good night, Jace

J: Good night, Zoey

J: And in case you were wondering, you get an A+

Chapter Twenty-Three

Zoey

"Little Griffin!" I'm walking out of class and stop when I hear my name. Leo's jogging through the hall to talk to me? "Thought that was you."

"Hey, what's up?"

He shrugs, "Not much. Have a break between classes."

"Wish I was that lucky. I have about ten minutes to get across campus."

Hey, look at me. I just said something to Leo without stuttering. Maybe this whole Jace helping me thing is working.

"Ouch. Sounds rough," he jokes

We both chuckle and when Leo's eyes drift over my head, I turn and see Jace walking by. I wiggle my fingers in a small wave. Jace nods back in acknowledgment before heading over my way. Randomly carrying a blueberry muffin.

"Stanford," Jace says, face expressionless.

Leo's smile falters. "Didn't know you two knew each other."

My gaze darts back and forth. Jace's jaw is clenched and he kind of looks like he's about to punch Leo. Why does Leo look like he would welcome the fight?

"We're old friends," I say, neither acknowledging me. My gaze darts between them like I'm at a tennis match.

"Yeah," Jace tosses his arm around my shoulders, "old friends."

Leo smiles at me, ignoring Jace's obvious caveman behavior, and walks away.

"What was that?"

"What was what?" Jace asks, walking us out the door.

"Seriously? What just happened with Leo?"

Jace shrugs.

"Next time, maybe you should just pee on me to assert your dominance." I bump Jace but he just pulls me closer to him.

"You'd be into that? I gotta say, I never pictured you as a golden shower kind of girl, but—"

This time I do push him off, but he grabs my wrist to stop me from leaving.

"I'm sorry, my little candy corn."

He's not even trying to hide his smile.

"No, you're not."

After a few moments of an intense stare off, Jace sighs. "I promise not to be so weird next time. Okay?"

"Not the best apology I've ever heard, but definitely not the worst either."

His smile is infectious. "I'm all about average."

I continue walking and Jace follows me. "My next class is a short one, but want to grab some dinner after?"

His shoulders stiffen. "Can't. Got plans."

"Oh. Plans with ..."

"Interested in my love life, lollipop?" Jace smirks at me as he clearly avoids the question. He's totally lying. I think.

"Love life? I didn't know you had one of those."

It was meant as a joke, but Jace's hard demeanor doesn't change.

"Um, okay then. I guess I'll see you later. Are you going to, like, eat that muffin? It's kind of weird that you're just carrying it around. And aren't you allergic to blueberries?"

"Uh, yeah. You should hurry up before you're late to Phonetics." And then he's gone. I swear he picks up his pace as he walks away from me.

When I register I'm staring, I hurry up and get to class. It's only when I finally sit in my seat that I realize Jace knew what class I had next even though I never told him.

Jace

After I finish at the gym and shower, I want to see Zoey but remember she's in class. I message her a few times, but when she stops responding I assume it's because I got her in trouble. She has class in Kelly Hall and it's a nice day, so I decide to take a walk.

I'm passing the library when I realize she still has twenty minutes left, so I decide to stop and grab a coffee. There's a small coffee shop right when you walk in that also has pastries and smoothies.

"How can I help you?" the lady behind the counter asks.

"I'll take a small black coffee."

"Anything else?"

My eyes scan the menu. Does Zoey like coffee? I've never seen her drink it before. Maybe a smoothie? But what kind of fruit does she like?

"I'll take a blueberry muffin, too. Thanks."

She hits a couple of buttons and I swipe my campus ID to pay. After pouring way too much cream and sugar in my coffee, I make my way to Kelly Hall. It's perfect timing too because it looks like Zoey's class is just letting out as I make my way into the building.

The hallway turns into chaos as students run from class to class. I finish my last few sips of coffee and throw the cup away. I set my sights on Zoey, but am not the first one to see her. Fucking Stanford? Really? That guy is such a tool. I stand off to the side and watch their interaction like the total creep I apparently am. She's smiling and giggling. I don't think I've ever heard Stanford say one thing worth smiling over, let alone laughing. I can't take it anymore and make my way towards them.

"Stanford," I nod in acknowledgement.

Leo's smile falters as he looks between Zoey and me. Then down at the blueberry muffin in my hand. "Didn't know you two knew each other."

What I wouldn't give to punch his smug-ass face right now.

"We're old friends," Zoey says.

"Yeah," I say, tossing my arm around her shoulders like a possessive jackass, "old friends."

Leo smiles at Zoey, ignoring me completely, and walks away.

Zoey waits until he's completely gone to say something. "What was that?"

"What was what?" I ask, guiding her out the door while I play dumb.

"Seriously? What just happened with Leo? That was weird."

I shrug, not wanting to think about Leo anymore than I already have.

"Next time, maybe you should just pee on me to assert your dominance." Zoey tries to push me away, but I just pull her closer.

"You'd be into that?" I tease. "I gotta say, I never pictured you as a golden shower kind of girl, but—"

This time I let her push me away, but I gently grab her wrist to stop her from leaving.

"I'm sorry, my little candy corn."

"No, you're not."

After a few moments of an intense stare off, I sigh. "I promise not to be so weird next time. Okay?"

"Not the best apology I've ever heard, but definitely not the worst either."

I smile at her. "I'm all about average."

She continues walking and I follow her. "My next class is a short one, but want to grab some dinner after?"

"Can't. Got plans," I quickly tell her, the lie easily rolling off my tongue. Seeing her with Stanford reminded me why we're doing this whole thing in the first place. Having dinner after class with her is something a boyfriend would do. Which I am not.

"Oh. Plans with…"

I give her my panty-melting smile that all the girls fall for. "Interested in my love life, lollipop?"

"Love life? I didn't know you had one of those," she teases. "Um, okay then. I guess I'll see you later. Are you going to, like, eat that muffin? It's kind of weird that you're just carrying it around. And aren't you allergic to blueberries?"

I chuckle to myself. I completely forgot about it once I saw her with Stanford. "Uh, yeah. You should hurry up before you're late to Phonetics." And then I walk away as fast as I possibly can without looking like a freak. Once I'm completely out of sight of Zoey, I toss the blueberry muffin on the ground. The birds can eat it. Such a stupid idea.

Am I a piece of shit for implying I have plans with a chick later? I know the right answer, but I'm trying not to think about it. After I get home, I take a nap. Once I get up, I realize throwing the muffin to the birds wasn't the most mature action I could've taken. This entire situation is because of Leo, so I should be a proud teacher that my lessons are working. Yeah, even that is too much of a stretch for me.

Chapter Twenty-Four

Jace

I'm walking back from the gym when I get a text from Conrad.

Sounds like some cryptic shit, but whatever. I'm curious. Instead of going in the front door, I walk through the gate on the side of the house. A bunch of the guys are hanging out and when I get closer to them, I see why.

A fucking trampoline is taking up half up our backyard.

"What the hell is going on?" I ask when I find Conrad. "Wait, are you waiting in line?"

He nods. "We figured only a few of us could be on the trampoline at once before we break it."

"Is no one wondering where the unsanctioned trampoline came

from?"

Caleb shrugs. "Who cares? Let's enjoy it before the cops find out."

The Ballentine House gets away with a lot. We're located just off campus, so campus security can't do shit to us and the local cops don't really care about us unless there are complaints from the nosey neighbors. Which has happened before. I laugh to myself as I head inside and up to my room.

After tossing my gym bag down, I find my phone, go to my favorites list and click on Zoey's name.

She answers after one ring, but doesn't say anything.

"A fucking trampoline?" I laugh. "Really?"

"I have no idea what you're talking about." She's trying so hard not to laugh. "I didn't think you'd be home for a while anyways."

My brows furrow in confusion. "And why is that?"

"I thought you had plans tonight?"

It dawns on me that my little lie might've hurt Zoey. I didn't mean to hurt her. I was only trying to distance myself from her, for both our sakes. Wait, is she ... jealous?

"Green isn't really your color," I tease.

She scoffs. "I am not jealous. You were just very insistent about your plans."

Changing topics, I start laughing about this ridiculous trampoline. "We're gonna get cited and it'll be all your fault, you know that, right?"

God, I love the sound of her laugh.

"Your housemates didn't seem to mind when they helped us set it up."

What a little shit. "You better get your ass over here to help take it down."

Is it possible to hear someone roll their eyes.

"I suppose I can stop over after practice later tonight."

"You better, or I'll come get you."

"That a promise?" she asks, her voice all low and seductive.

She hangs up before I can respond.

After practice, I walk back to Ballentine alone. Kai and some of the other guys went to grab drinks, but I said I needed to catch up on homework, aka see if Zoey actually shows. Instead of going through the front door, I walk through the side gate and around back. She's sitting on the porch, leaning back on her hands, staring at the sunset. I bite my lip knowing I shouldn't be thinking what I'm thinking—that she looks fucking beautiful. Her hair is in a messy ponytail and she's wearing a baggy shirt with biker shorts. She kind of looks like she rolled out of bed. God, I'm so screwed.

"You came," I say as I approach her.

She turns to look at me, a soft smile on her face. "How was practice?"

I groan, sitting down next to her. "Tiring. What'd you do tonight?"

She shakes her head, "Absolutely nothing. It was pretty boring all around."

Why is she smiling at me like that?

"Anyways, let's get to it. I don't want to be here all night."She jumps up and heads towards the trampoline while I grab the tool kit we keep in the small shed.

"I read something online that says you shouldn't just unscrew every-thing," she says.

"Huh?"

She crosses her arms over her chest. "I don't know. It was some article about how once trampolines are jumped on, it puts too much pressure on the screws."

I exhale sharply. "Well, what am I supposed to do then?"

"The article said to shake it."

"Shake it?" I ask, skeptically.

She nods vigorously. "Yeah. Like grab one of the rails and give it a good shake."

I stare at her. What the hell is she even talking about?

Zoey places her hands up in defeat. "Look, you can do it however you want. It's just what I read online. And you know they can't put anything online that isn't real."

I chuckle to myself and drop the tool kit.

I point a finger at her. "Fine, but when this doesn't work and I end up pulling a muscle, I'm telling Coach on you."

She shakes, pretending she's scared. Looking away from her, I grab one of the rails and plant my feet firmly in the grass. And God help me, I pull the bar to try and shake the trampoline.

And then I'm on my ass on the hard, cold ground.

"What the fuck?" I yell, staring down at the rod in my hand.

Zoey has fallen over on her knees, laughing so hard tears stream down her face. Between panting breaths, she admits, "That was so worth coming over an hour early."

I look at her in awe. That little shit pulled a prank on top of another prank? I toss the rod down and stand up.

"Oh, you think this is funny?"

Zoey scrambles back to her feet, but is still shaking with laughter.

"That," I point at the trampoline that has now collapsed on itself, "is what you were doing while I was at practice?"

She wipes a tear off her cheek and she's still freaking laughing! While she's distracted, I make a split decision and go for it. Zoey shrieks when I tackle her to the ground and we both start laughing.

"Say you're sorry," I yell, but there's no malice behind it.

She screams as I tickle her ribs, rolling us around in the grass.

"I can't breathe. I'm sorry! I'm sorry!"

"I don't believe you!"

We stop rolling with her on top of me and I relent my tickle attack. Fuck, she looks good on top. My hands come to rest on her waist and the slightest movement has her rubbing against my cock. Leaning down, she brushes my nose with hers and just as I close my eyes so I can kiss her, she whispers, "Good, because I'm not sorry."

Like a spider monkey, she jumps up and runs away from me. Is she serious? Does she know I actually like to run on the treadmill? I give her a five-second head start, then sprint after her.

The only reason I don't catch her is because she darts into the house and almost runs into Kai's back.

"What the—"

Kai turns around, his forehead creased. "Zo? What are you doing here?"

She struggles to breathe when I catch up with her. "I was helping, um, I was helping."

Kai turns to me, eyebrows raised for an explanation. "She unscrewed all the hardware on the trampoline and then had me pull it apart. She thinks she's funny or something."

Zoey smacks my arm. "I don't think I'm funny. I know I'm funny. That shit was hilarious."

We both laugh, but Kai looming over us dampens our spirit.

After a moment of uncomfortable silence, Zoey says, "I gotta head home. Early classes tomorrow."

"Need a ride?" Kai asks before I can.

She shakes her head, avoiding my eye contact. "I'm all good. Catch you guys later."

And then she's gone and Kai is staring at me like he wants to kill me, light my bones on fire and piss on the ashes.

"Everything good?" I ask with the most charming smile I can muster. It does nothing to diffuse the tension between us.

Kai crosses his arms. "Why was Zoey here?"

I stuff my hands in my pockets. "Little prankster set the trampoline up. Said she would help me take it dow—"

"I could've helped you," he interrupts.

"You didn't offer. Anyways, I need a shower," I pat Kai on the shoulder and head quickly upstairs. I can feel his eyes on me the entire way up to my room.

Zoey

The one thing I love about Winger University is how small it is. I love that I can walk around the entire campus in less than half an hour. I love that cozy small town vibe it gives off. What I do not love is running into people that you are trying to avoid.

Kai stares down at me with a less-than-happy expression. I slipped out of Ballentine pretty quick two nights ago and haven't seen Kai since. Clearly he's had time to think about why I was at his house. And why I was there with Jace.

"This seat taken?" he asks, pulling the chair out opposite me.

I shake my head and he plops down, dropping his backpack on the ground next to us. I chose to study at the coffee shop on campus because I needed to be close to some caffeine. I haven't slept well the past few nights and it's finally catching up with me. I want to say I have no idea why I can't sleep, but I know.

Kai nods to my papers spread out on the table. "Working hard?"

"Or hardly working?" I joke. It's something his dad always says, but he doesn't find it very funny now.

"What's got your panties in a twist?" I finally ask.

He leans forward. "Are you fucking Jace?"

I choke on my saliva and take a sip of water. "Excuse m-me?"

His eyes are dark and cold. "Are you messing around with my best friend?"

"No! We're not doing a-anything."

"Then why are you stuttering?" he presses.

"Because you're practically ye-yelling at me an-and making me nervous."

Kai's shoulders relax and he sits back in his chair. He rubs a hand over the scruff on his chin. "Because you could tell me if you were."

I laugh humorlessly, "Oh, I could?"

He blows out a breath. "I just, I knew you and Jace were becoming friends, but I don't think he's the guy for you."

I'm not exactly sure what this feeling is, but Kai's words land like a punch to the gut. I don't think I can even look at him right now. "Why would you say something like that?"

"Because he fucks anything with a big set of tits. He's the playboy of the team and that's not the kind of guy for you."

"That's not exactly the nicest thing to say about your best friend."

Kai sighs, running a hand through his hair. "I'm saying it *because* he's my best friend. I know him through and through. And he's a great friend to have, but he's not a relationship guy. I don't think I've ever even seen him sleep with the same person twice."

I hold my hands up. "My God, I get it. Jace is a man-whore and I'm some sc-scared prude who needs her step-brother to take care of he-her."

Good and pissed off, I shut my books and stuff everything into my bag. Kai jumps in front of me when I stand up.

"That's not at all what I meant. I just want the best for you, Zoey."

"And that's not your best friend?" Why am I getting so upset over this? It's not like there's anything going on between us.

We hold eye contact for several seconds before he says, "I thought you said there was nothing going on between you two?"

I swallow the gigantic lump in my throat. "There isn't."

Kai pinches the bridge of his nose. "I didn't come here to pick a fight. I actually had some good news."

Huffing like an angry toddler, I drop my bag and sit back down.

Once Kai falls back into his chair, an actual smile forms. "I got a call from one of the NHL scouts I've been in contact with. Remember that camp I was telling you about?"

"You mean the camp you told me about at the lunch that was a distraction for a juvenile prank?"

"Yeah," he slightly winces. "It's supposed to be super tough, but it gives you a taste of what it would be like to be in the NHL."

My frown slowly turns into a smile. "And you got in? Holy shit! That's amazing. So you're going, right?"

He nods his head. "Hell yeah, I am. I called dad on the way over here and already talked to Coach."

"Coach is okay with you missing two whole weeks?"

"For this training camp he is. I just have to make sure I don't disappoint."

I gently kick his leg under the table. "You won't. You're one of the best captains Winger U's team has ever had."

"Shucks, you do care," he teases.

"When do you leave?" I ask through a laugh.

"I head out to Pittsburgh at the end of the month."

"Wait, that's like really soon."

"I know. I have a ton of stuff to get done. I have to contact all my professors, get my ass back in the gym twice a day—"

"Do you have time for all of that?" I ask with genuine concern. Obviously, I want him to go to the camp, but not if it's going to cost him his mental health.

"I'll make time."

Ever since I met Kai, his dream has been to play in the NHL. This is absolutely crazy now that it might be an actual possibility.

Chapter Twenty-Five

Zoey

Later that night, I'm staring at my blank phone screen and thinking about what Kai said. About how mad he was when he thought Jace and I were messing around. I lied to him. To his face. Yes, Jace is only helping me, but something's been happening between us. I don't know if I'm just making it all up in my head or what, but things have felt different lately.

This is crap. All I want to do right now is ask my friend to come over and hang out with me. That's it! I'm going to do what I want and Kai can get over it.

Z: Movie night at my place?

J: Already on the way ;)

I've already selected the movie once Jace arrives twenty minutes later.

"I don't get a say?" Jace asks as I snuggle under my blanket on the couch.

"Not this time."

The couch dips with his weight and suddenly he's under the covers with me, his arm thrown around my shoulders. I look over at him in disbelief.

"What?" he asks, genuinely confused.

"How forward of you to think I want to cuddle."

He shrugs. "I'm known for my cuddling skills. Wouldn't want you to miss out."

I scoff. "Sometimes you can be so obnoxious."

"Just sometimes?"

We're watching the movie in total silence and it's nice. I'm wearing an off-the-shoulder sweater and Jace's thumb begins moving in circles on my bare skin. And it feels amazing. Why though? He's only touching my shoulder. Unless we're suddenly back in the 1800's when shoulders were erotic for men. When I glance over at him, he looks cool as a cucumber while I'm freaking out on the inside. I need to remember why I asked Jace to do this in the first place. Maybe he needs a reminder too.

"Um, so if L-Leo and I went to the mo-mo-movies, is there, like ..."

I scratch my head, letting my sentence fade away. Why am I having so much trouble thinking of what to say? "Is there stuff that's, um, supposed to hap-ppen while watching movies? Like Netflix and ch-chill?"

Jace's thumb stops moving and I swallow hard, knowing I just made everything super uncomfortable.

Jace turns to me and my breath hitches. "Baby Ruth? I really don't want to talk about Leo right now."

I think I'm leaning into him when I whisper, "Just right n-now?"

I'm barely able to form a coherent thought before Jace's lips are on mine. This kiss is not soft or sensual or anything like that. It's hungry and unforgiving. The hand that was resting on my shoulder, clamps on the nape of my neck and angles my mouth, giving him more access. His tongue tangles with mine and he tastes so incredibly good. He almost reminds me of chocolate; you can't ever just have a small taste. This doesn't feel like before. This doesn't feel like "practicing." Well, if I'm honest, our last kiss didn't really feel like "practicing" either.

I don't want to think right now. I don't want to do anything, but be in this moment. With Jace fucking Bennett. Without breaking apart, I move so I'm straddling him. His hands grip my hips while simultaneously pulling me down on his ... oh, holy crap! Did I do that to him? Is he hard because of me?

"Jace," I pant. I'm not sure if I'm asking if this is a bad idea or pleading for him to do it again.

His lips skim up the column of my neck and I grind down on him. I'm faintly aware of his hand moving to the top of my pants. I can't help the whimper that slips past my lips.

This is moving too fast. We should stop. But it feels so good. This wasn't supposed to happen. I want ... crap what's his name? At least I used to. Then there's Kai. He's going to be so pissed if he finds out what we're doing. That's it. I need to tell Jace to stop. But when I open my mouth, it's not to tell him to stop, it's to let out a satisfied moan as his fingers dip under my panties and inside me. My fingernails dig into his shoulders as my head falls back in pleasure.

"You're always so wet for me. So responsive to me."

Jace leans forward and runs his tongue along my neck as his fingers move in and out of me.

I'm a panting mess, struggling to catch my breath. It never feels like this when I'm doing it. Maybe I've been doing it wrong all along.

"You're so tight. I fucking love it," he moans. "Are you going to come all over my hand like a good girl?"

His words send shivers down my spine. Jace continues at—what should be—an orgasmic pace. But I can't get there. It's like I can see the finish line in the distance, but no matter how fast I run, I won't ever reach it.

"Dammit," I mumble.

"Are you okay?" Jace asks, his fingers slowing down.

"No. No. No. Don't stop! I just, I need..."

"Zoey," he whispers, completely stopping everything.

With an angry grunt, I jump off him. This could not be more em-barrassing. I head to my bedroom door, wanting to hide in the closet and hopefully disappear all together, but Jace's hand grabs my elbow and pulls me back.

"Did I hurt you? Are you okay?"

I shake my head, looking everywhere but at him as I feel the familiar burn of tears threatening to escape.

Jace cups my face, gently guiding me to look at him. "Talk to me."

"It's not working," I say like the pathetic loser I am.

"What's not working?"

"Me. I'm broken and I can't and it's not wor-wor-worth it for you. Please, just let me go."

Jace shakes his head. "How are you broken? Please help me under-stand what just happened."

Pushing away from him, I turn around and cross my arms over my chest. I can't look at him as I admit this. It's already humiliating enough.

When I don't speak, Jace quietly asks, "Baby, what's wrong?"

I close my eyes as I admit the most embarrassing thing about me. Something I've never told anyone. "I've never had an orgasm I didn't give myself."

"I thought you said you weren't a virgin."

God, I want to die right now. "I'm not."

Jace walks around so he can see my face. "I just want to be clear. Are you telling me the guys you've previously slept with have never—"

"Never," I interrupt. "And it's guy. Not plural. I've only slept with one guy and it was the worst experience of my life."

Jace ducks his head to look directly into my eyes. He looks angry. But not at me. For me. "Zoey. This is very important. I need you to tell me what happened."

It takes me a second to understand why he's so mad. And then it hits me. "No, it was nothing like that. It was consensual. I'd been dating this guy for a while. We were in high school and everyone else was doing it. It sounds so stupid to say it out loud now."

Jace is quiet as his gaze softens. He waits for me to continue.

"We tried, but it hurt. Like really hurt. It was so ungodly painful that I screamed for him to stop. He did and I've never had the desire to have sex again. I don't really get the hype around it. I know, I'm a freak! That's why I don't really talk about sex."

Jace's eyebrows shoot up into his hairline. "I don't know what he did, but he did it all wrong. Yes, your first time might be a little uncomfortable, but it shouldn't be like that. Come here."

Jace pulls me into his chest. His arms encircle me as I close my eyes and just breathe him in. I read somewhere that you have to hug someone for twenty seconds for oxytocin to release which can reduce stress. So for the next twenty seconds, that's what we do.

"I have an idea," Jace mumbles into my hair. We still haven't stopped hugging and I think this is the calmest I've ever felt.

"Oh, yeah?" I finally lean back and look up at him. A lone tear streaks down my face and he wipes it away with his thumb.

"You are not a freak. Sex is not a black and white thing like most people think."

I sniffle. "What does that mean?"

"I want to take you somewhere."

"Where?"

Jace's hand runs down my arm until he reaches my hand and intertwines our fingers. "Field Trip."

We drive for a while, out of town and onto the freeway. Instead of asking him where we're going, because I know he's not going to tell me, I put on some music and try to relax.

I start laughing when I catch Jace dancing to Taylor Swift. "AHA! I knew you liked her music!"

His body instantly stiffens to the point where he looks uncomfortable. "What are you talking about?"

"I saw you just now!"

"I was rolling a knot out of my neck, you crazy lady. See, this is what you crazy Taylor Swift people are like. You all need to calm down."

I narrow my eyes at him. Did he say that to me on purpose?

Once the Taylor Swift part of the playlist passes, the ride is quiet which means I'm trapped back in my head.

I don't understand what's happening anymore. I thought I wanted Leo. He's cute and sweet. But then why was I attracted to Jace back in the summer? Why did I kiss Jace? And why did I get so defensive when Kai tried to deter me away from Jace?

"We're here," Jace says as he turns off his car.

He walks over to open my door and when I get out and see where he's brought me, my mouth falls open. "You've got to be kidding me."

I have never been nor desired to go into a sex store. Let alone with my step-brother's best friend. Jace grabs my hand, but I stay glued to the cement.

"I can't go in there."

"Milkshake—"

"No. I'm twenty! I'm not even legal yet. It has to be some sort of crime for me to enter an Adult Store. Why would you think I would want to come here?"

Jace leans down to brush a kiss against my lips. "There are a lot of people out there who struggle to orgasm."

My eyes widen in horror and I look around to see if anyone can hear us. "Jace, we're in public."

"Orgasm is not a bad word. And it's not a bad thing. Some women don't just come at the drop of a hat. Sometimes the key is time and communication. And sex toys."

I shake my head vigorously and turn to get back in the car.

Jace places both hands on the door, caging me in. My backs to his front and I can feel his warm breath on my neck. "I'm man enough to admit that sometimes it takes more than just my fingers or my tongue or even my dick to make a woman come. There's a reason people make sex toys. It's because they can help. Tell me this, when my fingers were deep inside you, did it feel good?"

My eyes flutter shut, remembering how fantastic it felt. How it wasn't painful, but pleasurable.

"Yes," I admit.

"If you really don't want to do this, we don't have to. But you are too fucking sexy for me to keep my hands off. So if you want to leave, we can go back to your place and try again."

"It won't work," I mumble, my voice sounding small to even me.

He nips my ear. "Not with that attitude."

I laugh, but it's cut short when his lips land on my neck.

"I will spend all night between your legs if that's what it takes to get my girl off. So what do you say?"

I sigh heavily, "Okay. I'll try."

"That's my girl."

Chapter Twenty-Six

Jace

The door chimes overhead as I open the door for Zoey. She hesitates for a brief second before I grab her hand and walk her over the threshold.

"See," I whisper in her ear, "it's not that scary."

The store is small and cramped with dim lighting. The complete opposite of intimidating. Zoey's frantic eyes dart from a mannequin wearing BDSM chains to a display of multi-colored dildos.

"That seems a little ... excessive," she says when she spots the swing hanging from the ceiling.

"I don't think we're there. At least not yet," I joke.

"Yet?" Her eyes widen in horror. "When would I ever be ready for that?"

I chuckle, squeezing her hand for comfort and guiding her to the back of the store.

"Jace? Oh my God, I thought that was you!" Jessie shouts from the counter.

With a smile, I pull Zoey behind me.

"And you brought me someone? I love virgins."

Zoey squeezes my hand tight and I roll my eyes at Jessie. "She's kidding. Jessie, this is Zoey."

Zoey smiles tightly while Jessie is all loose and relaxed, her many face piercings shining when the light hits them.

I talk to Zoey, "Jessie used to go to Winger U, but dropped out."

Jessie shrugs. "It was that or be in debt until I'm dead."

"Is this your job then?" Zoey asks.

Jessie nods with a smile. "Sex is a completely normal action every human does. I believe that sex can build relationships. So I would much rather be working here than in some dusty old office."

Zoey nods, but doesn't say anything. So Jessie fills the silence. "What are you two looking for today? Are we thinking of a couples toy or some hot solo action?"

Zoey's eyebrows shoot up as she turns her gaze to me.

"Not sure yet," I answer for her.

"I'm here if you need me," Jessie says, then pops her bubblegum and goes back to the register.

Zoey follows me down an aisle to the left, towards the Women's Pleasure section.

"Oh my God!" Zoey shrieks, shielding her eyes from the mannequin wearing a purple glittery strap on. "Please say we are not buying that."

"I was thinking something more along the lines of this," I say, holding up a rose shaped vibrator.

"W-what is it?"

Looking at the label on the display, I read, "This rose twisting vibrator is a combination nipple and clit stimulator. Our special material is made to get wet, so don't worry about where and when you want to have some fun. The wetter the toy gets, the wetter you get."

Zoey's looking around, still heavily embarrassed. I didn't bring her here to humiliate her. I really wanted to help, but I think I pushed too far. I set the rose back down and head to the door.

"Maybe we should come back another time."

Still holding her hand, I start to walk away, but am pulled back when she refuses to move.

"Why does that rose have that thing attached to it?" she asks, pointing at the toy next to it.

I bite my cheek to hide my smile as I lean in to read the label. "Rose Licker and Thrusting Egg."

"What's that? The egg part?"

I lick my lips as I think about using this on her. Stepping behind her, I brush her hair over her shoulder and whisper in her ear, "It goes inside you. The egg fucks your tight little pussy, while the rose licks your clit until you see stars."

A slight pink tinges her cheeks. I bet she's now wondering the same thing as I am.

Zoey points to an all black display.

"And that one?" she asks through panted breaths.

"Woah. Let's walk before we run."

She looks back at me with that innocent look that makes me want to do very, very bad things. "What is it?"

"Do you really want to know?"

She nods without hesitation.

"That is a butt plug that has a remote control. So while I'm buried so deep inside you, I can fuck your tight ass at the same time. You won't just see stars with this, you'll see an entire galaxy."

Running my hand over her belly, I pull her back to my front. Her swallow is audible and I chuckle darkly. I would never want to make Zoey feel uncomfortable, but I am just a man and talking about using sex toys with her is turning me on.

"Is that what I think it is?" she gasps.

"I can't even pretend to be sorry."

"Maybe th-that's a little too much."

I smile as I kiss her cheek. "Maybe."

She sighs, spinning around in my hold and wrapping her arms around my neck. "You really think something like that rose thingy will help?"

I shrug. "Can't hurt. And even if it doesn't, we'll have a lot of fun trying."

Grabbing the rose—the one without the thrusting egg—Zoey and I make our way back to Jessie at the register.

"Great choice! Especially if you're just starting out. If you're asking for advice, get in a hot tub and go to town."

"No one was asking," I say dryly, but Jessie doesn't care.

Ignoring my remark, she winks at Zoey. "You know, this particular product is great because you can use it without grumpy gills over here."

A slight lift to the corner of Zoey's lips has me smiling. "Good to know."

Grabbing my credit card out of my wallet, I hand it over to Jessie and when my lips are next to Zoey's ears, I whisper, "The only way you're using that toy without me is if I'm watching you get yourself off."

Once we leave, I drive us back to Ballentine in record time. I can't wait to see her laid out before me, eyes twisted shut and fingers gripping the sheets as I eat her out while our new toy licks her senseless. Parking at the curb, I help her out of the car. She grabs the bag with her new toy and saunters into Ballentine. All confident and sexy. My smile falters when a passing thought flies through my brain. I just took my best friend's step-sister to a sex shop and bought her a toy I plan to use on her. Many, many times. I am definitely going to hell.

Zoey

A sex shop wasn't even on the list of places I thought Jace was going to take me. I've never even thought about toys before and now I'm the proud owner of a rose licker thingy. Holy shit! I bought a freaking sex toy ... that I plan to use with my step-brother's best friend. Oh, I am so going to hell.

Jace shuts the door to his bedroom and I toss the bag on his bed. We both just stare at it. How can this tiny little object make me feel this anxious? It's not that I'm even embarrassed anymore. Jessie's forwardness made me feel more at ease. Maybe it's because I don't want Jace to get his hopes up? What if the toy doesn't work? Or what if the batteries short circuit during use? It could also—

Jace walks over to me, grabbing my chin with his thumb and forefinger and guides me to his lips. It's a small kiss. Soft and sweet.

"Sorry. You were just thinking really loud," he says before he pulls me in for a hug.

I wrap my arms around his waist while he strokes my hair.

"We don't ever have to do anything you don't want to."

I push away from his hug and look up at him. "I can't waste your money like that. You bought me the toy, the least I could do is try it. Right?"

His hands rub up and down my arms. "Only if you want to. If you don't, it can stay in its packaging and the batteries can erode for all I care. I didn't take you to embarrass you. I just want you to feel comfortable with me."

"Sexually?" I tease.

Jace sighs, brushing a lock of hair behind my ear. "Emotionally, mentally."

Another soft, chaste kiss.

"What about this weekend?" I whisper against Jace's lips.

He groans, looking down at me. "I thought I told you. I'm heading out to Sharpsburg for a paintball tournament with some guys from high school."

"Oh. I say, slightly disappointed. "That's fine. I have to go to work later, but maybe when you come back?"

Jace nods a few times, grabbing my hips and walking backward before the backs of his knees hit the bed. He falls down, pulling me with him which forces me to straddle him.

"Why don't you just come with me?" His lips land on my neck and a moan squeaks out.

"To play or watch?"

"Either."

My head lolls back as his lips move down to my collarbone. "Are you sure you actually want me there?"

His kisses stop and I lift my head to give him a stern look. "Why'd you stop?"

"Because you asked a stupid question."

"There's no such thing as a stupid question," I say as I boop his nose.

"There is when you ask things like that. I agreed to this tourney at the beginning of the year and I'm not eager to go. But having you there to cheer me on? I might want to show off for you."

He winks and I giggle as I push his shoulders back and he falls onto the mattress.

"I've never gone paint balling before."

Grabbing the front of my neck, Jace pulls me down to him, "It's a good thing I'm such a great teacher."

Chapter Twenty-Seven
Jace

I notice Kai's door's open wide as I head up the stairs. I lean against his door frame and clear my throat. He turns around as he grabs some shirts out of his closet.

"You almost packed?" I ask, nodding to the open suitcase on his bed.

Kai chuckles, "I wish. Dad's been riding my ass all week to start packing."

He haphazardly throws his clothes in the empty suitcase and slams it shut.

"There. Done."

"Seems a little light for two weeks."

Kai shrugs. "It's an NHL camp. I'm going to be in my hockey gear most of the time."

"Still can't believe you got invited," I say walking in. "It's pretty fucking awesome. You know the team's proud of you?"

"Aw, shucks," he jokes, "I didn't know you cared about me like that."

"Fuck off," I laugh.

A brief thought flashes through my mind that he's going to be gone for two whole weeks. That gives him 336 hours to get comfortable with the idea of Zoey and I as a couple. Too bad I'm chicken shit and the second I open my mouth to try and tell him, I freeze.

"So, you're really going?"

A voice I've become very familiar with says from the doorway. I have to remind myself not to react because as far as my best friend knows, Zoey and I aren't romantically involved. And that's just another reminder of how I'm a shitty friend.

When she walks further into the room, her face is a mix of sadness and panic. Fuck. All I want to do right now is wrap her in my arms and hold her tight, but I can't. Because I'm the worst friend in the world.

Zoey flips open the suitcase and scoffs. "Who packs like this? You have like three shirts, one pair of shorts and no underwear? Ew."

"Don't talk about my underwear, Zo," Kai grimaces.

"You go commando on the ice? That's risky, dude," I add, knowing I'm not helping at all.

"Shut up," Kai says through a heavy sigh. "You two are exhausting."

Zoey crosses her arms, "It's not my fault Harold told me to check on you."

Kai scrubs a hand down his face. "I'll call dad on my way. My hockey stuff is already in the car."

Zoey's face relaxes and her eyes shine. Is she going to cry?

"It's only two weeks," Kai turns to Zoey, "I'll be back before you even have a chance to miss me."

She rolls her eyes. "Like I'm going to miss you."

A smile spreads across his lips. "Right back at ya."

Kai wraps Zoey in a hug and I hear her sniffle. It's killing me not to hug her right now.

"What about school?"

Kai zips up his suitcase and pulls it from his bed to the floor. "Coach is encouraging me to go and my professors gave me plenty of work to do while I'm gone. Don't worry, Zo."

Zoey and I follow Kai down the steps and to his car. He opens the trunk and hoists his suitcase in. When his back is turned, I take advantage of the moment and step closely in behind Zoey, brushing my hand against her lower back. She stiffens briefly then relaxes into my touch. I want to pull her into me and comfort her. Wrap my arms around her waist and press my lips to her skin as I tell her two weeks will fly by. But I can't. The second Kai slams the trunk, my hand falls away.

Zoey pulls the sleeves of her sweatshirt down over her hands. "It's just going to be weird. Being here without you."

"Two weeks," Kai says, wrapping her in a hug.

I swallow the words I really want to say. This is such a huge opportunity for Kai. If I tell him about Zoey and I before he leaves, who knows how he'll react and I won't take that chance with his future.

Kai and I bump fists. "Go show them what you're made of."

Zoey and I stand side-by-side as we watch Kai drive away. I've never seen Zoey so emotional before, but regardless of what's happening with us, I want her to know I'm here for her. I turn to wrap my arms around her ... but she's not there. I jog back into Ballentine and up into Kai's room to find Zoey taping pictures to his walls.

"What do you think you're doing?" I ask, leaning against the door frame.

She jumps at my question, not realizing I followed her.

A mischievous grin covers her face and I walk closer to see dozens of different sized heads of …

"Is that Michael Scott from *The Office*?"

Her shoulders shake with laughter. Zoey takes her time with each picture Kai has hung in his room and tapes a Michael head over the faces.

"Want to help?" she asks over her shoulder.

I'm already walking to grab some Michael heads before she even asks.

Chapter Twenty-Eight

Zoey

The number one mood killer in college has to be roommates. Jace and I were making out on his bed, his hand up my shirt with mine down his pants, when Conrad burst through the door. Without thinking, I pulled my hand away from Jace's hard dick and went to roll off him. But I rolled the wrong way and shouted in pain as my head collided with the floor.

Needless to say, the mood was ruined. I ended up heading back to my place—without my new toy—and got ready for work. Jace made sure to call me and give me my daily "North Side is a hell hole" speech, so that was fun. Once I got to North Side, I took some painkillers and held an ice pack to the welt on the back of my head. The ice definitely helped because when I woke up this morning, it wasn't as noticeable.

I'm hanging out on the steps near the bell tower, trying to get some homework done. So far I've done absolutely nothing because the only thing I can think about is Conrad busting Jace and me. I don't know Conrad which means I don't know if he's the kind of guy who would tattle on us to Kai. I grab my phone out of my backpack and send Jace a text.

> Z: Conrad knows something is going on between us

> J: Wow, detective. You should be on CSI

I roll my eyes.

> Z: I've never really hung out with Conrad, so I don't know if he and Kai are friends.

> J: They both live in the same house, but I don't think they hang out

> J: But Conrad's cool. He doesn't do drama

This is so confusing! How the hell did I end up liking Jace of all people? He's an asshole and a man-whore. But he's also really sweet and I feel safe around him. I don't even know if something is happening between us, but if there is, Kai can't find out about it from Jace's roommate.

> Z: Okay. Good.

My thumbs hover over the keys, debating on if I should type what

I'm thinking. I don't want to hurt Jace, but I want to be honest.

I drop my phone on the ground and wince. What if he agrees? Says there's nothing going on between us? Then I'm going to be the crazy one with these weird feelings that I have no clue how to navigate.

Scrunching my brows, I do as he says. But there's nothing. Just an empty lawn. My phone buzzes again.

I sigh heavily because Jace is an idiot, but when I look to the left, it's the same thing. An empty lot. This time I stand up, wondering if I'm missing something.

"Boo," Jace whispers from behind me and I jump. Quickly, I spin around and smack him in the chest.

"So not funny."

"A little funny," he says before kissing my cheek. "Why's your face look that way?"

I touch my cheek, suddenly self-conscious. "What way?"

"Like you ate a sour, rotten lemon."

"Ew. I don't look like that." He stares down at me and the next thing I know, the words are falling out of my mouth like word-vomit.

"I just don't know what's happening here. We were just messing around and you were trying to help me with Leo, but now you're kissing me and buying me ... things. I don't want to mess up your friendship with Kai. I'm not worth that."

Jace's jaw clenches as his hands grab onto my waist.

He lowers his voice for just me. "If you ever say anything disrespectful about my girl again, I will take you over my knee until your ass is raw and red. Do you understand me?"

A wave of heat pools in my belly and I think I forget to breathe.

Jace quirks an eyebrow. "Do you understand me? Or do you need a demonstration?"

My eyes go wide. "We're in the middle of campus."

"I don't care. You are the most amazing person, my little chocolate bon-bon. You are worth everything and more. Now, do you understand me?"

With one hand still gripping my waist, the other comes up to the front of my neck. His hold is loose but sturdy as he forces me to maintain eye contact with him. It's only when I nod that he releases me.

"I'm gonna be late for class, but I'll catch you later."

Then he's gone. And I'm wondering what the actual fuck just happened. My panties are soaked and I feel like I'm going to scream from him not touching me or kissing me or something! He can't just say something so hot and wicked and dirty and then walk away.

I practically fall back into my seat on the steps. There's no way I'm getting any work done today. I'm packing up my bag when I hear my name. I turn in time to see Leo sitting down next to me.

"Hey, Zoey. Haven't seen you lately."

"Yeah," I say as I zip up my backpack, "classes have been crazy. How's the semester been going for you?"

"Good. It's been good."

I nod in agreement. "That's good."

We both sit in silence and that's when I realize there are no butterflies in my stomach. Not even one. Maybe it's because now when I look at Leo, all I see is some cute college guy. Just cute, nothing special. Not like—

"I was wondering if you have plans this weekend?"

Jace's face floods my brain and I smile at the prospect of me spending the entire weekend with him. Just us two.

"I'm actually going out of town."

His smile falters. "Bummer. I was going to see if you wanted to go to the movies with me."

Am I dreaming? Did Leo just ask me out on a date? This is something I've wanted to happen since the beginning of the semester. The entire reason I asked Jace to help me out. I've dreamt of this moment so many times, but I never expected to feel like this. To feel ... absolutely nothing for him.

"Thank you, Leo. I'm flattered. But—"

Moments appear in my head; when Jace made me feel comfortable no matter how I looked, our first kiss, how he was so willing to help me even though we weren't even friends, if I stuttered, he would patiently wait for me to finish my sentence and not rush me or guess my next word.

"I think something's happening and—"

He holds up a hand to stop me as he stands up. "I gotta say, I'm surprised you're turning me down."

My head jerks back. That's a response I never thought I would get.

"I'm sorry? I don't really know what to say to that?"

He stands tall, like he's using his height to intimidate me. "It's no secret you had a crush on me, Zoey. I'm asking you out now, that should be like your dream come true, right?"

This has to be a joke, right?

I quickly finish packing up the rest of my stuff and stand up, so at least Leo isn't literally talking down to me. "I don't know what that's supposed to mean, but I'm seeing someone."

Leo starts laughing, like shoulders shaking laughing; it couldn't sound more fake though. "The fat girl with the stutter is turning me down? Yeah, okay."

My mouth drops open. Is he seriously trying to make me feel insecure because I turned him down? He's smirking down at me like he just said something hurtful now.

"What did you just say to me?"

"Hey, Leo," someone yells from behind him.

Leo turns around and Jace is standing there. "You were never good enough for her anyway."

And then me, along with the rest of the students on the steps, gasp in horror as Jace punches Leo so hard blood pours from his nose.

I'm still staring at Leo groaning in pain on the ground when Jace comes over to me and grabs my face. "Are you okay?"

My stunned gaze bounces between Leo and Jace. "Why did you get to be the one to hit him?"

Jace and I both start laughing together.

Chapter Twenty-Nine
Zoey

I didn't expect to be that upset Kai was leaving. It's only two weeks. But I've never had a sibling before and Kai feels like my actual brother. Decorating his room with a bunch of tiny Michael Scott heads definitely made me feel better. But what made me feel like I didn't want to cry, was Jace being there. He distracted me and we had fun together. Albeit it was vandalizing Kai's room, but that's neither here nor there.

Ever since Jace punched Leo, I haven't been able to stop thinking about him. Jace, that is. Wake up, think about Jace. Go to bed, think about Jace. Take a shower, think about if Jace is thinking about me. It's confusing and frustrating as hell.

I haven't talked to Becks or Corrine about it yet. Mainly because we've all been so busy, I haven't seen them. Becks and Trent are officially a couple and Corrine apparently doesn't like him, so Becks hasn't been home much lately. It hurts me because I've felt closer to

Becks from day one, but now it feels like there's a distance between us all.

Becks is painting her nails when I get home from class and the fumes make me dizzy the second I walk through the door.

"That's strong," I mutter.

She chuckles, focusing on designing a feather on her big toe. "How was class?"

"Weird," I mumble, walking over to open the small window in our living room. I feel like I'm in a daze as I drop my bag and flop down next to her.

"Weird how?" She turns to look at me and sets her brush down. "Woah. What happened?"

I know how I look. Pursed lips, unfocused gaze, brows pushed together into a frown.

"I'm just really confused. I think."

"What do you mean, 'you think'?"

When I don't answer, she yells and claps in my face. I flinch and snap out of it.

"What the hell is going on? Are you okay?"

So, I tell her. Everything.

"You remember when we went to that party a while ago and I made a fool of myself in front of Leo?"

Becks' brow furrows. "I have no memory of you making a fool of yourself, but I do know which party you are referring to."

I narrow my eyes. "Well, I was humiliated. It didn't help that I ran into Jace right after."

"Like Hockey Jace? Like your brother's best friend Jace?"

"Step-brother," I correct, not that it matters. "And yes. It was just a weird night all around because I actually had a lot of fun pretending to flirt with Jace at Cherry On Top. And it was so easy with Jace and not with Leo and I didn't understand why. I figured it was because I just needed practice."

I pause because I'm not sure Becks is going to be very receptive to my idea.

"And?" she prompts.

"And I asked Jace to help me."

She slowly nods her head, twisting the lid of her nail polish shut. "Help you, how exactly?"

I speak quickly, hoping it doesn't sound as stupid as I know it does.

"At first, I just wanted him to help me perfect my flirting, but then it kind of turned into us fake dating. I actually think we started becoming friends, and then he took me to a sex shop to try and help me orgasm. But the other day Leo was a total douche to me and Jace showed up out of nowhere and punched him. And now I have no idea where we stand."

I'm breathing fast and heavy when a slow smile forms on Becks' face.

"You have no idea?"

I shake my head. "None."

"You care about Jace." She doesn't phrase it as a question.

"I don't know. I mean ..."

Becks doesn't say anything. Just crosses her arms and stares at me. My foot starts shaking and my heart rate picks up.

"I don't know if I like Jace or not!" I shout.

I take a deep breath and continue. "We've just been hanging out so much and I feel like I can be myself around him. I don't have to pretend to be put together and perfect around him. Like the last time we were hanging out, I burped in front of him."

Becks pretends to look shocked.

"Shut up," I playfully swat her arm. "I know how silly that sounds, but I've never burped in front of a guy. My brain is all over the place."

I groan, burying my head in my hands. Becks rubs my back as my mind races.

My face is still hidden when I say, "What if I do like Jace and what if he likes me back? This could ruin his and Kai's friendship. I can't do that to them. I'm not that—"

My sentence is interrupted by a sharp pinch to my elbow. My head snaps up. "Ow!"

"Well, don't say stupid stuff if you don't want to get pinched."

I laugh to myself. "Jace called me stupid too."

Her face falls and I swear I can see fire in her eyes. "He called you what?"

I shake my head, realizing how that sounded. "No. He didn't call me stupid. He said I asked a stupid question when I asked ..."

"Asked what?"

"When I asked him if I was worth it?"

Becks' shoulders relax. "Oh. Well, then that's okay. Because that is stupid."

A smile spreads across my lips. "He asked me to go away with him this weekend."

"Then what the hell are you doing sitting here with me? You don't have toe nails that need to dry. Go pack some slutty lingerie!"

She practically pushes me away. I chuckle as I stand up and head to my room. "I don't have any slutty lingerie. I don't have any lingerie."

"Then just forget underwear. Men go feral if you tell them you're not wearing panties."

Chapter Thirty
Zoey

The next morning, Jace picks me up at my door, grabs my bags and guides me down to his car. He opens the door for me, loads my overnight bag into the trunk and after he buckles himself, turns on the radio.

I start laughing immediately. "I thought you hated Taylor Swift."

He shrugs, pulling away from the curb. "She's growing on me."

The drive isn't too long and we spend most of it talking about classes and hockey. After we park, Jace grabs our bags before I can.

"I can carry my own bag," I protest.

He ignores me and jumps away when I try to steal it back. "But can you catch it?"

Jace takes off running through the parking lot like a maniac. I have no choice but to follow him. He finally slows down once he reaches the double doors that open to the lobby. It takes me a few extra seconds to catch him, but I'm a panting mess by the time I catch up.

"You might need to start working on your cardio."

Jace opens his mouth to say something else, but dramatically doubles over when I playfully smack his stomach.

"Drama queen," I tease.

"Sore loser," he taunts.

We're both still laughing at each other when we approach the front desk.

"Room for Bennett."

Jace slides his ID and credit card over the counter while the staff clicks a few loud buttons on her keyboard.

The tall and slender blonde hands Jace back his things along with two room keys. "You booked a queen, cleaning service comes around every morning and there's complimentary breakfast in the lobby from 9:00-10:30. Oh, and the wifi password is your room number. If you need anything else, just press the 0 key on your room phone. Have a nice day."

Jace takes his things and we're in the elevator before I process what she said.

"Did she say *a* queen? As in one bed?"

The doors slide open and Jace is striding down the hall.

"Jace?"

"Hmm?" He only walks a few doors down and swipes the key. When the light turns green, he looks at me with a smirk and holds the door open. I walk past him into a cute little room ... with only one bed.

I nod towards the bed. "Did you know about this?"

Jace kisses my temple as he walks past. "It was supposed to just be me, remember?"

"Uhh—"

"What? Don't think you can keep your hands on your side of the bed?" he jokes as he drops his bag, grabs his toiletries, and heads to the bathroom.

I roll my eyes and pick up the bags off the ground to unpack. Jace's backpack crunches in my grasp. Huh? What the hell does he have in his bag? Being nosey, I pull the zipper down and frown in confusion. Jace's entire bag is filled with snacks. KitKats and sour patch kids and Reese's pieces. My reflexes take over and I dump out the bag on the white bedspread.

My little debbie cake.

Goodnight, my Milky Way.

You coming out with us tonight DumDum?

Merry Christmas, Reese's Pieces.

My little sour patch.

"Jace?" I call out.

"What's up?" he pops his head out of the bathroom.

I hold up a box of whoppers. "You have a backpack full of junk food."

He snorts. "I'm aware. It's some of my favorite things and there's no one here to rat on me to Coach. Unless you're going to?"

I can't even focus on him teasing me as my eyes scan over the contents. "But these are all things that you've called me."

Jace takes his time sauntering over to me. "I know. You're one of them too."

"One of what?" I ask, peering up at him.

Jace tucks a lock of hair behind my ear. "My favorite things."

His hand slides around to the back of my neck, pulling me closer to him. My lips pop open as his nose rubs against mine. "You are mine. Aren't you?"

A nervous laugh escapes my throat. "Who knew my boyfriend was such a sap."

His eyebrows shoot up. "Boyfriend?"

How did that just come out of my mouth? I wasn't even thinking about anything remotely close to that word.

"I di-didn't mean—"

"I like you calling me your boyfriend. Do it again."

"Really?" I giggle, melting into his embrace.

He nods, his lips ghosting over mine.

I stand taller on my tippy toes, but Jace pulls back with a wicked smile.

"Please, kiss me. Boyfriend."

The word is barely out of my mouth before his lips are on mine. A gasp escapes me, but is quickly replaced with a moan. Gripping his waist, I pull him closer to me. I want to feel every inch of him pressed against me. I'm done waiting, Jace Bennett. My hands sneak under his shirt, caressing the ridges and dips of his abs.

Jace shivers and I jump back. "Sorry. Are my hands cold?"

He chuckles as he leans his forehead against mine, holding my hands between us. "No. I told myself that if you came with me this weekend, I was going to be a gentleman the entire time. I don't want you to think this is just about the physical stuff."

God, this man is perfect.

"Jace?"

"Yeah?"

"Shut up and get naked."

Jace laughs, but the sound fades away when I fist his shirt and pull his mouth down to mine. A yelp escapes my throat when Jace grabs me by the back of my thighs, my legs instantly wrapping around him. He twists us around and sets me down on the wooden desk in the corner of the room. Our lips break apart only long enough for him to pull my shirt over my head. Jace's fingers tangle in my hair, angling my head exactly like he wants me.

He kisses the corner of my lips, my jaw, all the way over to my ear where he whispers, "You are in complete control of the situation. Remember, if you want to stop at any moment, you say the word."

"I promise," I pant. "But I don't. Please, don't."

Jace stands to his full height. My brow furrows, worried maybe he changed his mind when one arm reaches behind his head, grabs his shirt and pulls it off in the sexiest way I've ever seen.

Chapter Thirty-One

Jace

Fuck me. Every inch of this woman is incredible. Grabbing her hips, I pull her against me so she can feel what she does to me. Zoey's eyes widen in surprise and dart down between us.

"Are you—"

"And it's all because of you."

This is, hopefully, our first time. However, I don't want to push her. I want everything to be perfect and go at whatever speed she wants. But holy shit, does it hurt! I practically have to bite my tongue to keep myself from begging her to at least touch it when she slides her hand between us.

"Will you tell me what you like?" she asks. My girl is sexy and confident and just asked for something sexual without stuttering.

"Of course, baby. But I promise you, I'll like anything you do."

She uses both hands to undo the button and zipper on my jeans and when I notice the slight shake to her hands, I push the hair back from her neck. The slight brush of my lips on her skin sends a shiver through her body, so I do it again. I moan into the kiss when her fingers wrap around my cock. Fuuuuck. She's soft and gentle, but her touch is firm and commanding. Her strokes are agonizingly slow at first, but when my hand cups her jaw and turns her head to me, she quickens her movements. Her lips attack mine first. She tastes so goddamn good. My hand slips down to her neck and accidentally tightens when her grip on my cock does.

"Shit," I breathe, "Sorry. That was too much."

She shakes her head. "No. Do it again."

Zoey goes to kiss me again, but I pull back and just take a moment to look at her.

"What?" she asks. "What's wrong?"

"Who are you and what have you done with my shy little Zoey?"

She giggles playfully, sliding off the desk to stand in front of me, and unfortunately, removing her hand. "It's all your fault you know."

"My fault?"

"You helped make me feel comfortable in my own skin."

Cupping both her cheeks, I pull her mouth to mine. God, this woman is perfect. I feel the tug of my pants and laugh into our kiss as I step out of my jeans. Shock takes over when Zoey pushes my shoulders and I fall back on the bed. I slide up to the headboard and just take a moment to stare at her. Fuck, she's sexy.

"Do you remember what I said to you at the end of our first date?"

My sassy girl has the nerve to roll her eyes. "You mean our fake date."

Licking my lower lip, I crook my finger in a silent command: come here.

Her eyes widen in excitement at the memory. Just when I think I've taken it too far, Zoey leans down to place her hand on the mattress. I reach down to adjust myself because my dream girl is on her hands and knees crawling to me. I think I can die a happy man now. Her tits sway with every movements and I can't even keep track of all the things I want to do to her.

I reach out to grab for Zoey, but she bats my hand away as she straddles me. We both groan when she sits down and rubs against my straining cock. I don't try to grab her, though. I wait for her to take whatever control she needs.

Zoey guides both my hands to her hips before cupping my face and whispering, "Make it all better. Please."

Without warning, I flip us over. This way she's all laid out for me like my own personal feast.

"Hm, where to start? Maybe here?" I say, biting at one nipple through the fabric of her bra.

Zoey grunts in frustration and it only makes me chuckle.

"How about here?" I kiss her soft stomach as I slide down her body.

"I think I like this game," she says, wiggling in anticipation.

"Maybe here?" I kiss her ankle and the smile vanishes from her face.

"Jace Bennett, you are not funny."

Zoey tries to yank her ankle out of my grasp, but I hold on tight until she stops fighting. Only once she's done do I slide my hand up, up, up.

Her breathing turns shaky and I say, "You were saying?"

She tries to fake a laugh, but can't get it out. The air turns serious when my fingers reach the button of her pants and flick it open. My eyes never leave hers. Not when I lower the zipper, not when she lifts her hips to let me pull her pants off and not when she's laying in front of me in just her bra and panties. I wait for her to tell me that this is okay. That she's still okay with what we're doing. When she smiles and nods, I finally look down and my mouth falls open.

"Cat got your tongue?" Zoey teases.

"You are the sexiest woman I have ever seen. I think you might need to walk around like this forever now. Actually, new rule. Whenever we're together, no more clothing. It just gets in the way and you are way too fucking beautiful to be hiding behind all that fabric."

Pink stains her cheeks and I love that I make her do that.

"Only if you do the same," she adds.

"Deal."

Holding eye contact, I lower myself down to kiss Zoey's hip. She props herself up on her elbows to see me better as I kiss her other hip. With a smirk, I finally look away from Zoey and down to her cotton panties. They're nothing fancy or sexy, but they're absolutely perfect. I don't want her to feel shy, so I kiss her through the fabric, right over her clit. She inhales sharply, her legs instinctively tightening around my head. A cry falls from her lips when my fingers slide the fabric out of the way and my tongue licks one long languid stroke.

"Take it off," she pants.

I chuckle as she rips her panties off, tossing them across the room. I knew she would get comfortable soon enough. She just needed time.

"I want you to hold yourself open. Can you do that for me, baby?"

"Hold myself open?"

Placing my hands on her knees, I push them apart as far as they'll go. "Put your hands here and don't let your knees move. I promise this will feel good."

Her forehead creases. "Even better than that?"

"A million times better than that."

The fact that she is completely bared to me and isn't even a little shy is beyond fucking sexy. This time, I'm not as tentative. I dive in between her thighs like I haven't eaten in weeks and she's my four-course meal.

"Holy, I mean, Jace, what ..."

I thrust a finger inside her, curling it at just the right spot to get her moaning.

"Cat got your tongue?" I mock.

She doesn't respond because I don't think she can.

"Mmm. You're holding your legs open like such a good girl," I praise. She's definitely into it because I see her fingers dig into her skin, tightening her hold. My lips wrap around her clit, sucking and gently biting. Her legs begin shaking and that's when I shove a second finger in.

"You're soaked, baby. I think I could fit a third finger in you with how wet you are for me."

Zoey moans in response and within seconds, she grips my fingers like a vice.

"Would you like that? To be so full of me, you can barely stand it?"

"I'm so close," she cries.

"You're doing so good, baby," I praise, adding a third finger with ease. I wasn't kidding before.

"Yes, yes! Oh my God! Keep doing that! Please, don't stop!"

I listen and do exactly as she says. She's so close, I know she can cross that finish line and I know I can help her. I alternate licking and sucking while still fucking her with my fingers. I wait for the right moment and just as her back arches off the bed, I gently press my thumb against her asshole. The surprise of the action combined with how good it feels has her coming hard. Her body spasms, but I don't let up.

"I knew you could do it, baby. I'm so proud of you."

My mouth still on her, I lick up everything she has to give me as I help her ride out her orgasm.

I crawl up her body, wanting to check on her. Her head lolls to the side and she's giggling like a maniac. I join her because her laughter is infectious.

"I didn't just cross a line there, did I? I just knew you were so close and I really, really wanted you to come," I say quickly, worried that I might've destroyed some of the trust we've built.

"What? No. That was ..." She pants heavily. "Wow."

At my smile, she asks, "Why are you looking at me like that?"

"You're just so beautiful."

Reaching up, Zoey cups my face and brings it to hers. The kiss is anything but soft. Her hand falls to my shoulder and I allow her to push me until I'm lying on my back and she's straddling me. She pulls away from our kiss and when I open my eyes, she's reaching behind her back and unclasping her bra. Her tits bounce free and I don't hesitate. I sit up, sucking one hard nipple into my mouth while kneading the other with my hand.

Zoey arches her back and I swap tits, giving them each the same attention. I'm not sure if she's doing it on purpose or not, but Zoey grinds her hips back and forth over my rock hard dick and it has my eyes rolling to the back of my head. Only the cloth of my boxers separates my cock from her hot pussy and if she keeps doing what she's doing, I'm going to come.

"Baby, baby," I grip her hips to stop her movement. "You have to stop that."

"Stop what?"

I take a deep, steadying breath. "I've waited so long for you and if you keep grinding on me like that, I'm not going to last much longer."

Her breathing is fast and with every one, her tits are shoved in my face—not that I'm complaining.

Her next words take me by surprise. "Do you have a condom?"

Chapter Thirty-Two
Zoey

I yelp when Jace tosses me off him. He jumps off the bed, runs over to his suitcase in the corner of the room and pulls out a box—A BOX?!—of condoms.

"You brought a box? That seems a bit presumptuous. Don't you think?"

Jace tosses me his trademark smirk. "Not at all. I would say I feel hopeful that the sexy woman sharing my hotel room would finally let me know how tight she feels around my cock."

I raise one brow. "Finally?"

Jace chuckles nervously. "Finally? Who said that? Definitely not me."

Jace grabs a packet, rips off his boxer briefs and it's then that I get to see all of him. My mouth goes dry and I try to swallow the lump in my throat. Jace takes his time rolling on the condom and I think for the first time since he kissed me, I'm a little scared.

"That's not going to fi-fit."

With a smirk, he climbs on the bed and crawls towards me. I fall back and once he's completely on top of me, he whispers, "It'll fit. I promise you."

I think he's going to kiss me, but then his head falls to my neck and he bites me.

"Did you just bite me?" I shriek.

He chuckles, licking and sucking where he just nipped all while his hand slides down my body. "I can't help it. You taste delicious."

I gasp when he shoves his hand back between my thighs.

"Do you know how much of a turn on it is to feel how wet you are for me?"

I shake my head. I don't think I've ever been this wet in my entire life. I've never had someone be this careful, attentive or mindful of me.

"Jace," I moan as he slides a finger inside me.

"Fuck, baby." He nips at my ear. "What do you think? Can you take all of me?"

When I don't answer, his other hand comes to rest on my neck. When he did this earlier, I was shocked and surprised. Mainly because it turned me on even more.

"Yes. Yes."

I close my eyes to try and focus when I feel the tip of his dick try to enter me. I squeeze my eyes shut, preparing for the pain I felt the last time I had sex.

"Hey."

His voice is commanding, but soft at the same time. So, I open my eyes in curiosity.

"Eyes on me, baby. I'm not going to hurt you. I would never hurt you."

I nod. Bending my knees, I shift my hips up towards his. It's not pain that I'm feeling; more like an uncomfortable feeling of being so full, I fear I might burst.

"Jesus," he mutters. "You have to relax. Let me in, baby."

"You're not in?" I squeak.

His laughter calms me slightly, but my entire body is seizing up. The hand that was on my neck drifts down to my tit, pinching my nipple. The feeling of that, combined with him slowly filling me is too much. I forget how to breathe all together when he starts circling my clit.

"I've got you, Zoey. You know I'll take care of you, right?"

I nod, not having to even think about my answer.

"You are the most beautiful thing I've ever seen in my life. Let me in, please? Let me in, so I can see what you look like when you come on my cock."

Once he's fully seated inside me, we both exhale a sharp breath.

We stay like that for several moments and I'm wondering if Jace is going to move. I'm about to say something when I notice the vein in his neck looks like it's about the burst.

"Baby, I have to move. You're so tight. I have to move."

I nod. "Okay. Okay."

Jace slowly pulls out and pushes back in. His moans are low and dirty and I can tell by the shine of sweat on his forehead how much he's restraining himself. He applies more pressure to my clit, and I think I can feel another orgasm. But there's no way that's possible, right? Reaching up, I twist my fingers in his hair and bring his mouth down to mine. The more he moves, the more natural this feels. Jace's teeth clamp onto my bottom lip and I moan.

"You feel so good, Zoey."

"I, I want …"

"Yeah? What do you want?" he asks, his thrusts picking up speed. "Tell me. I'll give you anything."

"I think I want to come again."

His movements halt and I freeze, thinking I said something wrong.

His breathing is heavy and hot and I run my hand down his chest, over his racing heart.

"Can you?" he pants. "I really want to try."

"Really?"

He nods vigorously. "I think I can get you to come again."

"Wow," I swallow hard. "That's some positive thinking."

"Hold on to me."

I wrap my arms around his neck and shriek when he rolls us over. Now I'm straddling him and somehow he's still inside me.

"Put your hands on the headboard," he instructs. "And just relax."

I do as he says and try to calm my breathing. After a few moments, his hips thrust up into me and the new position has me gasping for air. I tighten my grip when his lips find my nipple. I try to move my hips to meet his, but then his thumb finds my clit and I turn into a pile of jello. It's like my entire body has shut down on me and with his mouth on my nipple, finger on my clit, and dick inside me, I come so hard that I break a nail from my grip on the headboard. My vision blurs and I swear I feel every nerve in my body spasm. Jace continues his thrusts and it's only when he freezes and grunts do I realize that he's spilled into the condom.

We both fall over on the bed and after a kiss to the side of my head, Jace says, "I'll be right back."

He rolls off me and disappears to the bathroom for a few minutes.

"Now, that is a sight I could get used to."

I'm still trying to calm my breathing as I lay motionless on my stomach. At Jace's voice, I turn my head and see him leaning against the wall, sans condom, staring at my ass.

"I think you killed me."

"Imagine reading that in an obituary," he teases.

I chuckle into the sheets, trying to muster up the energy to move. Jace saunters over, pulls the covers back so I can crawl up the bed and snuggle under them with him. He tucks me under his arm, so I'm laying on his chest and everything just feels ... right.

I wasn't able to get a proper look of the room before, but it really is nice. A giant television is mounted on the wall with wooden dressers and a desk underneath. Next to the dresser is a mini-fridge and microwave. Right when you walk in is the bathroom. It's all white and pristine and across from that is a closet with mirrors for doors.

"What are you thinking?" Jace asks, running his fingers up and down my arm. Goosebumps erupt over my entire body and I cuddle further into him.

"I'm glad you invited me," I mumble into his chest.

"You're not sore, are you?"

"Not really. Should I be?"

"You might be." Jace turns and presses his lips to the side of my head. "I tried to be gentle."

I run my hand up his chest. "I'm not complaining."

His pursed lips worry me, so I cup his cheek in my hand. "I'm really okay. That was the best moment of my entire life, Jace."

Chapter Thirty-Three
Jace

The giant lump under the covers whines as I turn off her alarm. For the second time.

"It's time to get up, Sleeping Beauty," I say in a soothing voice. I try to grab the duvet when Zoey tightens her grip.

"If you rip these covers off me, it will be the last thing you ever do."

Her tone is eerily calm, so I do as she says and back away.

"Jesus. Maybe you're more like the Beast in the morning," I mutter to myself.

She throws off her covers and pops up like a Jack-in-the-box from hell. "What did you just call me?"

I always knew my mouth would get me in trouble one day, I just never thought it would be over something like this.

"There are energy drinks in the mini-fridge," I say with a smile, trying to tame the wild animal that has taken over my girlfriend.

"Why are we up so early? I just want to sleep," she whines.

"Why don't you stay here and rest and I'll come back and get you after I'm done playing?"

She rears back like I slapped her. "You don't want me to come?"

Wait, what?

"Huh? That's not what I said."

"That's exactly what you just said."

"No. I just know you're really tired—"

"I am really tired!" She falls back onto the bed.

"I know that."

I flinch when she pops back up.

"But I want to come."

"So come then."

"Fine! I will!"

"Good!" I exhale, absolutely exhausted.

The room falls silent for a few seconds and I'm wondering what in the fuck just happened. Her chest is heaving and her brow is creased like she's mad ... at me?

"I'm not a morning person," she finally says.

"Obviously," I mumble.

Her cold stare cuts through me and I offer her a smile. Zoey just rolls her eyes before stomping off into the bathroom. I stare at the closed door for a solid minute, almost afraid to move. It's only when my phone starts ringing from the other side of the room that I'm brought back to reality. I swipe to answer my phone, putting it on speaker so I can continue getting dressed.

"Dane, it's been a while."

"Too long, man. You still coming today?"

"Yeah. I actually brought someone from school with me."

I toss on a shirt and then grab my water bottle.

"Really?" He perks up immediately. "That's actually what I was calling you about. Big Blue has the flu and now we have an open spot."

I choke on the water and bang on my chest a few times to cough it up.

"You okay over there?" Dane asks.

"Yeah," I mumble through a cough. "I'm fine, but she can't. No, uh, she can't take his spot."

Dane sighs. "Can you just ask her? We need one more player or we forfeit."

I'm about to refuse again when Zoey clears her throat right behind me. Holy shit, who showers that quickly? She's wrapped in just a towel and I have to clench my fists to keep from pulling her to me. Clearly that would be a mistake because even though she looks less beast-like, her eyes could burn down cities.

"She would love to play," she says loud enough so Dane hears.

"Hell yeah! I'll let the other guys know."

"No! Don't do that!" I run to grab my phone, but he's already hung up.

With her head held high, she drops her towel and walks over to the closet to start getting dressed. My mouth drops open and I don't even care I'm drooling like a dog as I take her in. She's a goddamn masterpiece. From her huge tits that barely fit my hand to her curves that I want to sink my teeth into to her soft belly, all the way down to her ass which is currently pushed out while she bends down to pick out a pair of pants. I can't hold back anymore. Fuck her grumpy morning behavior.

Walking up behind her, I run my hands along her hips, taking in her sexy as sin stretch marks. I want to lick every single one and I will when we have more time.

"I'm trying to get ready," she huffs out.

"Stand up," I say in a more dark and commanding tone.

I feel her body tense against me, but she listens.

"What a good girl."

I shut the closet she was digging through so she's forced to see her—us—in the reflection. Taking my time, my hands slide up her naked waist, her ribs, ghosting past her hard nipples. Her whine has my cock twitching in my shorts and I shift my stand so I'm sitting right in between her perfect ass cheeks. Not wanting to completely torture her, I use one had to play with her nipple while the other slides up to her neck. She's looking down at her body and that's not going to do, so using my hand on her neck, I guide her face up and she gets the hint.

"Are you done yet?" I ask with one raised brow.

She narrows her eyes in protest until I pinch her nipple. A yelp escapes her lips and I swipe my thumb along her lower lip.

"I asked you a question. I said, are you done with the attitude?"

When she doesn't answer immediately, I shove my thumb into her mouth. Somehow I get even harder when she starts sucking on it.

Only when I pull it out does she say, "Maybe."

"Maybe?"

"I told you," she mumbles, "I don't like mornings."

My hand still on her neck, I tilt her head to the side. Leaning down, I bite her ear, making her shiver.

"Then maybe we need to do something to change that," I whisper.

Zoey's nodding frantically as I release her and shove my pants and boxers down.

"Bend over and keep your eyes open. I want you to watch what I'm going to do to you."

She seems too stunned to move, so I help her by gently pressing between her shoulder blades. Her hands come up to brace herself against the mirror as her ass pushes into my erection. She gasps in surprise as I shift my hips against her.

"Again?" she pants. "We just had sex last night."

I chuckle darkly, letting my hands roam over her perfect ass. "I don't think you understood just how serious I was when I said I would spend all day between your beautiful thighs."

Bending down, I grab a condom out of my pants pocket, but can't help myself. Zoey curses when my teeth sink into her ass then I kiss to soothe the spot.

"Did you just bite my ass?"

Chapter Thirty-Four

Zoey

Jace chuckles darkly as he rolls on the condom, all while keeping his eyes on me. I shift my weight from side to side in anticipation of what's to come. The bite mark on my butt still stings, but in such a good way. I can't believe he bit me; I can't believe I kind of liked it.

My breaths are heavy as I wait for his next move when suddenly he drops to his knees. A loud moan escapes me when his tongue instantly finds my clit. Jace's fingers dig into my ass cheeks as he spreads me, licking me from clit to—

"Holy shit!"

My arms threaten to give out underneath me at the unexpected pleasure. Jace's laugh vibrates against my skin as I struggle to stand.

"How about now?" he asks.

"What?" I pant, having no clue what the hell he's talking about.

Does he really think I'm able to hold a conversation while he's doing that to me?!

"How are you feeling now? Feeling less cranky?"

I start laughing to myself, but am abruptly cut off when one finger is shoved into me.

"Yes! God, yes!"

Jace's fingers continue to pump in and out as he stands to his full height. I whimper at the loss when he backs away moments later.

Seeing out of the corner of my eye that he's walking towards the bed, I push myself to stand.

"You're lucky we have somewhere to be this morning or else your ass would be mine all day long," he threatens.

"Oh, no. That sounds terrible," I deadpan.

Jace crooks a finger at me. "Come here."

Completely helpless, I do as he says. By the time I get to him, he's grabbed something out of his backpack and is hiding it behind his back.

I try to peek behind him, but he turns his body. "Are you going to tell me what you're hiding?"

Using his thumb and forefinger, Jace grabs my chin and forces me to look him in the eyes.

"You are always in charge. You know that, right? If we ever do anything that makes you uncomfortable, you just say the word and everything stops."

I nod. "I know that. I trust you."

His smile is beautiful and sexy and I can't help but lean forward and kiss him.

Finally, Jace shows me what he was hiding behind his back.

"You brought it with you?"

He shrugs, probably nervous of my reaction. I turn the rose toy we bought at the sex shop over in my hand.

"Huh. It's actually kind of cute. Not as intimidating as I remember."

"Well, the last time you saw it, it was surrounded by butt plugs and sex swings, so that would make sense."

I laugh humorlessly. "Yeah. That must be it."

I bite my lower lip, wondering what it will feel like. The material is rubbery; that can't be comfortable, can it?

"You've never used a toy before, so it's normal to be scared or nervous. But we also don't have to use it today."

The gigantic ball of tension in my chest slowly begins to unravel. I wasn't lying before. I trust Jace with my whole heart. Woah. When did that happen?

Walking over to the bed, I pull back the sheets and turn to Jace. "Show me how to use it?"

It takes him a minute to register what I said, but when he does, he makes his way to me. Tossing the toy on the bed, Jace's fingers get lost in my hair as his lips devour mine. I press my naked chest against his as our tongues meet. I groan when Jace bites my bottom lip and then start giggling when he gently pushes my shoulders so I fall back onto the bed. With him still standing, he wraps my legs around his waist and explores my body with his hands.

"Baby, you're so fucking tight," he groans as he slides into me.

Digging my feet into his ass, I try to pull him further in which makes him laugh.

Jace's hands wrap around my thighs, helping himself control his pace. "Eager for my cock, huh?"

I nod, completely unashamed. "I need you."

I start to whine when he pulls out, but stop when he thrusts fully back into me. It shocks both of us and I forget how to breathe for a second.

"Were, wait, were you this big last night?" I finally ask.

Jace lets out a shaky laugh. "Fuck the tournament. I'm staying like this all day."

Jace begins moving his hips at a steady pace that feels so freaking good. It's like when you have an itch and you finally scratch it and it feels so good that you never want to stop. I don't say it back, but I could easily stay like this all day too. His movements pick up speed and I feel the beginning of an orgasm. I'm so worked up and so close, we might not even need the toy. Just as I think that though, the feeling fades slightly and I want to scream. It's like Jace knows exactly what's going on in my head because while his one hand is on my tit, the other grabs our new toy.

"Are you sure you want to do this?" he asks.

I swallow the lump in my throat. I know I can easily back out and Jace won't care, but then I feel like I'll spend the rest of the day wondering how it feels. What if this is the little extra boost I need?

"Yeah," I whisper, "I still want to do it."

The hum from the vibration is so quiet, you probably wouldn't even be able to hear it if we were talking. Jace moves to my other nipple, trying to distract me which is semi-working. I'm trying to stay still, but it's as if he's moving at a snail's pace. I just want to know what it feels like already! I just want to know if—

"Holy Jesus Mary and Joseph!" I yell when he places the rose toy on my clit.

"Shit!" Jace shouts. "Fuck, your pussy is squeezing me like a vice."

I have no idea who I even should be praying to at this point, but it's like a bolt of lightning has just zapped my clit and launched me into another dimension. Still holding the toy to me, Jace leans down and takes one of my nipples into his mouth. The suction of the rose is too much and I explode. My mouth is open and I know I'm screaming, but I can't hear anything. It's like I'm in another world. It's just pure euphoria. I have never in my life come this hard or fast before. Jace spills into the condom while I'm still coming down from the best orgasm anyone has ever had.

Once I can move, I toss the rose off me and finally start to breathe again. Jace falls forward, collapsing on me and I wrap my arms around him. I run my fingers up and down his back, a light coat of sweat covering it.

"Okay, I'm ready," he says.

"Ready for what?"

He pushes himself back up, pulling himself out of me. "For you to admit I was right."

Chapter Thirty-Five
Zoey

Due to our morning ... activities, we end up running late. Jace's high school friends are decked out in masks and pads and are loading their guns by the time we arrive at the paintball course. It's in the middle of the woods with a few obstacles added; a small, empty wooden cabin, barricades made from sand bags and big oil drums scattered around.

"And here we were thinking you forgot about us," a short, stocky guy with a buzz cut taunts Jace.

Jace pulls him in for a hug, patting him twice on the back. "We got held up a little. Guys, this is my girlfriend, Zoey. Zoey, this is Dane, Moose, Martin and Harrison."

I smile, knowing I will need to be reminded of who is who in about five minutes. "It's nice to meet you all."

"Everything starts in ten. Go get your shit," Moose says.

Jace grabs my hand and guides me over to a tent where we check in and get our protective gear.

"Do I really have to wear that? It looks like it's never been cleaned," I say when Jace shows me the mask then quickly realize how whiny it sounded.

Jace laughs, placing said mask on me. "Well, I'm kind of fond of your head, so yes. It's one of the many parts of you that I like."

I roll my eyes when he winks at me. Next, he helps me put on a chest protector. Jace's hands begin roaming around my belly, ribs, and just under my boobs.

"Jace," I scold, slapping his hands away.

"What? I just needed to make sure it was on properly."

"Competitors to your starting positions," a deep voice says over the loudspeakers.

"Already?" I panic. "I've never paintballed before. Paintballed? Am a paintballer? Went paintballing? Whatever it is, I've never done it before!"

Jace's eyes widen. "Baby, I mean my next few words in the nicest possible way, so don't take them personally. But why in the fuck did you volunteer to take Big Blue's place?"

"I don't know! I was annoyed with you and I knew it would piss you off."

Jace looks as if he's about to have a heart attack or something.

"I know it wasn't smart or logical, but we're here now."

"Right," he says, running his hands through his hair. "Here's the CliffNotes. Our team color is Yellow, so don't shoot anyone on our team. When we grab our guns, they'll give you extra paintballs for when you run out. Those go into the hopper—"

"What the hell's a hopper?" I blurt out.

Jace looks like he's about to burst a blood vessel. I haven't even had a boyfriend for a full 24 hours and he's most likely already regretting his decision. That has to be some kind of a record.

"A hopper is the container on top of your gun. The object is to shoot anyone who is not wearing yellow. If you get shot, you're out. The best bet is to hide behind the big obstacles until you have a clear shot because even with protective gear, getting shot can hurt like a bitch."

I start laughing nervously and I think I might even be sweating. Is it getting hot in here or is it just this stupid mask I'm wearing? Jesus, I feel like Darth Vader.

Jace quickly gets himself dressed, we grab our guns and then we head to the course. Jace instructs me to crouch down and hide with him behind one of the oil drums. Who am I to disagree? The loud voice is back, counting down from five.

"Five, four, three, two, one."

A loud buzzer goes off and I feel as if I've momentarily entered the Hunger Games.

With a blink of an eye, the Jace that is supposed to be my boyfriend is gone. This new Jace puts his back against the oil drum like he's in some military movie. "Okay. Watch my six."

"Watch your—"

He's running in a crouched position to another oil drum before I can even ask what that means. When he reaches his destination, he looks at me and tosses his hands to the side like he's saying, "What the hell was that?"

"I don't know what watch my six means," I whisper-yell.

I yelp when paintballs hit the other side of the oil drum I'm sitting against. I quickly cover my mouth, but it's obviously too late. I look over to see Jace holding his forefinger to his lips.

Yeah, no shit Sherlock.

"I know you're over here," the person who is basically hunting me says. "Come out, come out, wherever you are."

Oh my God! This is terrifying! My heart feels as if it's going to beat out of my chest. Jace is trying to mouth something at me, but my mask is fogging up and I can't see a damned thing. My hands start shaking and I'm trying to remind my body that this is a game and it's all fake, but for some reason it's not listening. A whooshing sound echoes through the woods before the guy mumbles a few curse words. I look over and find Jace peeking out from behind his drum, his gun trained on the guy who was after me.

Now, I'm no damsel in distress and I can take care of myself. But holy shit, was watching my boyfriend save me from the big, bad wolf sexy as hell. I'm still insanely sensitive from the rose too. Maybe we could sneak off and no one would notice?

A snap brings me back to the present and I register that Jace is gesturing me to come over to his oil drum.

"What?" I mouth. "No!"

Is he kidding? I'm safe and sound right where I am. Well, as long as he's out there protecting my hiding spot. God, this is the dumbest game ever.

He crooks a finger at me in a more aggressive manner and I sigh heavily, giving up.

Jace holds up five fingers which I assume means run when he counts to five. Okay, sounds easy enough. One finger goes up, then two.

Three, four, and before he puts up five, he makes sure the coast is clear. His fifth finger pops up, but then his whole hand quickly turns into a fist. I've already unsquished myself from the position I've been stuck in for the last few minutes and am running towards him when he's shaking his fist at me. I don't have time to tell him I don't know what that means because pain shoots up my left side as green paint splatters all over my chest piece.

I fall to the ground and start choking and coughing to add dramatic flare.

"What the hell are you doing?" Jace whispers.

I push myself up onto my elbows. "It's called acting."

"That's definitely not acting. More like a dying fish looking for water."

My eyes narrow and I want to drag him out in the open just to mess with him when a staff member comes over to escort me off the field.

"You're out."

"Yeah," I say, standing up and dusting off my clothes. "I got that."

I'm surprised when I get to the viewing area that I'm not the first of our team there.

"What happened?" I ask Harrison.

He runs a hand through his sweat soaked hair. It may be early, but the sun is intense. "Someone from the red team was waiting and ambushed Dane and I,"

"Fuckers," Dane mutters.

"Good thing it's just a fun, friendly competition," I add, attempting to get rid of any tension.

Dane's smile is forced and that's when I decide to keep my mouth shut until Jace comes back.

When Jace finds me the first thing he does is grab my face and kiss me. The second is not as nice as the first.

"I told you to stop. Why did you keep coming towards me?"

My brow furrows in confusion. "What are you talking about? You held up five fingers which I took as run when you counted to five. Which is what I did."

"Yes, but then someone jumped out of one of the bushes, so I told you to stop."

"How?"

He makes a fist again.

"Are you kidding me right now?"

"I couldn't exactly scream it to you. I was trying to make sure you didn't get shot."

"I'm out," Martin says as he passes us. He collapses in a folding chair next to Dane.

"You gotta go grab some popcorn or something. These two are like watching a reality show," Dane adds.

Jace looks around at the five of us and laughs. "So Moose's our only hope?"

They all nod and groan collectively.

We're not even finished with our unspoken minute of silence when Moose stumbles in, covered in blue paint. My hands fly to my mouth to hold in a laugh that wants to break free.

"Bro," Harrison starts.

Moose puts his hand up to stop Harrison. I'm not sure what happened out there, but it feels ominous. As if he really did come back from war.

"I need a drink. Who's buying?"

Everyone laughs, but Dane's the only one who volunteers to pay.

Martin directs his question to us. "You two coming?"

"Next time," Jace says before I can answer.

I feel bad Jace didn't have any actual time to hang out with his high school friends. I guarantee if I didn't come this weekend, he would've seen them way more than just for a morning of paintball.

Chapter Thirty-Six

Jace

Once I'm done saying goodbye to the guys, I turn to find Zoey with a sad expression on her face. Where the hell did that come from?

I grab her chin, forcing her to look up at me. "Why so glum?"

She sighs. "You came here to hang out with your high school friends and you barely saw them because of me. I shouldn't have—"

"Don't even think about finishing that sentence unless you want to leave here with your ass covered in my handprints," I warn. Her eyes darken at my words and my cock twitches a little.

"You keep threatening me with that like it's a bad thing."

I pause, debating on following through with my threat right here and now.

I cup her face, rubbing my thumb back and forth over her cheekbone. "Baby, I wanted you here. I'm so fucking happy you came with me this weekend. And I'm happy with how I got to hang out with the guys. I'm good."

"Really?"

"Yes, really," I promise. "But, we're not leaving here until you shoot that gun at least once."

Her eyes widen like a cartoon character. "What? No, I don't need to. I took part in the tournament thingy. I definitely feel like I can cross this off my bucket list."

I shake my head.

"You said you wanted to play. Let's play."

Twenty minutes later, I'm hiding behind a fallen down tree trunk, waiting and ready.

"When do we start?" Zoey shouts, giving away her hiding spot.

"Depends," I yell back, "what are you going to give me when I win?"

Her fake laugh echoes throughout the trees. "Well, when I win, I want a full body massage. Complete with scented lotion and candles. And no wandering hands."

I laugh to myself. She's cute, thinking she's going to best me.

"That's a nice dream. But when I take you out first, we're giving that rose another try. But this time, we're kicking things up a notch."

"Up a notch?!" she shrieks.

"I was taking it easy on you before, Oreo. When we get back to our room, I want to hear you scream."

I wish I could see her right now. Touch her. Feel how fucking wet she is just by my words. I can't sit and wait for her any longer, so I click the side button on my watch that sets off a blaring alarm.

"Go!" I yell.

Peering over the trunk and to my right, I find Zoey looking around the smallest tree. My girl is also bad at hide and seek. She's looking to her left and I take the opportunity to creep around the opposite way. Walking on the balls of my feet, I'm careful to avoid stepping on fallen leaves and branches that will give away my location. I have her in my sights now. Her chest is rising and falling rapidly and I know the prospect of me catching her is turning her on.

She quickly spins in my direction and I duck behind a pile of wood. I'm counting to five in my head when I hear a splat to my left. She actually shot at me. Half of me is proud as hell of her while the other half can't wait to bend her over my knee for that. Tonight is going to be so much fun when I win. After a few more seconds of waiting, I slowly emerge from my hiding area. Zoey's finally made her way out from behind her tree and that's the moment I choose to strike. I run up to her, my foot stepping on a branch in the process. Before she can turn around, I carefully grab the front of her throat and press my gun against her back.

"Looks like I won."

Within the next few seconds, I drop my gun and mask, help Zoey take off hers and have her thighs wrapped around my waist as I press her against a tree.

"I guess congratulations are in order," she says as she thrusts her hips into me.

I groan low and deep. Even with all our clothes on, I can still feel how hot and needy she is for me.

"And I think it's time for me to claim my prize."

Twisting my fingers in her hair, I pull her lips down to mine. Her tongue finds mine as she moans into me. I feel her about to slip out of my grasp, so I try to adjust my hold when my foot slips on something. It's like we're moving in slow motion and I turn our bodies so I take the force of the fall. Luckily for me, I end up with a super hot woman straddling me.

"Oh my God! Are you okay?" she asks in a panic.

"Fine," I grunt. "I just slipped on that damn root."

I kick it for good measure. That'll teach it.

"Are you sure? That was a pretty hard fall."

Seeing the worry in her eyes, an idea comes to mind. I might be a total asshole for this.

"Actually, I think I might've landed on something hard," I say, grabbing my neck like I'm in pain.

"Are you serious? Here, let me look at it."

She gives me her hand to help me up, but once I'm in a sitting position, I use the opportunity to shove the handful of mud all over her chest protector. Her mouth falls open in horror.

"You did not just do that."

I flick the remaining mud from my hand. "That's for shooting at me."

Using both hands, she shoves at my shoulders and stands up. "You told me to! We were playing a game."

I quirk a brow as I reach for another pile of mud. "Yeah? And what about now?"

She holds up her hand like it will protect her. "You wouldn't dare."

"Wanna bet on it?"

Zoey shrieks and starts running the second I launch the mud at her. I run after her, but freeze when she finds her own handfuls of mud.

"Baby, let's talk about this." The look in her eye is mischievous and I take a step back.

"No," she says simply before she hits me square in the forehead.

Zoey instantly starts cracking up and that's when I decide this game is over. I straight up tackle her to the ground.

Chapter Thirty-Seven

Zoey

Rolling around in the mud and dirt didn't seem like a horrible idea at the time. Now that we're back at the hotel, I don't think I've ever felt so filthy.

"Dibs on first shower," I shout, running the final steps to the hotel door.

I swipe my key, but the light turns red. I frown and swipe again, but shriek when Jace catches me by the waist.

"But I like you dirty."

He presses his lips against my neck as the light turns green. I shimmy him off and rush through the door.

"That's disgusting. We were rolling around in the woods. I could have some obscure disease that's transmitted through touch and by coming near me, you're dooming yourself."

Jace stalks towards me as I walk backwards. "I think that's a risk I'm willing to take."

I turn to run into the bathroom, barely making it to the walk-in shower when Jace grabs me by the waist and pulls me to him. Thankfully there's no mud around his mouth, so I lean into the kiss. His tongue swipes into my mouth and I can't help it. I melt the second his lips touch mine.

"You know, I think you have a point." His fingers grip the hem of my shirt. "You are filthy. We should get these clothes off you immediately."

A little too eagerly, I lift my arms and allow him to undress me. His hand bumps the water faucet and I shriek in surprise when the freezing cold water sprays us.

"Shit," he mumbles. Jace turns to adjust the nozzle to a much warmer temperature and once we're both no longer shivering, he turns his attention back to me. Jace's fingers almost rip the clasps off of my sports bra as he tears it from my body.

His eyes drift down to my tits and he groans. "I'll never tire of this sight."

Before I can make a witty remark, he drops to his knees. His mouth sucks my nipple into his mouth while his hands pull my pants and underwear off.

"Hold on," he says.

"To wha—"

I don't get a chance to finish my question. He tosses one of my legs over his shoulder and shoves his head between my thighs.

"Oh!" Instinctively, my hands go into his hair, but my other leg quickly begins to shake. I feel around for something to hold onto, but only find the tile wall. Jace's tongue alternates from slow and steady to fast and frantic and I can feel my body turning into a pile of mush. I'm so close it's almost painful. My hips are moving against Jace's face when the most intense feeling takes over me. I look down at Jace's evil grin and him holding the rose toy. Where the heck did that come from?

"I told you, I want to hear you scream."

Jace has to adjust his head to account for the toy and when he finds the perfect angle, he turns up the vibrations. I swear my eyes almost pop out of my head. He dives back in, his tongue thrusting in and out of me and I swear I can feel every nerve ending in my body. Jace grabs onto one of my hands and guides it up to my tits. I follow his cue and play with one of my nipples. Jace gets his wish and I scream, while my entire body spasms as my orgasm overtakes me.

I'm still coming down when Jace carefully lowers my leg, stands and says, "It really is water-proof." While I'm laughing in my orgasm induced fog, I notice he's naked.

"Let's get you clean," he says. How does he make everything sound so damn dirty?

Jace gestures for me to turn around and he begins lathering the shampoo in my hair. I let my eyes flutter shut and accidentally let out a moan. I'm not even embarrassed; this feels too damn good.

"I love it when you make that sound," he mutters.

Suddenly, a hand is wrapped around the front of my neck while his thumb is forcing my chin to the left where his mouth is. Jace's tongue takes control and I try to spin around, but he pulls back. When I pout, he just continues to wash me. I roll my eyes at him, but yelp when his hand collides with my ass.

"Did you just spank me?"

"Roll your eyes at me again and find out."

I don't, but I definitely think about it.

I let him take his time soaping me up because I know I'll get my turn soon. It doesn't make sense how unbelievably sexy he is. Piercing blue eyes, incredibly beautiful face, a body with more muscles than I can count and a cock that is ... very excited to see me right now.

"I think it's my turn."

I hold out my hand for the bar of soap. After covering my hands in suds, I immediately reach down and wrap my fingers around his dick. He jerks and I tighten my grip.

"I just thought since you did such a good job getting me cleaned, I could return the favor."

"The favor?"

Letting go, I push him back into the water, so the soap runs off. Am I cold from standing here naked? A little. But I am so hot with how Jace makes me feel, I don't really notice it.

Once he's rinsed cleaned, I lower down onto my knees and dart my tongue out to lick his crown. He inhales sharply. I look up and watch him as I open my mouth to suck the tip in. His fists clench at his side. I suck his cock deeper in my mouth, flattening my tongue along the bottom.

"Zoey," he groans.

I love how he says my name.

Finally, I dig my nails into his ass and take him back as far as I can. I hear Jace's hand hit the shower wall and remind myself to breathe through my nose. Maybe this was a little ambitious, but oh well. Jace moves my wet hair away from my face and watches me as I hollow my cheeks. I bob up and down, letting the noises he makes guide me. I may be on my knees, but the fact that I'm controlling someone like

Jace Bennett is such a turn on.

"Zo-Zo-Zoey, you really have to stop that—"

"Or what?" I say with the most innocent smile.

"You know what."

Holding his gaze, my tongue licks the small amount of liquid on his dick.

Jace's smirk is evil. "Don't say I didn't warn you."

I lean back in to get another taste and within seconds Jace pulls out of my mouth and is coming all over my chest. Hot liquid slides over my tits and down my stomach all while his eyes squeeze shut and his mouth opens in a silent cry. It might be the most beautiful thing I've ever seen. Curiosity getting the best of me, I swipe my finger through a bit of liquid below my nipple and suck it into my mouth. Jace audibly swallows and I smile when his cock twitches.

"Tastes kind of sweet."

Jace holds his hand out and I take it. Once he helps me up, his lips press to the side of my mouth. I inhale sharply when he pinches my nipple.

"I should get out or you'll never get clean," he growls.

"You say that like it's a bad thing," I tease.

I'm about to kiss him again when—I swear to God—I think I hear a Taylor Swift song start playing.

"Do you hear that?"

"Shit." Jace stubs his toe as he stumbles out of the shower. He quickly grabs a towel, wraps it around his hips and runs out into the room.

"Is Taylor Swift your ringtone?" I shout after him.

"What? I can't hear you? I'm on the phone."

It was hard to hear over the shower, but I swear I heard "... Ready For It" from her Reputation album.

Chapter Thirty-Eight

Jace

Zoey saunters out in a fluffy white towel and I force myself to look away. I cannot have dirty thoughts about my girlfriend while I'm on the phone with my nana.

"I have some free time later today," I tell her.

"Gramps is making enough burgers to feed the entire neighborhood for lunch. Will we see you then?" She sounds hopeful and it's been a while since I've seen her.

"Of course. I'll see you then."

"Okay, dear. I love you."

"I love you, too."

I hang up the phone with a huge smile on my face. I haven't talked to my nana in awhile. We've both been so busy that we've been playing phone tag, so I wanted to make sure I didn't miss this call.

"Who were you just talking to?"

I look down at my phone and register that I said the words "I love you" while I was on the call.

"Was that your other girlfriend?" she teases. "I'm just telling you now, if I find out you invited me to your paintball weekend while she gets a spa weekend, I'm gonna be pissed."

Tossing my phone on the bed, I walk up to her and cup her face. "There's only you."

She's the one who kisses me and I realize this is the happiest I've ever been.

"It was my nana."

"Like your grandmother?"

I walk over to sit down on the bed and let her finish getting dressed. "We've never really talked about my family, have we?"

She shakes her head while squeezing water from sections of her hair with her towel.

"It's a pretty complicated story, but I'm willing to share. That is, if you want to hear it?"

"Of course. I would love to." Zoey tosses her towel on the dresser, walks the few steps to me and intertwines our fingers. She doesn't push me when I don't immediately start talking, so I begin rubbing circles on her skin with my thumb.

"My mom was really young when she got pregnant with me. Like way too young to be a fit mother. She was also into a bunch of bad shit; drugs, alcohol, men. I guess she wanted to get rid of me, but her parents wouldn't allow it, so she went through with the pregnancy."

I finally manage to look up. Her eyes are shiny with tears, but she doesn't say anything.

"I didn't exactly fit in with the lifestyle my parents had always dreamed of. Anyways, my mom gave birth and the second I was out of her, my parents ding-dong ditched me at my grandparents and hit the road."

"They what?" she asked, her tone dark and dangerous.

"I think it's called Wanderlust? My nana told me that she never wanted to go to college and they always planned to travel once they graduated high school. But then I came and just sped up the process."

"Oh, Jace. I am so—"

"Please don't say you're sorry. I don't tell people this about my life because I don't want them to feel bad for me. I told you because

... well, because I want you to know everything about me. Is that weird?"

She shakes her head and slides closer to me on the bed. "No. That's not weird at all."

A tear finally falls and I swipe it away with my thumb.

"That was my nana who called. I told her I was back in town."

This makes her smile. "Good. Do you want me to clean up while you go visit her or—"

"You're coming with me. Obviously."

Zoey's eyes widen in shock. Did she really not think I was going to invite her?

"Excuse me, but my nana raised me to be a gentleman. What will she think of me if she knows I brought my girlfriend home and didn't introduce her to my family?"

Zoey's cheeks turn pink. "I like it when you call me your girlfriend."

I thread my hand in her hair and ghost my lips over hers. "Good because I like calling you my girlfriend."

I wait another second, just to torture her a bit, but Zoey's not having it. She jumps forward, pressing her lips to mine in a searing kiss.

Walking up to the faded red front door brings back the memory of helping gramps paint it when I was six. I was adamant about being a man and doing it on my own. That lasted about one hour in the June heat until I was begging him to come back and help me. My fist bangs on the door three times and I have a huge smile on my face when my nana answers the door.

"Nana! I've missed—"

"It's about time some pretty girl makes an honest man out of my grandson."

"Nana—"

Ignoring me, my nana links arms with Zoey and pulls her into the house. "You know, my Jacey thinks we don't know what he's up to, but we know. He thought he was sneaky in high school when he would come home covered in hickies with glassy eyes. But you look like a good girl. What's your name, dear?"

"Um," she stifles her laugh, "Zoey."

"Nana! You make me sound like a degenerate."

"Well, if the shoe fits," she says over her shoulder.

"When did you get so mean?" I ask dramatically, even though her words hurt a little. How is it possible a woman who is barely five feet is able to be so mean?

"When they cancelled my soap. Now, who wants lemonade?"

I blindly follow them into the kitchen, letting the front door slam shut behind me. Our house layout is kind of weird. The front door opens into the kitchen which is attached to my grandparents bedroom. I've always said the person who built this house must've been stoned out of their mind.

Nana hands a glass of lemonade to Zoey, "So, how did you meet my perfect angel of a grandson?" Then she turns and looks at me. "There. Did that sound convincing enough?"

Zoey chokes on her lemonade and starts coughing. Or maybe she's laughing? It's hard to tell.

"I smell homemade cookies," Gramps announces as he struts in wearing his usual suspenders and bowtie. Never mattered if he and Nana were going out on a date night or staying in for a movie night with me; he was always dressed to the nines.

"Oh!" Nana grabs a plate covered in foil off the stove and sets it in front of Zoey. "My specialty is chocolate chip, but I wasn't sure if you had any allergies or dislikes, so I still have some fresh dough in the fridge if you want something else."

Zoey's eyes meet mine and I know I made the right choice in having her come with me. When Nana called, it wasn't even a question. She looks comfortable being here with my family. I can't pinpoint the exact moment when everything between us changed. Maybe it was the move-in party when she punched that asshole in the face. Or when our lessons turned into excuses to be around each other. I don't know. But I do know I'm falling for Zoey.

"I'll just grab one of those," Gramps reaches over the counter, but quickly retracts his hand when Nana swats at it.

"Those are for after lunch."

Gramps holds his hand to his chest like it's broken. "But you said Zoey could have one."

"She's our guest. And the first girl Jace has willingly ever brought around. I would like to keep this one a little longer."

"Willingly? What does that mean?" I finally chime in.

Nana waves me off. "Oh, nothing to worry about. Just that one girl. Oh, goodness. What was her name? Hazel or Haley or—"

My eyes widen in horror. "Hayden?"

Gramps snaps his fingers. "That's the one. She was something."

Oh my God. Hayden was the first girl I ever had sex with. It was the night of senior prom and after I dropped her off, she snuck back over to my house a few hours later. I was terrified the entire time we were going to get caught. Needless to say, it was not a night to remember.

Zoey tries to hide her smile. "Who's Hayden?"

Before I can answer, Nana chimes in. "His prom date. They never dated though. She was a bit of an oddball, if you ask me."

I scrub a hand down my face. "Nana, you can't say things like that."

"Things like what?"

"She wasn't an oddball." Gramps adds. "She was just quiet."

Zoey's eyes are on me, waiting for me to elaborate. There's a few moments of silence where Nana, Gramps, and I all exchange glances, wondering who is going to tell her.

Gramps opens his mouth first, but Nana grabs a cookie and shoves it towards him. "You shush. It's Jace's story to tell."

"So?" Zoey prompts.

"Um. Well, she was—"

"If you're not sure how to answer, you should ask Hayden's girl-friend," Gramps grumbles around a mouthful of cookie. "Poor Jace made the girl switch teams."

Zoey's mouth drops open as Nana grabs a wooden spoon and chases Gramps out of the kitchen with it.

"No!"

Leaning over the counter, I grab a cookie and pop it into my mouth. "Yes."

Zoey stares at me, waiting for me to elaborate. Once I'm done chewing, I put her out of her misery. "She didn't know at the time. Hayden and I never dated, but were always friends. We liked to flirt and it was fun and casual. Then prom night she came over and we finally had sex and that was ... not fun and casual. Not long after that, she told me she wanted to figure out who she was and I told her I thought it was really cool."

"Wow. Hayden sounds like a badass."

"She is. We still talk from time to time. She has a serious girlfriend now and seems really happy. To be clear, nana and gramps don't think she's odd because she's dating a girl. They only met Hayden a few times and she was always so quiet. And, well, you've met nana and gramps."

We both chuckle.

"They're amazing," she says.

"Yeah. They really are."

I scratch my head and look back down the hallway Gramps and Nana went. They must've gone outside because the house has gone silent. "I can't believe they saw Hayden leave the next day and never said anything."

Zoey jumps off her stool and looks around the kitchen. Nana loves the concept of ancient Italy and since she never got to visit, she figured decorating her house like that was the next best thing.

"Show me the rest of the house?"

I nod for her to follow me. Our fingers intertwine as I take her further into the house towards the family room. We see Nana scolding Gramps through the front window and both laugh.

"They've been married 43 years," I tell her, pointing to the family pictures covering the mantel.

"That sounds magical."

She already saw the kitchen, so I take her upstairs to show her my bedroom next.

"Are you sure you're ready for this?" I ask.

She looks up at me. "I mean, I was until you said that."

"Too late." I open the door and pull her in.

Zoey narrows her eyes at me. "You made it seem like you were hiding dead bodies in here or something."

Is she serious?

I gesture to one of my biggest secrets growing up. "You don't think this all looks a little crazy?"

"What? Oh, are you talking about the fact that you have a Spiderman bedspread, Spiderman sheets, Spiderman posters, a Spiderman rug, a Spiderman snow globe, a Spiderman night light, and a raging boner for Spiderman? Tell me, which Peter Parker is your favorite? Because that might determine the future of our relationship."

When she takes her eyes off me, I use that to my advantage and tackle her on said bedspread. She's not quick enough and I grab both her wrists and pin them above her head. The fight slowly dies inside her when our lips are barely an inch apart.

"I also have a Spiderman mask."

She tries to capture my lips, but I lean back.

Her smile doesn't falter when she says, "So put it on."

I can't take it anymore. I press my lips to hers and groan as her hips meet mine. Fuck, I bet she's wet for me. Holding both her wrists with one hand, I let the other slide down her body. I have to know or I'm going to go insane.

My fingers make it to the edge of her jeans when we hear, "Jace? Zoey? Lunch is ready!"

Well, shit. I'm not even living at home and still getting cock-blocked by my family. I fall off Zoey and onto the bed beside her.

Apparently we're not moving fast enough because the next voice is Gramps. "Remember son, no glove no love!"

"Don't say something like that! What is Zoey going to think of us!" Nana chides.

"Uh," Gramps shouts up, "No offense, Zoey?"

We look at each other and burst out laughing. I can practically see Nana's death glare right now.

Even with Nana and Gramps chirping me the whole time, lunch goes by way too fast. Our goodbyes are quick and before I know it, we're on our way back to the hotel.

"You were really good with them. Gramps and Nana," I tell her.

She's holding the hand I'm resting on her knee. "Lunch was amazing. Thank you for inviting me."

"Thank you for coming," I say, lightly squeezing her leg three times.

"I really love ... your family."

I bring her hand up to my mouth, brush a kiss against it and then return it to her knee. Fuck, she's perfect.

Chapter Thirty-Nine

Jace

The weekend went by too fast. I wasn't worried about Kai or any of that other shit at Winger U when it was just Zoey and I. I don't know what's gonna happen now though. Zoey and I are together, that much is clear. But Kai isn't here, he's off at camp and it's not like we can casually call him up and tell him that we're seeing each other. He'd lose his mind. Conrad knows, but no one else does. I think. I know it's a big issue with Zoey too and the last thing I want is for her to be worried.

I place my hand on the gear shift on the drive back and she threads her fingers through mine. She ends up sleeping through most of the ride, but never lets go of my hand. Jesus, I've turned into such a sap.

"You ready for practice without your Captain?" she asks once she gets up. She doesn't look at me when she asks it.

I shrug. "It's definitely going to be weird. He's only gone for another week."

"One more week," she echoes.

Neither of us say it out loud, but we're both thinking it. When this thing started out, we never thought it would turn into us actually caring about each other. And now we're dating and we've been sneaking around behind his back. What the fuck are we going to do?

Zoey

I stumble back into my dorm room, my overnight bag bouncing off the door and trying to knock me over.

"Ow," I say, rubbing my elbow where I just banged it on the door knob.

If I could only use one word to describe the drive back to Winger U, it would be weird. The entire time Jace and I were thinking the exact same thing, but refusing to say it. That we need to tell Kai as soon as possible. Before we're caught or worse, someone else tells him.

"Well, well, well. Look who's back from their filthy weekend of debauchery," Corrine teases.

I breathe out a laugh and collapse onto the chair in the living room. Truthfully, I'm exhausted. Between the guilt from keeping this a secret from Kai and the non-stop orgasms, I feel as if I could sleep for a week.

"I'm supposed to go help The Good Neighbor Program mulch tonight," I groan as my eyelids flutter shut.

"Tell Regina to do it herself. She can use the stick that's usually shoved up her ass," Becks says without even looking up from her magazine.

"That's mean," I say through a laugh.

She shrugs. "Maybe I would be nicer if when I volunteered my time to dig in the dirt, she didn't comment on how to improve my technique."

"She did not," Corrine laughs. "You are so lying."

"You would know if you came and helped," Becks taunts Corrine.

Corrine pretends to gag. "Manual labor is just not really my thing."

Taking a deep breath, I muster up all the energy I have and force myself to stand.

"Is no one coming with me then?"

Becks finally looks up at me. "I didn't know you signed up or I wouldn't have made plans with Trent. Sorry."

Corrine's face falls and she rolls her eyes.

So, that's a no for Corrine, too. Not wanting to get in the middle of that fight, I head into my room to unpack. I'm the kind of person who has to unpack their bag the second they get home. I hate letting my clothes sit and get all musty and gross. I was only gone for two days, so I'm unpacked in no time. After washing my face and changing into clothes I don't mind getting dirty, I grab my university ID and head out.

The weather's been slowly getting colder and colder lately, so I dressed in leggings and an oversized sweatshirt. On my way, I decide to send a quick text to Millie to see if she wants to come help me dig in the dirt. Her response is a bunch of laughing emojis, but I'm relieved when she actually does show up.

"No roommates today?" she asks.

I shake my head. "Not today. I actually forgot I told Regina I would help out, so thank you for coming."

"No problem. The space is coming along nicely. Think it will be ready before we leave for Thanksgiving break?"

"For sure. We only have a few more weeks of stuff to get done depending on how many people help."

After being shown bags and bags and more bags of mulch, Millie and I grab our gloves and get to work. Sweat starts dripping down my face as my phone vibrates in my pants pocket.

J: Bonfire at Ballentine tonight. You in?

Z: You aren't sick of me yet?

J: Watch your tone when you're talking about my girlfriend

"Is he sending you dirty pictures or something? Your face looks like a tomato right now," Millie laughs.

Z: Volunteering now. Maybe I'll stop by if you're lucky...

I tuck my phone away and try to get back to work, but Millie's eyes are solely on me.

"Are you two an actual couple now?"

I pull my bottom lip between my teeth. "Yeah. He called me his girlfriend. God, I'm acting like such a fool."

She shakes her head. "No, you are not. You're excited, which is a good thing."

"We haven't to-told Kai," I say hesitantly.

Millie's eyes widen. "Oh."

"Yeah." I sigh, "it's kind of messing with my head."

"He's your brother. You don't think he'll be happy for you?"

"Considering he told me to stay very far away from Jace, I doubt it. Plus, I don't want to tell him while he's at camp. This is a huge deal for him and I don't want to distract him."

Millie grunts as she picks up a bag and dumps it out in the flower bed. "It's impressive, you know? You tamed the man-whore. They're going to write studies about you."

I burst out laughing, thankful for the change in topic. "Who is they?"

"Mythbusters."

Jace

Practice without Kai is weird. I'm happy for him, though. If anyone deserves an opportunity like this, it's him. The first half of practice is focused on getting the blood flowing, warming up our muscles and sharpening our reflexes. Each of us have our own stretching routine and once I've finished mine, I snag a puck and aim for the net. Gomez stops a good chunk of the shots sent his way, a few sneak past, but majority of them go wide and pepper the glass.

The rest of practice, Coach sets up a few different stations and has us switch from drill to drill whenever he blows the whistle. We work on breakouts, power plays and penalty kills. Practice wraps up with the team lining up and taking shots on goal. Gomez stops next to none, so like the good buddy I am, I have to mess with him.

Circling the net, I slap his leg pad with my stick. "Damn, Gomez. I've seen coupons that save more than you."

"And I've heard better chirps from a dead bird," he taunts back.

The collective oohs of the guys echo through the rink. I fist bump Gomez, giving credit where credit is due.

After I shower and am getting changed, Caleb approaches me. "You're coming back to Ballentine for the bonfire, right?"

I nod, slipping my shirt over my head. "Yeah. I'm heading back with you guys. I, uh, invited Zoey, too."

"Who?"

I clear my throat. "Um, Little Griffin."

I don't have to look at Caleb to see the judgmental stare he's giving me. "Kai's sister?"

"Step-sister."

Caleb's lips twitch and I know he's not buying my bullshit. I run my hand through my wet hair, avoiding Caleb's eyes.

"She's volunteering right now, but said she might stop by later. If she has time."

He crosses his arms over his chest and starts laughing. "I'm sure she will."

Chapter Forty

Zoey

It feels weird to be hanging out at Ballentine without Kai here. Especially because I only know a handful of people at the bonfire. I've met Conrad and Caleb, Caleb's sister Bonnie and Millie and everyone knows Buzz, but then there's Oliver, a basketball player named Zeke and a bunch of girls. There's a fire pit in the backyard surrounded by Adirondack chairs and a cooler. It's one of the more tame nights I've seen at Ballentine. Without Kai here, Jace is able to be close to me, but not too close. I know Conrad knows about us, but I don't know about the rest of the guys. Kai's pretty close with Caleb too.

It doesn't matter because Jace and I talked about it and decided now that we're officially a couple, it's time to tell Kai. And it's definitely not something I could tell him over text. So once Kai is back from camp, I'm going to tell him. Or Jace and I will. Regardless, Jace and I are serious. And I've never been happier.

I'm talking with Jace and Caleb when I feel something in the deepest part of me. It's like a drip, drip, drip. My eyes widen and I grab my phone out of my pocket, making sure I have the date right. I do. Fuck!

"Excuse me," I mumble, pushing past Jace. I drop my solo cup on the lawn and run as fast as possible until I find the first available bathroom.

"No. No. No. No. No!"

I pull down my pants and underwear and mutter as many curses as I know. I got my period early? It's never early! I'm like clockwork. And I had to get it at a party at Jace's house? I'm not due for another week, so I don't have anything with me. Oh my God! This could not be more embarrassing. The sting in the back of my eyes is wanting me to cry, but I stomp down those hormones.

No! It's not time for you! You are a week early and no one is happy about that!

A knock on the door has me quickly pulling my pants back up and wondering what the actual fuck I am going to do? How am I going to leave with a giant period stain on my shorts?!

Another knock. "Zoey? It's me. Are you okay?"

"I'm fine," I say through a sob and then clamp a hand down on my mouth.

I hate you, hormones! Go back to hell where you belong!

The next thing I know, the door knob is turning and Jace walks into the bathroom before I can even move.

"Are you okay?"

"Do I look okay?" I snap. I gasp, covering my mouth. I always forget how Aunt Flo makes me one big, giant bitch. "I'm sorry."

Jace carefully walks towards me, like he's approaching a bomb, which I guess he kind of is. "Did something happen?"

A tear slides down my cheek and I lose it. "I got my fucking period and it's a week early!" My tears suddenly disappear and rage fills my veins. "The stupid bitch is never early, so of course she's going to show up when I have no pads or tampons. And I bled through my underwear and pants. These are my favorite pants! Do you know how hard it is to get blood stains out?"

Jace's face pales. This is it. This is the moment he realizes I'm a crazy person and breaks up with me.

Jace holds up a finger, "Wait here. I'll be right back."

When he shuts the door behind him, I say, "Yeah, because I was so eager to go back to the party like this."

Jace

Okay. Everything's okay. Zoey's okay. Right? She isn't going to like bleed out in the bathroom if I take too long? No, that's a stupid thought. Shit, I'm trying to remember what my health class teacher taught us about periods, but my mind is blank. I hope she's able to clean her pants. I've never thought about how hard it is to clean blood stains. Holy shit, is this why so many women serial killers never get caught? I'm walking fast and almost trip on my way outside.

"You drunk already?" Conrad jokes.

Ignoring him, I turn to the few women here. "Who has a pad?"

The women all look at each other while Buzz laughs. "That time of the month already?"

I point to Buzz. "Fuck off." And then turn my attention back to the women. "Ladies?"

Bonnie shakes her head. "I didn't bring my purse. Sorry."

I turn to Millie who is searching through her bag. "I must've used my last one. I can run back home and grab one."

I look at the random bunnies with pleading eyes.

"Let me check," the blonde one says, standing up to grab her purse. "I have some tampons? Do you know what size she needs?"

"I don't know, vagina sized?"

All the guys bust out laughing and I look at them. "What other fucking sizes are there?"

Blondie walks across the lawn to me, handing me three tampons. "The sizing depends on how heavy her flow is."

"I don't understand what you're saying. What flow?"

I think I'm starting to sweat now. Blondie rolls her eyes before going back to the bonfire. Zoey said she bled through her pants. That has to be uncomfortable as shit. I stare down at the tampons and run up to my room. I hurry back down to the bathroom and stop at the door to take a few deep breaths before I knock.

"Occupied," Zoey says, her voice all nice and fake.

I jiggle the handle, hoping it's unlocked.

"I said someone's in here," she snaps. I jerk away. Those must be the hormones from her period. Right? Is that how it works? I really should have paid more attention in high school. But it's not my fault the health teacher had huge tits and insisted everyone learn how to put a condom on a banana. Spank bank material for years.

I blink back to reality, registering how much of a creep I was in high school, and knock again.

Before she can yell at me, I say in my most soothing voice, "It's me, Goldfish. Open up."

The door opens slightly and then her hand darts out to yank me into the bathroom.

I'm not sure if I'm staring into the eyes of my Zoey or the demon who seems to be possessing her, but before she can tear my head off, I hold out my offerings.

"None of the women had pads, but one gave me a few tampons. She said they're different sizes and asked for your flow. I still don't know what that means. And then I got you some sweatpants since you said you bled through yours. I also grabbed you a pair of my boxer briefs. They're clean and all, but I didn't know what would be more comfortable for you. If you really do need a pad, I only had one beer and that was like an hour ago. I can drive to the Pharmacy on Main Street and get you some. Or I could just walk. Yeah, I'll just walk. That's the safest—"

My words are cut off by Zoey's lips. She wraps her arms around my neck, pulling me closer. Her tongue darts out first. Just a little taste. I want to deepen the kiss and stay in this bathroom with her the rest of the night, but then she pulls away. Her eyes are shiny with tears and I start to panic. What did I do wrong? Did I hurt her when I kissed her?

"Baby, are you okay? Did I do something?"

She shakes her head and then laughs. Not a little giggle either. She starts cackling and I'm extremely terrified that my Zoey has gone to the dark side.

After a few moments, she composes herself. "Thank you. This is …"

Her sentence fades away. I am so confused right now.

"It's just tampons and some clothes."

She shakes her head, cupping my cheek and smiling at me. "It's more than that. Thank you."

We don't go back to the bonfire. Instead, we go up to my room and cuddle while watching TV on my laptop. My fingers dance up and down her spine as we watch fisherman after fisherman try to catch Jaws. And by the time they do, she's quietly snoring next to me. I turn off my computer and snuggle into her as I drift off. I could get used to this.

Chapter Forty-One
Zoey

It's twenty past closing, but one of the regulars got here late and needed to finish his set, so I said I would stay behind to lock up. I wiped down the equipment, swept the floor and am about to bag up the trash when he comes out of the locker room, a cloud of steam following him.

"Sorry, I tried to make it fast."

"No problem. Have a nice night."

He's almost at the door when he stops and turns around, "Want me to walk you out? It's kind of late."

I shake my head. "I'm good. Nothing bad ever happens here."

Once he's gone, I grab the trash from the men's locker room. I'm combining it all into one giant bag to take out to the dumpster when I think I hear footsteps. I'm about to turn around when a sharp pain reverberates through my skull as I drop to the floor.

"Where is it?" is shouted at me. The words sound like they're being yelled through a wind tunnel. "I said where the fuck is it?"

I open my eyes in time to see a boot colliding with my ribs. I gasp for air, unable to breathe as his foot rears back for another kick. The need to vomit is strong when I'm grabbed by my shirt, and slapped hard across the face. My mouth fills with blood and I think I'm crying, but I'm not sure I can feel anything besides blinding pain anymore.

"I said where is it?" the person yells at me, this time shaking me in the process. My vision is blurry, so I'm not sure if they're a man or woman. More like a giant blob. When their hand lifts, I squeeze my eyes shut and brace for impact when I hear another voice.

"What the hell are you doing?"

"She might know where it's at!"

"How the hell is she going to tell you when you've beaten the living shit out of her? Besides, I can't find it. We have to go. Now."

I may not be able to hold my head on my own right now, but I can tell the person beating me to death is not in charge. Oh my God, am I going to die?

Suddenly I'm dropped and I cry as my skull cracks against the hardwood. I lay there for what feels like hours. Am I bleeding? I feel like I am. But how much? Is it bad? I should call someone. I should do something. I need to get up. But I'm just so tired.

Jace

"Who wants to kick my ass," Buzz announces to the party.

I smack him on the shoulder, "So many people. Should we start a list?"

"In Mario Kart." He hits me in the chest with his PS5 controller.

I shake my head. "I'm out. I have plans tonight and they should be here soon."

"Just say you're a pussy. Don't make up shitty excuses."

Buzz walks away as my phone starts to vibrate. I grab it out of my pants but point to him before I answer it, "You say that now, but wait until you see why they call me King of The Rainbow Road."

I'm still laughing when I answer Zoey's call. "Hey, Candy Cane you almost here?"

The call is silent except for a few odd noises. "Zoey? Zoey, are you there?"

Something in my gut twists and I run out of the party, "Hang on, baby. Do you hear me? I'll be right there."

When I get outside and see that I'm blocked in by hoards of people, I start my car and lay on my horn. Everyone moves out of my way and I haul ass. She was supposed to close and then head straight to the party. Something had to have happened at work. I tighten my hold on my phone while focusing on the road.

"Zoey? Baby, are you there?"

"Ja-Jace?"

"It's me. I'm here. I'm coming for you. Just stay with me."

My car can't go fast enough as I speed through town. I barely put the car in park before jumping out and running into the run-down building, its front door wide open. I have no idea what I thought I was going to find. But I didn't think it would be my girlfriend covered in blood and struggling to breathe.

"Oh my God." I feel the first tear fall as I run to her.

"Zoey, baby. It's me. It's Jace."

Her eyes widen in panic before she registers who it is. Then she grabs onto me and sobs. I wrap my arms around her, but pull back slightly when I realize my hand is now covered in her blood. The back of her head is bleeding. I clench my fist to try and stop the shaking.

"An ambulance. You need help."

She tightens her hold on me as I call 911 and report an attack. The words sound so bizarre to say. My girlfriend was attacked at work. And I wasn't there to protect her.

Once the ambulance and the police arrived, Zoey and I were separated. I hate every fucking second of this, but the sooner she gets looked at, the sooner she can come home. With me. Because if she thinks she's going home alone, she's even crazier than I thought.

"Jace?" I turn around and bring Conrad into a tight hug. I called him not long after they hooked Zoey up to an IV. He's my roommate and I either needed his okay for her to stay over or time to reserve a hotel room for us.

"What the hell happened?"

Pulling back, I sniff. "She, um, she was closing and I- I don't know. This is all so—Fuck!"

Walking away from the scene, I run my hands through my hair. "This is so fucked!" I scream.

Conrad follows me, but doesn't say anything.

"She was all alone, man," I start crying. "She was all alone and I was at some fucking party. She needed me and I wasn't there. She was in pain and—"

Conrad's hug comes out of nowhere. He holds me tight and I can't hold the tears in anymore.

"I almost lost her. I almost lost my Zoey."

Conrad doesn't talk. He doesn't tell me I'm wrong or right. He just lets me feel what I need to feel. I pull back after a few minutes and then start to laugh.

"What are you laughing at?"

I point to the stain on his shirt, "The giant tear stain I left on your shirt."

He shrugs, "What are roommates for?"

I pat his back in thanks, but as I'm walking away, he stops me. "You know you did everything you could, right?"

I nod.

My beautiful girl is nothing if not stubborn. Once she told the paramedics that she was hit in the head, they insisted she go to the hospital for scans to make sure there was no internal bleeding. Thank God they all came back clean and I was able to take her home. But that leads to a whole new argument. She was determined to stay at her own place. Alone. That shit wasn't happening no matter what she thought. I practically had to pack her bag for her, but now we're back at Ballentine and Conrad is helping get her situated in our room.

"Are you sure you don't mind?" she asks Conrad. Her voice is so quiet and meek. Not like my Zoey at all. I don't like it.

"You know we all love you, Zo. Just rest and get better."

She smiles, but winces at the cut in her lip.

Holding out my hand, I wait for her to grab it and then bring her to bed. After I tuck her in, she looks up and asks, "Where are you going?"

"Just going to get you something to drink. I'll be right back."

I give her a kiss on her temple and head out the door with Conrad.

"You gotta tell him."

I groan. "I know."

"Do you?" Conrad scoffs. "You've been sneaking around your best friend's back for months, and now you just moved his sister into your room—"

"Step-sister."

"You need to tell him. Sooner rather than later. Because if he finds out from someone who isn't you or Zoey, it isn't gonna be pretty."

Chapter Forty-Two

Zoey

It's been four days since the attack. That's four days I've haven't told Kai about what happened. I've basically lied to one of the most important people in my life. I've tried to text him. I've brought up our message thread multiple times, but I never can seem to send him anything. I know he would drop everything and come back, but then I would have to explain everything with Jace and I don't know if I could do that. Plus, this camp is a huge opportunity for him. I can't mess that up for him. I've even been dodging calls from my mom and Harold.

I did get a few calls from my boss. Obviously he knows I won't be in, but part of me wonders if he called because he wants to know if I told the burglars anything. They obviously were looking for something. If I'm being honest, it kind of drives me crazy that I don't know what "it" is. It doesn't help that Jace won't let me do more than go to the bathroom alone.

I'm attempting to close my eyes when the sound of shouting fills the house. I'm about to get out of bed to see what's going on when the door to Jace and Conrad's room is thrown open. Kai's angry form fills the doorway.

Oh, fuck.

Conrad, Jace and a few of the other guys are enjoying the show as Kai runs to me, gently grabbing my face and turning it side to side to examine my injuries. "Holy shit! Are you okay? Why didn't you call me?"

"Kai, wh-what are you doing here? Y-you can't ju-just leave camp."

Kai clenches his jaw before turning back around and pointing at Jace. "You're done."

"What the hell does that mean?" Jace asks.

"I want you out of my house."

"That's not how that fucking works. I'm not leaving."

Kai stomps towards Jace. "Yeah. You really fucking are."

I quickly—well, as quick as I can—jump up and get in between Kai and Jace.

"Go to my room, Zoey," Kai tells me.

"I'm not doing that," I say. That has him breaking eye contact with Jace and looking down at me.

It's at that moment that I know things between Kai and me will never be the same.

"Wait. Is this—Have you and Jace …"

He knows. He knows everything. He knows that we lied. He knows that we've been keeping things from him. He's never going to trust us again. He's never going to trust me again.

Kai looks over my shoulder and says, "Get out before I throw you out." Then he storms out of Jace's room and is gone.

I'm frozen to the spot. Kai could barely look at me once I stood up for Jace. Is this how it's going to be from now? As much as I want to sulk and feel bad for myself, Jace essentially just lost his best friend and his housing. Because of me. I turn around and open my mouth to apologize when his lips slam down on mine. We haven't really been intimate in the past couple days because of how sore I've been, but my lip has finally started to heal. His tongue invades my mouth and I moan into his.

"What was that for?" I pant when he pulls away.

"I know how you think. And I don't want you for one second thinking I'm regretting any of this. Do you understand me?"

I nod.

Walking over to his closet, I grab his suitcase and toss it on his bed.

"What are you doing?"

"It's my turn to save you," I tell him. "Pack up and come stay with me for a little. Give Kai some time to cool off."

He shakes his head. "He doesn't get to kick me out of my home because he has his panties in a twist."

Placing my hands on my hips, I turn to him. "And while I agree, you can still be my big, bad protector at my place. Just for a while."

When Jace continues to stare at me, I add, "Kai's only known about us for thirty minutes. Let's give him some time to adjust."

I smile victoriously as I get him to pack and temporarily move-in with me. It's the next two weeks that get complicated. Jace tries over and over to reach out to Kai, but he ignores every call, message and voicemail. At first, I was really sad, but now I'm just pissed off. Yes, Kai didn't find out about us in the best way, but he's being a bit dramatic about the whole thing. It's not like Jace and I devised this secret plan behind his back to be together. Well, I guess we kind of did, but it wasn't on purpose. He was just helping me. It was all innocent back then. Gah! This is all so messy.

"You should call him," Jace says.

I pause doing my mascara and look at him through the reflection in the mirror. "Who?"

He chuckles, "You know who?"

I shrug and finish my eyelashes. Once I'm done, he wraps his arms around my waist and twists me around. Finally, I'm all healed up and feel better than ever. Jace's lips hover above mine as his hands slowly slide up my sides, stopping just underneath my tits.

"Your brother. You should call your brother."

"Step-brother. And do you really want to talk about him while you're trying to feel me up?"

I lean forward to capture his lips when he backs away.

Jace clears his throat. "I'm serious."

"I'm serious too. I'm finally healed and it's been a while since I've seen you on your knees."

We both laugh out loud and he kisses me on the cheek before walking over and grabbing his backpack.

"Jace," I whine.

"I gotta go to class, but you two need to talk."

I scoff. "And he can call me when he's ready."

"You're so fucking stubborn."

"One of the many reasons you're with me," I say and then blow him a kiss.

Jace's smile slowly spreads across his lips then he leaves and once again, I'm alone.

I want to call Kai. I want things to go back to normal. But how he barged in and kicked Jace out was messed up. If he wants to talk to me, he knows where to find me.

Jace

I shouldn't need an excuse to go to *my* house. I know we fucked up, but Kai's blowing this way out of proportion. I walk up the steps of Ballentine and take a deep breath before I open the door. No one is in the hallway, but the second I shut the door, I hear him. Kai charges out of the kitchen with his sight set on me.

"What the fuck are you doing here?"

I place my hands up in defense. "I'm just here to grab some clean clothes."

"I hope you have a big ass suitcase with you because you're out."

I laugh humorlessly. "You can't kick me out. I'm staying with Zoey to give you time to calm the hell down."

"Calm down? You think I need to just calm down from the fact that my best friend was fucking my step sister—"

"Watch how you talk about her in front of me," I snap.

Kai's eyes are a dark endless pit and it's all my fault. I know that and I own it, but that doesn't give Kai the right to try and kick me out of my house. And it definitely doesn't give him the right to talk about Zoey like she's just another bunny.

"Let's get the guys together," Kai says.

My brows pull together, "Why?"

"I'm tired of this shit." He crosses his arms over his chest. "I'm putting it to a vote."

"You can't kick me out because you're pissed—"

"Cut the shit!" Conrad yells from the top of the stairs. A few of the guys surround him, staring down on Kai and me.

"You two are friends. You need to get over—"

"I'm not getting over shit. I didn't do anything wrong except have faith in someone I thought was my best friend."

"Jesus, how fucking old are you two?" Beaver shouts. "It's time for the shirt."

"Fuck no!" Kai scoffs.

Oliver walks down the steps holding a XXXXL white t-shirt with the neckline cut. "No one is voting anything. No one is getting kicked out. Now work this shit out like men."

He tosses the shirt at my feet and I reluctantly put it on. I turn to Kai, waiting to see what he does.

Do I want to wear this stupid ass shirt with Kai? No. But he won't listen to me, so maybe this is the only option. With what sounds like a growl, Kai walks up to me. I can't tell if he's about to hit me or not. He surprises me when he ducks under the shirt with me. The two of us stand side-by-side in this stupid shirt that has "The Get-Along Shirt" written on it in blue sharpie across the chest.

"Now," Conrad and the rest of the guys surround us, "Talk it out."

"I don't want to talk it out. I want to punch him in the face and permanently alter it."

"That seems a bit dramatic," I mumble.

A sharp sting on my side has me trying to jerk away from Kai. "Did you just fucking pinch me?"

When he doesn't even look at me, let alone answer me, I do what any rational adult would do. I pinch him back.

"This is better than reality shows," Caleb comments.

Beaver laughs at him and Caleb clears his throat. "Millie makes me watch them."

"Sure, she does," Buzz taunts.

"This is fucking stupid," Kai shouts. He slides out of the shirt and stomps up the stairs, not looking at anyone. The crowd around us dwindles down until it's just me and Conrad.

"I didn't mean for this to happen," I say to Conrad.

"I still don't understand why you and Zoey kept it a secret?"

I rip the stupid shirt off and toss it. "I don't know, man. It's not like we planned this. Him and Zoey aren't even talking."

Conrad rubs at the back of his neck. "He might just need some time. He left camp because he heard Zoey was attacked and then he found you two together. He's dealing with a lot right now."

I nod, hating myself for being the wedge between Zoey and Kai.

"I can grab you some clothes," Conrad says.

I smile tightly, "Thanks, man. I guess I'll wait outside."

Conrad winces. "That's probably best."

Conrad takes the backpack I brought and fills it with random clothes. I thank him before walking away. How did we let everything get so messed up?

Chapter Forty-Three
Zoey

Jace is lounging on the couch in our living room when I approach him.

"Can you help me with something?"

Not even fifteen minutes later, we're parked on the edge of town in front of North Side. Jace is still pissed I asked him to bring me here. He's trying hard to be supportive which is all I can ask for.

Roy, my ex-boss, must see me because he's heading out the front door, waving at us.

I turn towards Jace, placing my hand on his chest, "Wait here."

"Are you sure?"

I nod. "I n-need to do it." Of course, my stutter chooses to come back right now.

Jace's thumb swipes my cheekbone as he says, "You got this."

I turn to meet Roy head on.

"Woah. Look at you, showstopper. From what those cops said, I didn't think I'd be seeing you anytime soon. You coming back to work? Nah, I'm just messing with you. Why don't you come inside and we can talk?"

I know it hasn't been that long, but somehow Roy looks different. He's balding, but looks like he's trying to hold onto those last few remaining hair follicles. His beer gut sticks out from under his shirt, where the top two buttons are undone. He's decked out in fake gold jewelry and missing three teeth. Maybe the rose colored glasses were shattered with the first punch I took.

"I'm not going back in the building ever again."

My words have their desired effect and disturb his customer service personality. "I, um, I don't really know what to say to that."

The wind begins picking up and I can still see some of the yellow crime scene tape stuck to the edge of the front door.

I shut my eyes tight, almost thinking I can feel the pistol hitting me in the back of the head again. The repeated kicks to my ribs. What did I ever do to deserve this?

"You can tell me why it really happened?" My voice shakes, but I don't stutter. I'm not nervous or scared anymore. I'm pissed.

"What do you mean?"

"Why was I almost beaten to death, Roy? What were they looking for?"

He shakes his head like I'm confusing him. "I don't know what you're—"

"It wasn't money because they said they couldn't find "it." What was the "it" they were talking about?"

Roy glances behind me and I don't have to turn around to know what he sees. Jace borrowed Conrad's bike because he knew that would look more intimidating. It's clearly doing its job, because Roy looks scared shitless. I always liked Roy. He was a nice boss and was always super flexible with my schedule. But knowing that he has something to do with what happened to me makes me sick to my stomach.

Roy begins shifting from foot to foot and now I'm starting to get nervous.

"Jesus, Roy. What are you into?"

"It's just a bit of gambling. Nothing like drugs or anything bad like that."

"Nothing bad? Are you fucking kidding me, Roy? Look what happened to me!" I shout a little too loudly. Roy's eyes move behind me and I turn to find Jace moving closer to me. I shake my head, silently telling him to stand down. I can do this.

"What were they looking for?" I ask Roy when I turn back to face him.

Roy groans like he's in pain.

"Fine, I'll just go find it myself."

I go to walk around him, but Roy jumps in my path, calling my bluff. Thank God too because there was no way I would actually be able to step through that front door.

"It's this gaudy, old piece of shit ring. It's worth a couple thousand and I won it in a game. The guys I won it from were pissed and I knew they would come looking for it."

"You won it in a game? So, you're saying all of this was because these guys were sore losers?"

He winces. "Well, I won in a sense."

"Roy!"

"I needed a win, so I hustled 'em. I've done it to a few guys before. It's never been a big deal. I was gonna pawn the ugly thing, but then shit started happening, so I had to lay low. I knew they were looking for it, so I kept it on my person at all times."

I turn away when the first tear falls.

"Oh, dear. You weren't even supposed to still be there. It was after hours."

"Are you serious? I stayed late to help out one of our loyal customers and get my ass beaten half to death because you have a pathetic gambling addiction?"

Suddenly, there are arms being wrapped around my stomach, gently pulling me away from Roy. I didn't even realize I had been advancing on him.

"You are a sorry excuse for a man," I finally shout.

"I've got you," Jace whispers over and over in my ear.

Once we're back at the bike and I'm a sobbing mess, I look up to see Jace on the phone.

"Hello? Yeah, I need to talk to someone about an ongoing investigation."

Right after Kai caught me in Jace's room, he told mom to call me. I obviously couldn't lie to her about the attack, so I told her everything. I just happened to leave the part about my boyfriend out. I know! I'm the worst at confrontation. Luckily, I was able to convince her everything sounded worse than it actually was—only half a lie—and that she didn't need to come to campus to check on me. As mad as I want to be at Kai for involving my mom, I don't think I can be. But that was a few weeks ago and now it's time to face reality.

I pull up to the house and park on the curb. Alone. It took everything I had in me to get Jace to stay back on campus. I know he just wants to protect me, but facing Kai is something I have to do alone. He's my brother and as messed up as things are now, they can't stay like this forever.

I'm walking up the front steps when I hear a car screech to a stop. I don't know what to do here. Should I wait for Kai or meet him inside? This is so uncomfortable and I haven't even walked through the door. Before I can even make up my mind, the front door is flung open and my mom is standing there with a bright smile.

"You're here!"

My step-dad and mom don't know about this big fight between Kai and me. They don't know about Jace. They don't really know about anything except for the attack. So they're probably wondering what the hell is happening because neither of us have spoken a word since entering the house twenty-seven minutes ago. Yes, I'm counting. Every time I muster up the courage to say something, Kai makes a grunting noise and I deflate instantly.

"You look good," Harold says to me. "Have you seen any specialists since the hospital?"

I shake my head.

"I could make some calls. My buddy golfs with a great neurosurgeon-"

"Surgeon?! She doesn't need brain surgery!" My mom fans herself. Now I see where I get my dramatics from.

I go to open my mouth when Kai speaks up. "She's fine. All healed up. When's dinner? I'm starving."

"Just a few minutes left on the veggies."

More silence. Once we hit the thirty minute mark, mom opens up the wine.

After the first sip, the oven timer goes off and she jumps up. "Let's move to the dining table."

One of the main things Kai's dad and my mom bonded over was their love of cooking. So, I'm not surprised when they bring out a feast for just us four.

"Dig in," Kai's dad announces. "And after that you can tell us all about camp."

"The food looks delicious," I say just as Kai coughs.

"Thank you, sweetheart. It's Gnocchi and Peppers with Thyme Frico with some extra veggies on the side. Your dad's become quite the gardener lately."

"Step-dad," Kai corrects.

I clench my jaw in irritation. Part of me wants to kick him under the table the next time he speaks up, but that would be childish.

The sounds of silverware clanking echoes throughout the room and Kai still won't make eye contact with me.

"Can you pass the veggies?" I ask mom. It just so happens I ask at the same time Kai has a coughing fit.

I kick him. Fine, I'm childish. Whatever. He's asking for it at this point.

My mom clears her throat. "Anywho, tell us about camp."

"It was fine."

This time it's Kai's dad who grunts. "We paid all that money for you to play with NHL stars and it was just fine?"

Kai shrugs. "I didn't get to finish the entire thing, so maybe the end was the best. I'll never know."

Kai finally looks at me with his last few words. I break eye contact first and continue pushing food around my plate. It doesn't hurt to eat anymore, I'm just not hungry. I can't really stomach anything right now. Honestly, I kind of feel like I want to vomit knowing not only does Kai hate me, but that I ruined a once in a lifetime opportunity for him. My eyes begin to burn and I quickly blink away the tears. I will not cry here.

"Such bullshit," Kai mutters. I'm not sure if either of our parents hear it, but I sure do. And as upset as I am, that pisses me off.

"You could've gone back," I say before I can stop myself.

Kai jerks his head back. "Excuse me?"

Screw this. "I said, you could've gone back. You didn't have to stay."

Kai practically throws his silverware on his plate. "I came back because of you."

"Which was clearly such an inconvenience." I cover my mouth. Who am I? I've never talked like this to Kai before. I've never talked to anyone like this before. Is this how I really feel? Maybe it is.

Kai sucks on his teeth. "I was trying to help."

"And you did. But you obviously resent me for it. You could've checked on me, seen I was fine and then gone back to your fancy camp—"

"You were beaten and could've died!" he shouts, pushing back from the table.

I follow suit with our parents looking on in horror. "You don't think I know that? That's why I called Jace!"

"Next time, call 911," he spits.

The room is silent enough to hear a mouse. Kai and I are in a stare down when my mom chimes in.

"Like your friend, Jace?" She says to Kai and then looks at me. "I didn't know he helped you."

I tear my gaze away from Kai. "He was the one to call 911."

Her hands are covering her mouth in horror.

"Um, sorry for ruining dinner. I think I need to go now." And then I walk out of my house as fast as possible.

I make it to my car and am about to open the driver door when Kai comes down the front walkway towards me, hands in his pocket.

"I knew it."

I spin around. "So now you're talking to me?"

"I knew something was going on with you and that asshole—"

"You mean your best friend?"

Kai shakes his head. "A best friend would've told me what he was—no. This is bullshit. Why didn't you say anything? My fucking sister."

I open my mouth, but nothing comes out. He's right. I should've been the one to tell him. "I don't know. I think I didn't know what was happening between Jace and I and then you left and—"

"You're blaming my once in a lifetime NHL camp again?"

"What?! No, Kai! We messed up. Big time. And we're so sorry. I'm so sorry to put you through this. But I care about Jace. And I know how bizarre that sounds. But I do. And he cares about me."

Kai scrubs a hand down his face. "I can't deal with this right now."

"Kai!" I call after him, but he's in his car and gone within seconds.

Chapter Forty-Four

Jace

By some miracle, I was able to get Zoey to agree to go to the game today. I think part of it was her mom and step-dad are going, but it doesn't matter. This stupid Zoey and Jace vs. Kai thing has to end.

The locker room looks a little different on game day. Everyone has their own superstitions such as Gomez putting his gear on in a specific order, Caleb tapping his stick on the ice thirteen times—his number—before taking his first practice shot, or something as simple as listening to their favorite song before they get dressed. That one works for me and no one knows the song either. The guys would never shut up about it if they did. Scrolling on my phone, I find Taylor Swift's Reputation album and click the first track. I close my eyes and let the beat flow through me. *Are you ready for it? Bum, bum, bum.*

Okay, so I'm a closet swiftie. It's not my fault that she just happened to be on the radio before the best game I've ever had. I thought it was a fluke until it kept happening and now it's become a habit. My head bobs along with the music when my eyes land on Kai, fully dressed and ready to go. He quickly looks away, still pissed. This is bullshit. He needs to take out his tampon and get over it. Not finishing the song, I toss my headphones and phone in my hockey bag, throw on my gear and rush out to join the rest of the team.

Just as I muscle my way through, Kai jumps on the ice and zooms away from me. I catch up to him in seconds.

"Come on, man. I know you're pissed. Just hit me and get it over with."

"Fuck off," he mutters as he chews on his mouth guard. Kai snags a puck from the pile, practicing his stick handling all while avoiding me.

"Stop being a dick," I taunt, smacking his skate with my stick. "We made a mistake not telling you and we feel like shit about it."

"Back off, Jace. I mean it."

Instead of listening, I keep messing with him until he comes to an abrupt stop. Kai drops his gloves, turns around and tackles me to the ice. We're surrounded by the team and I grunt when Kai sucker punches me. I grab onto his jersey, but don't fight back. This has been building up and he needs this.

"Be a man and fight back," Kai shouts as his fist connects with my jaw.

I hold on tighter to his jersey. "I'm not going to hit my best friend."

"Are you trying to embarrass the entire school right now? Get the hell up!" Coach yells.

It takes three guys to pull Kai off me and we're both thrown out of the game before it even starts. I guess that's what I get for not finishing my pregame song.

Kai and I sit on opposite sides of the locker room, just staring at the ground. Waiting. An ice pack is thrown my way and I manage to catch it just before it hits me in the eye.

"Thanks, Coach."

"Don't thank me. And take off those jerseys. You two don't deserve to wear them."

When neither of us move, he shouts, "I said take them off!"

Kai and I strip off our jerseys in shame.

Coach stands tall, shaking his head in disappointment. "I don't even have fucking words for whatever that was out there. Fix whatever shit is going on between you two, then kiss and makeup. You both are on laundry duty for the next month."

We both groan, but shut up when Coach pins us with a look.

"Are we clear?" he asks.

"Yes, sir," we mutter.

Coach rubs the back of his neck. "Once you're done, get your shit and get out. I don't want to see either of you for the rest of the game."

The door slams behind Coach and the room is so quiet, you could hear a pin drop. I need to fix this for Zoey. I have to do this for her.

"Kai—"

"You fucked my sister and didn't think to mention it to me?"

"Step-sister," I mumble. Not the smartest move either because if looks could kill, Kai's would be burning me alive right now.

"Who cares? She's family now. You both went behind my back and made me look like a fool. What kind of friend does that?"

Kai stands up and I can tell he's done with the conversation, but he can't leave. Not yet. This can't be over. I have to fix it.

"A shitty one," I admit as I jump up. I wobble over to him, still in my skates. "I know I messed up, but it wasn't anything serious at first."

His jaw clenches and I think he might take another swing at me. "Are you telling me Zoey's like one of your puck bunnies?"

"What? God, no! I would never treat her like that. I don't even know how to explain it, but one day something clicked and I couldn't stop thinking of her."

Kai's frown deepens. I've already dug my grave, so I continue.

"Yeah, I know. I want to punch myself in the face for saying cheesy shit like that too. Here's the deal. You can hate me as much as you want. You can use me as a human punching bag every time you see me, turn the entire team against me, even make a voodoo doll of me. Whatever. I don't care. I just—"

I cut myself off when it dawns on me. "Holy shit."

"You just what?"

"I think I'm in love with her."

"This is a sick and twisted joke, right?"

I run my hands through my hair and laugh. "I don't know how she did it, but she got me to fall in love with her."

My laughing slowly dies when Kai takes two steps closer to me. His hand rests on my cheek and I don't think I've ever been this scared of him before.

"You're serious? You're really in love with her?"

"Yeah. I'm really in love with her."

"You know if you hurt her, I'll kill you and they'll never find the body, right?"

We both smile, his more sinister than mine. Kai pats my cheek a bit rougher than necessary, but I think we might actually be okay.

"I can't believe you sucker punched me out there," I say.

Kai chuckles, "I can't believe that's all I did."

Zoey

"What on Earth just happened?" Mom is holding onto Harold's hand for dear life as we make our way out of the rink and into the lobby. "I thought Kai and Jace were friends."

"It's, um, a long story," I say, navigating through the crowd. It's insane that some people haven't even found their seats yet and we're already leaving.

"I can't believe Kai," his dad grunts as we make it to the lobby. "He knows better. What the hell was he thinking?"

"He's probably been so stressed, dear. School is hard on a young man. Add hockey and that camp—"

"I only signed the permission form for that camp because he promised me he had a level head on his shoulders. Fighting with your own teammate is a surefire way to keep scouts from never wanting to look at you again."

Jesus, I can't take it anymore!

"It's because of me," I blurt out once we reach the double doors that lead to the lockers. I instantly cover my mouth, regretting my outburst. The silence is loud and just as I think my mom might say something to break the tension, the doors to the locker room open.

My step-dad's features harden when Jace walks out and I can only imagine what he thinks.

"No, no, dad!" I try to stop him as he stomps towards Jace, but it's Kai who jumps in between the two. The two men size each other up and my mom has to be completely lost by now.

"Kai?" I look at Kai who just protected Jace. With a smile he nods at me and as silly as it sounds, I know that our fight is officially over.

Jace starts talking first, "Sir, I would really like to say something before I get hit by another Masterson."

Neither Masterson moves, but Jace directs his next question to me, "Can we go somewhere private to talk?"

"No," my step-dad answers quickly.

"I don't think he was talking to you, honey," my mom whisper-yells.

Jace steps around Kai and his dad to get closer to me. Well, as close as my step-dad- allows him.

"Okay. Um, I didn't really think before I went out on the ice tonight. I just wanted to make everything better for you. Fighting with Kai obviously wasn't the right thing to do. I was goading him, but I didn't actually think he would do it. But live and learn." He chuckles nervously. "Shit, um," Jace sees my step-dad's disapproving glare, "I mean shoot."

Jace sighs heavily. "Screw it. I love you, Zoey. I love you so much that I'm completely okay with making a fool of myself in front of your parents. I love you so much that I go to sleep thinking of you and wake up missing you. I love you so much that I'll finally admit the truth: that I really do love Taylor Swift and of course Reputation was her best album. I love you so much that I am willing to do whatever I can to make you not hate me for fighting with Kai tonight. I can clean your bathroom with my toothbrush or I can make you dinner every night for the next month. Or—"

Closing the few remaining steps between us, I grab Jace's face and press my lips to his. It takes him a moment to register what's happening, but when he does, his hands slowly envelop me. He loves me! Jace freaking Bennett loves me! My hands slide to the back of his neck, my fingers tangling in his hair. I vaguely hear my mom say something and guide my step-dad away.

Jace tries to kiss me again, but before I let him, I say, "Me too."

"You too what?"

"I am so completely and utterly in love with you too."

His lips are back on mine and I completely forget about the fact that we're in public. I moan into our kiss as our tongues meet.

"This is worse than laundry duty," Kai pretends to gag.

I start laughing, but refuse to stop kissing Jace. One of his hands leaves my waist and I can only assume it's to flip Kai off. Jace playfully nips at my bottom lip one last time before he tosses his arm around my shoulder.

"I knew you always loved me. Hate to tell you, but you're pretty transparent my little debbie cake," he says, tapping my nose in the process.

"Oh, really?"

He nods, a satisfied smile on his face.

"Well, I always knew you liked Taylor Swift."

Epilogue - Zoey

The Good Neighbor Program was something I decided to do because I like to help people. I like the nitty gritty of getting to help implement changes, but my favorite part is when a project is over and you get to unveil the final result. Jace, myself and a few other friends came out today for the ribbon cutting ceremony.

"You all really didn't have to come with me," I tell them.

"Shut up," Becks says. "I still have dirt under my nails from this place. I'm just here to make sure it's at least getting used and all our hard work didn't go to waste."

I roll my eyes. Becks has such a hard exterior, but is such a big teddy bear on the inside.

Jace wraps his arms around my waist from behind. "This place looks amazing, baby."

"Dude, don't call her baby," Kai whines.

Just to piss him off further, Jace grabs the front of my throat, turns my head and crashes his lips onto mine.

"This is a family place," Millie tsks.

I giggle as I pull away from Jace. "Seriously though. Thank you for all your help. I know there were a lot of other people in the club and this park would've gotten done anyways, but it was really awesome how you all stepped up and helped."

Becks nudges my shoulder with hers. "It is a pretty cool park."

"I know, right?"

Everyone disperses to go check out the rest of the equipment when Jace and I see a family with the cutest little baby head into the park.

Jace rests his chin on my shoulder and says, "That could be us one day."

My body stiffens, "I'm sorry. What did you just say?"

"A family. Me, you and a bunch of little mini-Zoey's running around."

"Woah, woah. Who are you and what have you done with my boyfriend? You know, the one who used to screw anything that—"

My words become muffled when Jace puts his hand over my mouth and I start to laugh. I pull his hand away from my mouth and turn around so I'm facing him.

Wrapping my arms around his neck, I look up at him. "You're serious."

"Not any time soon, obviously. But don't you think that would be nice? And we'd get to have a hell of a lot of fun trying."

"Only if they would all be mini-Jace's. I was not a cute kid."

Jace taps my nose. "I don't believe that for one second, my honey bun."

Acknowledgements

Here we are again, after my third book! Can you believe it, because I can't! Back before The Twelve Swipes, I never even thought about creating a world where a series would take place, but here we are. It's all so exciting and crazy and overwhelming (in a good way).

I have to start off by giving a huge shout-out to my editor, Esther, and proofreader, Jenna. You both helped twist and mold Zoey and Jace's story into what I get to share with the world, and I will be forever grateful for that.

To all of my friends who were constantly bothered by my messages about correct grammar, if Jace was enough of a green flag, and late-night messages, thank you for still being my friends. We're still friends, right? Right?!

Yummy Book Covers, you've done it again! Thank you so much! I could not be more obsessed with my beautiful cover! After working with them for three books, I believe Enni and her partners are miracle workers. Being able to understand my gibberish throughout multiple e-mails and produce a spectacular cover is definitely a superpower!

To all my ARC readers, you're the best! I knew I could trust you with my baby!

The entire online community of Booktok and Bookstagram — thank you for following me, engaging with me, and helping me celebrate the release of my third book. Being an Indie Author means I am responsible for all of my own marketing, and I heavily rely on social media. Everyone has been so inviting and accepting that it has made my journey a lot more enjoyable.

And as always, the biggest thank you goes out to my family. Without you, this book would not exist. My husband, daughter, and son are my biggest cheerleaders, and they are the real reason I can do what I love.

Also by

The Twelve Swipes of Christmas

<u>The Ballentine Boys Series</u>

The Power Move